ALLERGIC TO MISTLETOE
Neighborlee Book 10

Michelle L. Levigne

www.YeOldeDragonBooks.com

Previously released as
Have Yourself a Faerie Little Christmas, 2010
Revised

Ye Olde Dragon Books
P.O. Box 30802
Middleburg Hts., OH 44130

www.YeOldeDragonBooks.com

2OldeDragons@gmail.com

Published in the United States of America
Publication Date: November 1, 2021

Cover Art Copyright by Ye Olde Dragon Books 2020

Welcome to Neighborlee, Ohio.

Where? Somewhere on the North Coast of Ohio, south of Cleveland, right off I-71, north of Medina, in the heart of Cuyahoga County.

What is it? That's a little harder to explain.

Neighborlee is a place you need to experience.

The most important thing you need to understand: Neighborlee is *magic*. Some people say the town is alive. It exists to protect the weird and wonderful (and sometimes a little bit scary) from the cold, practical, material world.

More important, Neighborlee protects the outside world from the weird and wonderful that come to visit … and sometimes come to stay.

First stop: Divine's Emporium, a four-story Victorian house sitting on a hill overlooking the Metroparks. Whatever you really need, you can find at Divine's. Even if you don't know what you're looking for when you walk in the door. The shop is often bigger inside than it is outside. Angela is the proprietor. Please stay on the first floor. You don't want to find out what is hidden and locked safely away upstairs. Like Aslan, Angela is good, but that doesn't mean she's safe. And neither are the secrets and wonders and doorways to other worlds that she protects … and keeps securely locked.

Come in and explore. Meet the people who help Angela guard Neighborlee. Share their adventures of magic and wonder, danger and sacrifice. You never know who or what you'll run into as you walk the streets and listen to the stories of their lives.

Chapter One

Saturday, December 1

"Happy anniversary to me," Maurice half-sang as he flew through the rooms on the first floor of Divine's Emporium. "Happy anniversary to me." He curled into a ball and bounced off an expanding wall of magic that swelled with power, ready to bloom into wonders. "Happy anniversary, dear--"

What could he say about himself? Despite having been exiled for nearly a year now from the Fae Realms, he wasn't that bad off. Sure, he had no communication whatsoever with any of his old friends, his relatives, but time passed differently for the Fae. For all Maurice knew, no one had even started to miss him yet. And if truth be told, he sort of liked living on reduced magic and among Humans. They had to be pretty clever to survive without magic at their beck and call. He liked their inventions, and he sure liked hanging around with Angela and her friends who could see and hear him.

"Happy anniversary, dear rehabilitated-joker-who's-learning-his-lesson-and-isn't-a-moronic-loser," he sang at the top of his lungs. He folded his wings to do a dive bomb roll into the main room of the house-turned-shop. "Happy anniversary to -- Oh, dang, Angela, why'd you let them in here?"

Maurice tried not to pout, but the ceiling of the main room swarmed with the twinkling blue, green, pink, and gold lights of winkies. When he was a child, he liked the winkies, the tiny, sparkling, nearly mindless little creatures that were the basis for most of the false stories about the Fae in the Human world. They were fun playmates, and they made great lights for reading at midnight, when his mother or his nanny or his older sister thought he should have been asleep. Then Maurice had grown up and learned winkies also made great spies for his mother or nanny or older sister, to ensure he behaved himself.

The Fae Disciplinary Council probably used winkies to keep track of him while they were gathering evidence to have him hauled in for trial and punishment, and exile here to Divine's Emporium and the Human realms: shrunk down to five inches tall, with magic shrunk to match, and glittery, fluttery, sparkly, enough-colors-and-glitz-to-rival-Las-Vegas wings embedded in his back.

"Everybody gets to enjoy Christmas." Angela tugged on the gold-trimmed sleeve of her crimson gown, reserved for the Christmas decorating party. She tipped her head to one side and studied Maurice. "You look especially dashing today."

"Thank you very much, mi'lady." He bowed extravagantly, and nearly turned a somersault. It was hard to bow while hovering in mid-air. His head tended to overbalance his wings. Maurice was especially proud of his midnight blue frock coat, trousers, and vest, an ascot with a dusting of diamond essence, a crisp white shirt with diamond cufflinks, and a blue diamond pin in the ascot.

"I don't suppose I could talk you into volunteering to be the angel again this year?" Angela mused. She held onto her thoughtful expression for two heartbeats, while Maurice swallowed down half a dozen pleading or vitriolic comments. "Don't worry, I was just teasing. You've come a long way in the last year, Maurice. I want you able to mingle and enjoy the party this time."

"Great." He heard quite clearly the unspoken words: *As much as you're able.*

Maurice enjoyed being able to visit with the regulars at Divine's who had enough inherent magic to see and hear him. Unfortunately, that left the other 99.9 percent of the population of Neighborlee who were totally oblivious to the fact that a shrunken, exiled Fae flew around Divine's Emporium.

The protective net of magic around Divine's chimed pleasantly just then. Maurice had grown sensitive enough to the magic resonance of the people who regularly came into Divine's to identify them before he saw them.

"Lanie's first." He spun around in mid-air to follow Angela as she moved out of the room to the main entryway of the store.

The door swung open without anyone touching it -- courtesy of Lanie Zephyr's telekinetic talent -- and a moment later her wheelchair bumped up the last two shallow steps to enter the shop. The dark-haired woman paused a moment to shake the damp from her hair before rolling through the open doorway.

The weather was cold, but not cold enough to produce snow

or even ice yet. The air was filled with a thick, icy fog. Maurice looked past Lanie at the street. So far, her Jeep was the only vehicle parked out there yet. Soon, the entire dead end street would be jammed with cars. Hopefully, the soil of the empty lots on either side of Divine's was frozen hard enough to allow parking. Angela's decorating party was the annual kick-off for the Christmas season in Neighborlee.

"So, how's it going, Wheels?" Maurice swooped around to keep pace with Lanie as she rolled down the aisle between the shelves to the main room. "Are your folks coming?"

He had been especially pleased to discover that the experience of being yanked through time from the Bermuda Triangle had given Lanie's parents, Charlie and Rainbow Zephyr, enough magic to see and hear him. They were having a good time comparing all the bizarre and amusing tales of the Fae in the world with what Maurice remembered of his Fae history lessons. He was handicapped in being unable to call up the Ether Lexicon, the Fae repository of all knowledge and answers to most questions. Still, it was a fun project.

The three settled at the little bistro table in the main room of the shop with cappuccinos, to chat and catch up until more helpers and friends showed up.

The next arrivals were Jo August and Ken Jenkins, bringing the tree. Maurice flew circles around them, feasting his eyes on their happy faces and congratulating himself on doing something right. There were other couples he had nudged in the right direction -- or, as Angela put it, tripped up those who stood in the way of their happiness -- but Jo and Ken were special to him because they were the first. He watched them as two more carloads of helpers showed up, including Lanie's brothers and parents, and students from Willis-Brooks College. Jo and Ken were greatly changed from last year, when he had mistaken her for a skinny boy, dressed in baggy clothes. Ken had been aching from the shattering of his marriage. In Maurice's opinion, Ken had been the only one who had been married. Jo had been working three part-time jobs to pay off her aunt's hospital bills and funeral expenses, too busy to take any time for herself. It had been a major miracle that she showed up at the decorating party last year.

"And the rest is history," Maurice said, settling down on his usual shelf behind the counter, to stay out of the way as everyone got to work. He liked the sense of everything coming full circle.

Within half an hour, the shop was full of people running in all directions. Half the crew went down into the cellar to haul dozens of boxes of decorations out of storage. The other half emptied those boxes and hung decorations everywhere inside and outside the shop. Maurice wished he could help, but it was smartest to just sit on the sidelines and watch, rather than risk getting swept aside or even knocked to the floor and trampled by people who couldn't see or hear him. He was having fun, feeling a little impatient for the hustle and bustle to slow down and the celebrating to begin. Especially when Angela had everyone make their wishes for the year with miniature Wishing Ball decorations. Maybe he could help make some of those wishes come true.

John Stanzer showed up with Dawn Dover. Maurice had been spending a lot of time watching over Meggie Richards and Lanie's brother, Pete, who were becoming an "item," overseeing the preparations for Diane and Troy's wedding, and spending all the time he could in Holly's dreams. He had missed most of the times that Dawn had come into the shop since moving to Neighborlee. Mostly because the interdimensional beasts who protected Stanzer and Dawn, the Hounds of Hamin, created an energy clash that made his wings itch. The Hounds didn't seem to like the sensation, either, and it wasn't smart to irritate something that could swallow him in one gulp and not even notice.

Dawn was a senior at Neighborlee High, and lived on the top floor of the building Stanzer owned, where he had his private investigator offices. He lived on the bottom floor and rented out the apartments in between them. Maurice felt kind of sorry for them, and privately felt the Hounds had messed up big-time, when they separated Dawn and Stanzer in time, as well as distance. They would have been married by now, if she hadn't arrived on Earth eight years after him, but not a day older than when she left home. Maurice thought he had it rough, waiting for the day (if ever) when Holly would be able to see and talk to him when she was awake. For now, Dawn and Stanzer were stuck waiting, too.

They came through the door, carrying cartons of eggnog and brightly colored fruit pastries to contribute to the party. *Something else* came with them.

Maurice's first instinct was to duck, because he knew what that *something else* was. If his exile spell hadn't bound him to the Human realms, he would have streaked for the nearest slit in reality and taken his chance on whatever dimension he landed in.

The *something else* coalesced into being, walking behind Dawn and Stanzer as they approached the long refreshment table between the counter and the tree. Big, silvery teeth. Electric blue eyes. Power sizzling over dark fur. An enormous dog, its head level with Dawn's shoulder, coalesced into being, walking behind her and Stanzer. Two people walked right *through* the Hound. It didn't flicker like a bad hologram, and the people didn't react.

Maurice swallowed hard and wished he had been a smart-mouth again so Angela had exiled him to be the angel at the top of the tree. What good would that do? An inter-dimensional big bad wolf could find him at the top of the tree, without any trouble.

The Hound nudged Stanzer's arm. He followed where the big blue eyes gazed: right at Maurice. Then to Maurice's relief the Hound faded out. The tingling and sizzling and especially the itching in his wings faded out too.

"I have a message for you, Maurice." Stanzer and Dawn stepped aside, out of the traffic.

Maurice flew down to perch on Dawn's shoulder. If there was going to be any trouble, she was most likely to defend him.

"The Hounds have decided that you're friendly, and they'll try not to show up when you're around, because it makes you so uncomfortable."

"Oh, hey … tell them thanks." Maurice could think of a couple dozen smart-alec remarks he could make, but that was the old him. He really was a much better person than he had been at this time last year. So he kept his mouth shut and decided to be grateful rather than snarky.

Then a big part of the reason for his change walked into the shop, with another group of volunteer decorators.

Holly.

Maurice kept watch on her as she opened the boxes of new decorations he had kept hidden until her arrival. He perched on the branches of the tree just below her eye level, anxious for some flicker of reaction. Other than delight in the golden spun glass stars, delicate as thistledown, she showed no hint of recognition.

Last night in her dreams, they had decorated a tree using those ornaments. Maurice had hoped something would remain from her dream, to come into the light of day and brush against her conscious thoughts. He consoled himself that he would have time with her on Christmas Eve day, when he was full-size, an ordinary man. When she could see him. He planned to meet Holly at the library, ask her to walk with him through Neighborlee and look at the decorations, and sit beside her for Christmas Eve dinner.

For now, though, all he could do was watch her and brush against her fingers when she reached up to hang the ornaments. Their ornaments, from their shared tree, even if only a dream tree.

At least Holly had been happy last night, so excited about Christmas and the decorating party at Divine's. She had only mentioned once that she wished he could come to the party. He thought maybe there had been a tear in one eye, while they sang songs. He told her about his cousin Angeloria, who was allergic to holly and mistletoe, thanks to being present when Charles Dickens wrote Scrooge's infamous line, hoping Christmas well-wishers died with a stake of holly through their hearts.

Maurice didn't visit Holly as often as he would have liked. At fall equinox, he had managed to spend three hours in the library, talking with her, and then he went to a movie with her, Meggie, Diane and Troy. Ever since then, Holly hadn't been as happy in her dreams. It hurt her that she couldn't remember him during the day.

Sometimes he thought about going away, leaving her dreams alone from now on, but he admitted he was too selfish to make that kind of sacrifice. He had no idea how much longer he could go on, showing up at equinox and solstice and Christmas Eve, tormenting himself with the hope that this time, when he looked into her eyes and she could see him, she would remember him from her dreams.

"Maurice." Angela stepped up behind the counter and lightly brushed a fingertip along the top of his folded wings.

"Huh? Oh." Maurice blushed, despite knowing only a few people could see him, sitting and moping on the bent leg of the dragon stand that held the Wishing Ball. "Sorry. Wishing time already?" He leaped up into the air and gained enough altitude for a good view as the members of the decorating party took their turns picking up an ornament and making their wishes.

When Jo stepped up to take her ornament, Ken offered her a

slightly larger ball, crystal and gold instead of the dark, metallic rainbow swirls. Maurice saw the ball's seam and hinge. He turned a triple somersault in mid-air. Something was inside the ornament.

"It's about time, you big goof!" he crowed, and earned some soft laughter from Diane, Troy, and Lanie, who were close enough to hear him.

"You're breaking tradition," Jo said, laughing, as she took the ornament from Ken.

"This is a new tradition." He bent to kiss her softly and quickly on the lips. "Just open it, okay?"

Jo blushed and opened the ornament. A diamond ring nestled among glittery silver and white cotton. Pale, her eyes went wide. She dropped the ornament and ring, but Ken caught them. He was on one knee in front of her.

"Ken--" Jo choked, and pressed trembling hands to her face as it flushed cherry red.

"Say yes?"

Everyone cheered as Jo held out her hand, and he slipped the ring on her finger.

Maurice cheered with the rest of them, but it was an effort. The sound caught in his throat and he wilted a little inside. He retreated to the edge of the counter, to sit and kick his legs and watch the decorating party turn into an engagement party.

"Maurice." Lanie wheeled over and pivoted her chair so she could watch everyone else gathered around Jo and Ken. With all the noise of talk and laughter, it was a given no one could hear her talking to him. "Tell me something."

"Sure." He could barely tear his gaze away from Holly, who had her arm around Jo and nearly bounced up and down with excitement, chattering away.

"How serious are you about Holly?"

He thought about making a joke, but that defense no longer worked. He wilted a little more. "Serious enough to hurt."

"I think you're just what Holly needs."

"Hah! Five inches tall, invisible and impossible to hear, and we can only talk four times a year, if we're lucky. Yeah, she needs me like a..." He couldn't think of something miserable enough to compare himself to.

"Holly needs an enchanted prince, and you're pretty close. The question is if you'll stick around after you get your size and your magic back. I don't want you hurting her."

"Never!"

Lanie studied him solemnly for several long moments, then a slow smile graced her face. She nodded. "That's good enough for me. Let's see what we can do to get the two of you together."

"It's gonna take a miracle, that's all I can say. "

"Maurice..." Mischief lit her dark eyes. "It's Christmas. It's the season of miracles."

Sunday, December 2

They -- whoever "they" were -- lied.

It was not lonely at the top.

Bethany Miller found it danged crowded. The number of people who gathered around her growing stardom made her feel downright claustrophobic. What had made her think she wanted this?

Oh, yeah. To show all those idiots in school who made her feel invisible. Other than a few friends, starting with Athena Longfellow, it was like an invisibility cloak had been wrapped around her all her life. Except when she got on stage. Then she became visible, and audible -- everybody watched her, everybody listened. Meaning no sense of privacy. Sometimes she felt like her godmother, Angela, was a faerie godmother who had gone too far with a spell designed to protect her. The same sense of "go away, we don't like you here," that drove most troublemakers away from Neighborlee seemed to make her invisible to everyone in town.

When she won a talent competition, got an agent, started doing commercials and small recurring roles on networks like Nickelodeon, then she became visible.

Which wasn't all it was cracked up to be.

With shooting wrapped on her third feature film, she looked back on those days of invisibility and anonymity with nostalgia. What insanity had driven her here? She could be perfectly happy right now, flipping burgers at her father's diner, being a perpetual student at Willis-Brooks College, clerking for Angela, spending her weekends hanging with Athena and her gang of computer geeks.

And yes, trying not to be jealous that Athena was now engaged and deliriously happy. But no, she had taken the path that meant she couldn't even walk to the corner drugstore to get the paper without being recognized and mobbed.

"I don't suppose you two could help me go invisible for a few weeks?" she said, half-joking, to Alexi and Megan Ambrosius.

Her Las Vegas magician friends were real friends, met and made in her days of living from commercial to commercial. They had taken a nervous, first-time-away-from-home adolescent under their wings and had remained friends ever since.

Bethany could only go home to Neighborlee for Christmas if she could lose the press and scandalmongers who chased her. Athena's Artificial Intelligence friend, London Holiday, arranged for airplane tickets for her father and a condo in the middle of the desert. No one would know when Ben Miller was leaving to spend Christmas with Bethany this year. Not like the disaster of last year, when every time they turned around someone was flashing a camera at them or banging on their door. If they spent the entire holiday indoors, they would be safe. Bethany knew better than to trust to luck. Sometimes it felt like the whole planet was focused on finding her. And honestly, she didn't want to sit in the condo for three solid weeks.

She wanted to go home to Neighborlee, sleep in her own bed, eat at the family diner, hang with Athena, and make sure Wallace was good enough for her. Bethany was happy for her best friend, and jealous. Because honestly, the more successful she got, the more miserable she felt. Which made no sense.

Okay, just be happy with a peaceful Christmas with Dad. Leave it at that. Don't ruin things by wishing for more.

"And invisibility for my dad, too," Bethany added on a sigh.

"Sweetheart, you know our magic is little more than illusions," Megan began. She squeaked and turned red when Alexi nudged her hard enough she nearly fell out of the booth in the dark corner of the casino where they were currently working.

"I don't know any such thing." Bethany pulled out her ace card. She had held it to herself, a secret treasure, for the past five years. "I know you can do real magic. I saw you."

"Real magic?" Alexi gave her a convincing frown of confusion.

"Just as real as your pointed ears." Bethany smirked when he reached up to yank his tangled mane of silky blond hair down around his ears. "I've seen you two working real magic. Of course, I've been looking for it." She played all her cards. "So, are you like witches or wizards? Is there a real Hogwarts?"

"Actually--" Alexi jerked at a hard nudge from Megan now. He grinned at his wife. "Whether there is or isn't, that doesn't matter. What makes you want an invisibility spell, in particular?"

"You two seem to have some kind of force field or invisibility spell, so nobody ever mobs you." Bethany sat back in the booth and crossed her arms. "I've seen the groupies come after you, when you finish a show. It's like a switch is flipped or something. One minute they're circling you like vultures. The next, they just don't see you, and they go wandering off. And when we're out like this?" She gestured around the room. "When I'm with you, nobody sees me, either."

"She's good," Megan murmured.

"We're magicians. Illusion is what we do," Alexi said with another grin.

"You're more than magicians. So, what are you?" Bethany sat forward, elbows planted on the table, projecting belligerence and determination as hard as she could.

"Faeries." He jumped from the force of the elbow in his side, but laughed, totally destroying the scowl he directed at Megan. "All right. Fae. Just wanted to see if I could shock you."

"She's beyond shocking," Megan said. "She needs our help. Bethy ... think Faire Folk. Lords and ladies. Tam Lin."

"Are we talking *Lord of the Rings* stuff?" Bethany said.

"Well ... that's a good analogy. But instead of going into the West, our ancestors created the Enclaves, where time passes differently and you can cram a whole lot into what seems like a crack in the sidewalk." She shrugged. "The simplified explanation."

"Then why are you out here?"

"It's not really that great in there." Alexi linked hands with Megan, intertwining their fingers. "We like it out here. We have jobs out here, things to do. And believe it or not, sometimes it's more fun to do things the non-magical way."

"What Alexi is so delicately avoiding saying is that I'm a Halfling. That means my father is Fae, but my mother was Human. My Fae relatives like me a whole lot more once we married --"

"My family has a lot of clout," he muttered.

"But they weren't so welcoming for the last two centuries. Old habits die hard."

"Two centuries." Bethany took a few seconds to get her breath back, but she was relatively talented at thinking on her feet. That gift had gotten her through some really wretched scripts.

"Okay, so you make like the Cheshire Cat and vanish when things get heavy. I envy you." She chewed on that idea for a few moments. "So, how can I get some of that without making you hang with me? Do I have to get a bodyguard? I just want my freedom of movement, some privacy for the holidays." She sighed. "Am I whining too much?"

"Not at all," Megan said, and reached across the booth to catch hold of Bethany's hand. "You're sensitive enough to be miserable."

"A bodyguard might be a good idea," Alexi said slowly. He leaned back in the booth and slouched, arms crossed over his chest, his eyes going cloudy and distant.

"You can't just give me a bracelet or necklace or anything to wear, when I want to vanish?" Bethany felt a little queasy all of a sudden. She honestly hadn't expected to get answers so quickly. She had been mostly joking when she asked about magic.

Note to self: Don't joke about things you don't understand, in case they turn out to be real.

Bodyguard, Alexi had said. Something made Bethany think there were other kinds of bodyguards than the ones in dark suits with radio plugs in their ears, shoulder harnesses, and James Bond gizmos. She didn't want one. The studio had hired a bodyguard for her when she went to Greece for some location shooting. The jerk decided he needed to guard her body full-time, day and night, with as much physical contact as possible.

Bethany wondered if he was still singing soprano.

"My cousin, Hargrove." Alexi snapped his finger.

"Hargrove?" Megan shook her head. "I don't remember him."

"He has a medical condition." He leaned across the table and lowered his voice. "He can't permanently turn off an invisibility spell he triggered when he was a kid."

"And that helps me how?" Bethany said slowly, while her mind raced through dozens of implausible scenarios. "Can he, like, infect me with it? But how do I turn it off so I can work? And how would that help me go home for Christmas? That's what I really want."

"He can wrap the invisibility field around you, enough to just blur you so you can still talk to people but nobody recognizes you. Or he can turn you... Well, the field is so strong, if he let it go full force, people could walk through you."

"That's more like phased out into another dimension," she murmured.

"Almost. Harry has a lot of control, except for turning the whole thing off. If he wants to be seen, he can be. And he can do the same for you."

"Sounds like a good idea."

Questions immediately sprang to mind:

Would he mind spending the holidays with strangers?

Would he mind going to Neighborlee?

She had always believed magic protected Neighborlee, but would that magic work against someone who had real magic?

Most important: Did Harry know who she was, and would he turn out to be an irritating fan?

Chapter Two

Monday, December 3

"Hargrove? Hargrove! Wake up, boy!"

The admonishment, in the tired, worried voice of Uncle Mortimer, was punctuated with a slap that served quite adequately to bring Harry back to consciousness.

He lay still, trying to remember what had knocked him unconscious. A few cautious sniffs answered him. The stink of Human gunpowder and several sophisticated Fae explosives filled his sinuses. Memory streamed back into his head. He had been playing with a new kind of controlled explosive device, to help in archaeological excavations. Obviously, the charm controlling the direction of the explosion had malfunctioned.

Why were people hitting him?

"He must be conscious now. He's fading out," said his sister, Hera-Jane.

That yanked his attention off trying to figure out what he did wrong. "Fading out?"

"You were visible, the entire time you were unconscious." She fumbled across his chest until she found his shoulders, then shook him. "Come on, Harry, rise and shine."

"I'm always invisible when I sleep. I have to concentrate to be seen." He opened his eyes, relieved he could still see. That explosion had felt uncomfortably close to his face.

Uncle Mortimer patted his cheek. "I wish gunpowder had been around when I was your age. It's quite the thing to make messes when you're only 100 years old. When you're pushing nine centuries, well, you have to pretend to have some dignity."

"Especially when your cloaking spells aren't what they used to be and you can't hide the evidence," Hera-Jane added. "Uncle Morty...the Chinese had gunpowder back when you were a child."

"Hmm, yes, but the Asian Fae Enclaves were quite isolationist back then. They wouldn't share anything, least of all such clever

Human toys." Their wild-haired uncle nodded once more for punctuation. "Quite all right now, lad? Back to normal?"

"Close enough. How much can you see me?" Harry asked.

"Not a speck. We can smell you, though." His sister sat back and wrinkled up her nose. "Well, are you any closer to success?"

"I think so. Not much, but at least I didn't trip any of the fire suppression and reconstruction spells." Harry allowed himself a few flickers of triumph over that, before diving into the new puzzle. "You say I was *visible* when I was unconscious?"

"Something disrupted the invisibility spell for a little while. It just proves my theory that the malfunction lies in the Ether connection that powers this particular invisibility spell. You need more research, lad." Uncle Mortimer slapped in the general direction of Harry's invisible shoulder and heaved himself to his feet. Chuckling, he tottered out of the laboratory. Standard housecleaning spells had cleared the damage while they talked.

"I'd much rather you concentrated on doing new things," his sister said, "rather than fiddling with spells that are nearly as old as time itself. Less chance of something semi-sentient deciding to punish you. The really old spells have a life of their own. They don't like being tweaked." She reached out with her unerring sisterly sense, caught the sides of his face in her hands, and bent down to kiss his forehead. "Please wash up and come to breakfast visible." As she got to her feet, she made a face. "Bleah. Gunpowder. It tastes even worse than it smells."

"Well, you've learned something new before breakfast, just like me." Harry grinned when Hera-Jane strolled out of the laboratory, muffling giggles that sounded like nightingales.

The communications sphere shimmered into being while Harry relaxed in the hot tub -- another wonderful invention of Humans. Fortunately for him, and whoever might be calling at this time of the morning, the sphere remained opaque.

"I gave at the office," Harry said.

Alexi's rich, rolling laughter made him grin. Nothing like a call from his favorite rebellious cousin to take a morning from interesting and frustrating to fun.

"How's that non-magical betting system working out for you?" Harry snapped his fingers to bring a towel over and got out of the hot tub. He tapped the communications sphere, activating it so it shimmered into transparency. Alexi and Megan's faces appeared before him. He was glad he had opted for the towel.

Harry wasn't a skinny geek by any means, but Alexi had inherited the family build and good looks, along with the family curse. Harry was white-blond and buff, but Alexi had it cubed. Still, despite all the advantages Alexi had in looks and freedom and a real job in the Human world, along with a smart, fun wife who hadn't needed to trap him by going into Need, Harry preferred his smaller troubles. Alexi had nearly been doomed to spending eternity without magic. Megan had rescued him from that. While Harry wouldn't have minded being rescued by someone like her, he knew it would still rankle from time to time. He had a ridiculous longing to be the White Knight, rescuing damsels in distress.

"What's up, Cuz?" He gave an extra yank to his towel.

"We have a job for you," Megan said.

"You and your invisibility spell," Alexi added with that grin that had always meant really cool, really loud, really messy adventures when they were boys.

"I'm there." Harry snapped clothes onto himself. "Just tell me where and when."

Tuesday, December 4

Angeloria had a highly inconvenient allergy to mistletoe and holly. Usually, that wouldn't be much of a problem. How many months of the year did mistletoe flourish, after all?

Unfortunately, Lori's need to flee the Fae Enclaves coincided with Christmas. The last thing she wanted was to retreat back into the shelter of the Enclave where she had grown up, because that would leave her prey to her matchmaking great-aunts and their odious choices of the perfect husband for her. Lori didn't want to get married to someone who would keep her anchored in the Enclaves for the rest of her life. She wanted an adventurer who explored the Human world on a regular basis. Someone who thought satellite feed and a DVD collection to rival all the major studios were basic necessities of life.

If she went back to the Fae Enclaves, her great-aunts would force her into dreary formal wear. Then they would drag her through a long chain of visits and teas and social functions that made Socrates' public execution sound like a jolly good time.

Besides, regular contact with the Human world provided her with a fresh, ongoing supply of dark chocolate and diet cherry cola. To do that, though, she needed to get out of the hotel. She had retreated here to hide from the mad proliferation of holiday decorations before she sneezed herself to death, while generating rainbow-streaked light shows three yards in diameter.

"It's not even something a doctor could help me with," Lori explained, when her two best friends snapped their fingers and conjured up boxes of allergy medicine and calamine lotion, and settled down in her favorite suite at the Waldorf-Astoria. "It's psychosomatic. I was traumatized as a child, when Dickens had Scrooge talk about a stake of holly through the heart. I was there when he read it aloud and laughed at what a clever line it was." She shuddered. "You can't imagine the mental image."

"So it's all in your head," Wilfred murmured. He glanced at Philomena.

Lori certainly envied them when they grinned and slapped hands in congratulations before turning to her with their idea. When was she ever going to find someone who knew what she was thinking almost before she did?

Then again, she didn't completely envy them. How dense could anyone be, not to realize they had already found their soul mates and didn't need to hunt? The two of them were arrested adolescents in some ways. She needed the cleverness of adolescents to hide from her matchmaking aunts, and stay itch-free.

"Distraction," Will said, with a nod for punctuation.

"We'll just keep you busy to keep your mind off it," Phill added.

"How?" Lori demanded, and reached for water to wash down the first allergy pill.

"That's gonna take some thinking. Stay here, have fun with room service, sleep late, and catch up on *Stargate* episodes." She shrugged. "And give us a few days."

"Days?" she nearly shrieked.

"We have to throw your family off your trail. They're going to watch us. If you can't be found, people will expect you to be with us," Will said, getting up and pacing a little. "So we go home, go to our separate homes, do some heavy-duty thinking, and then in a few days we'll come back for you when the heat is off."

"And we'll have some fun, whatever we do, wherever we go," Phill added, nodding for emphasis.

Wednesday, December 5

Will worried about Phill, while his aunties and uncles and matchmaking cousins all worried about him. The pressure was incredible.

Not the pressure to get out of the Enclaves and adventure in the Human realms. Admittedly, that was pretty strong, but not at the point of discomfort. In fact, the other pressures and strains Will felt made the wanderlust itch well nigh pleasantly ticklish.

"Wilfred, it is your duty to talk Philomena into having a thorough examination." Aunt Gustaphina sailed into Will's library that afternoon.

It took a massive outlay of magic to shut down the TV and DVD player so Aunt Gustaphina wouldn't see *Chuck* playing. She was charmed by good-hearted Chuck, his geeky misfit friends and the federal agents sent to protect him, and Will was terrified she would insist on watching the entire season with him. Right now.

Will needed his alone time. Mostly because he was worried about Phill as well. She was his best friend. They had known each other since their nannies met in the park and parked their perambulators next to each other. Will could hardly think straight when Phill was around, but when she wasn't around, he was a total failure. It was like the current powering his brain changed whenever she entered or left the room, and it took him a day or two to adjust. Which meant his life was a mess.

The only solution was to either never go near Phill again, or never let her out of his sight.

"Examination, Aunt Gusty?" he said, dragging his mind away from the addictive subject of Phill. "What kind of examination?"

Actually, Will would be delighted to spend the rest of his existence, every day and night in Phill's company. But he lived in dread of the day Need grabbed hold of her by the hormones and she targeted some lucky young Fae male to bond with him, body and soul and mind. Will couldn't stand the thought of a third member of their team.

Sometimes a Fae woman had total control over the targeting mechanism of Need. Other times, she had no control, and it dragged her wherever the unseen forces of the universe chose. When that happened, she might just leave her intended sweetheart in the dust, wondering if he really was nothing but week-old chopped liver.

"A physical examination, and a charting of her currents." Aunt Gustaphina settled her ethereal, five-century-old, doesn't-look-a-decade-over-two-fifty figure into a chair usually reserved for one of Will's many nieces and nephews.

"Her currents?" Will sank down into his favorite overstuffed leather recliner.

"Men." Mischief sparkled in her eyes. "I will never understand how a man who so thoroughly enjoys being bonded to your mother could raise all his sons to be terrified of Need."

"It's not Need in general, Aunt Gusty." He shook his head, fighting off the image of Philomena tackling some idiot who had never been outside the Enclaves. How could they go on their adventures if she shackled herself to an Enclave-bound weakling? How could he get her to go on any more year-long anthropological studies all over the constantly changing Human world?

"Ah ha! Just as I thought." She slapped her knee with enough force to break it in anyone else as delicate-looking. Aunt Gustaphina made the Man of Steel look like he was made of wet tissue paper.

"What did you thought -- think?"

"You're stuck on Philomena, aren't you?"

"She's my best friend and I don't want her to get shackled to someone who isn't good enough for her."

"You don't want to be left behind. I have a theory, my dear." She stood up with enough force to topple the chair. "I think Philomena is unconsciously holding off the final stage of maturity because she doesn't want to hurt you."

Will swallowed hard and took a few deep breaths to fight the surges of nausea that rolled up through him, large enough to dwarf the waves in *A Perfect Storm*. He had been skirting that idea for years now, trying not to put his deepest darkest fear into words.

If Phill was holding back her maturity for his sake, that meant she was not just an uncommonly strong Fae, but she had recognized, even if only subconsciously, that she and Will weren't meant for each other.

"So what am I gonna do?" He stood up as well, fighting the urge to hide his face in his hands and wail. Maybe slide down to the floor and kick in a temper tantrum he hadn't indulged in for nearly two centuries.

"Let her go. If you have to, get the girl so angry with you that she vows she never wants to see you again. That might just do the trick, dislodge whatever roadblock her mind has created, and get the natural processes rolling." She nodded and looked him over, head to foot and foot to head. "And it wouldn't do you any harm to get out there and throw yourself into the path of a couple girls on the verge of Need. If someone's radar latches onto you, that might jolt Philomena enough to do the trick." She patted Will's arm, then floated up high enough to pat his cheek. "It's for your own good, lovey. You need to settle down. Put down roots. Get yourself bonded to a nice girl and find something useful to do with your life. Studying Humans and bringing back interesting artifacts from their world is fine and dandy when you're only a dozen or so decades old, but you have to grow up. Put away that hobby and do something useful. Your cousin Kevyn was a scatterbrain for the longest time, pretending to be a Human actor. Then he found a nice girl and settled down, and now he's on his way to becoming a fine advocate."

"I hate paperwork and legal briefs and--"

"Yes, I know. Agriculture is a respectable occupation for a Fae, my dear. Consider that." She patted his cheek again, floated down to the floor, and bustled out of the room.

Will sank down into his recliner and sighed. "Anthropology is a respectable career, too." He looked around his comfortable library. Bringing back artifacts for scholars and scientists to study, and all sorts of supplies to feed the Fae addiction to Human-made toys, had made him richer than all the rest of his family put together. Not that he had ever flaunted his wealth. Will lived for the adventure, not the rewards. Telling his interfering, matchmaking relatives that he was set for the rest of his long life wouldn't do him any good. They would still nag him about settling down, getting a job that would keep him in the Enclaves, and finding a wife.

Someone who wasn't Phill.

What Will wanted more than anything else was to just run away. Back to the Human realms.

If he and Phill escorted Angeloria through the Human realms to get her away from her family problems, that would give him lots of time in Phill's company, away from his relatives. And that equaled lots of time to think and get his head on straight.

That was it. Will felt as if several hundred pounds of weight had slid off his shoulders. He would get away, to a place where the air was clearer and there wasn't as much magical static buzzing and ringing through the atmosphere. He loved the rarified air of the Human realms, where a Fae could hear another Fae work magic and pinpoint where it took place. He would get time away, time alone with Phill, and they would figure out this problem together.

How did an adult Fae male approach an adult Fae female and bring up that subject without shocking or horrifying or embarrassing her?

Will wasn't an old-fashioned prude, but some things just weren't done. Discussing Need and why a Fae woman hadn't gone into Need phase yet, at the mature age of 243, was one of them.

~~~~~

"If you ask me," Great-great-uncle Throckmorton wheezed, "it's all that time spent away from the Enclaves. It can't be good for you. It puts a strain on your whole system. Maybe even shuts down essential functions." He stepped away from the scrying globe that currently displayed a slowly rotating image of Phill's body, with all sorts of writhing, swirling, intertwining colors displaying her various physical and magical functions and statistics.

"So I'm doomed?" Phill sighed, sitting on the edge of the examination table, and kicked her legs.

Thank goodness she didn't have to put on a ridiculous never-meets-in-the-back Human examination gown. Sitting on the examination table in her great-great-uncle's medical office simply meant putting herself into the reading field.

"Hardly." He squinted once more at the globe, then took off his spectacles--an affectation, because as one of the premier healers in the ten surrounding Enclaves, he could fix his eyes or any other ailment with little more than a thought. He turned to face her. "My
~~~~~

dear girl, when are you going to take the plunge? I never thought I'd see the day when someone of my bloodline displays such cowardice."

"But I don't want to ruin things." Phill blushed as soon as those words left her lips. It sounded just as lame coming from her as it did in every single movie and book when the hero or heroine refused to take the crucial step to move best friend into true love.

"Uh huh. And what happens when some desperate idiot steps over the line and invades your territory to snatch up Willfred and steals him out of your life forever?" He sank down in his old-fashioned wooden swivel chair, supposedly a gift from Doc Holiday. "It's been my opinion for the last 600 years that the happiest, most stable marriage bondings are the ones where the man and woman choose each other *before* Need strikes. I can't imagine anyone better suited for each other than you and Willfred."

"Me, neither. But you know how the men in his family are mortally terrified of even the mention of Need. His brother nearly had a heart attack when Sephrinia appeared out of nowhere and nearly dragged him off and seduced him."

"Good thing she knew mouth-to-mouth resuscitation," he muttered. Holding an antique Meerschaum pipe tight in his teeth, he poured spearmint-scented bubble solution into the bowl. He winked.

"You're a dirty old...dear." Phill managed a crooked smile. "The thing is, I don't want to kill my best friend with terror if I just come out and say I want to try bonding before Need hits." She sighed again. "If it ever hits. Is something wrong with me?"

"Nothing a good strong dose of romance won't cure. Or a good kick in the pants, whichever is easier to procure."

Phill's pager chimed. A rosy haze surrounded her as she read Will's number and his message on her screen. When it grew thick enough to impede half the message, she impatiently waved the tinted air away.

Found a solution for Lori and whatever ails us. Meet me at the doorway into Neighborlee, one hour.

"Gotta run. Thanks!" She brushed a kiss across Uncle Throckmorton's shiny bald head and dashed from the room.

"My pleasure, kitten." He settled back, making his chair creak and groan. He blew a long streamer of spearmint-scented bubbles that spun around the room, forming dragons that frolicked like puppies. "There is none so blind as she who will not see."

~~~~~

Will loved the town of Neighborlee, and not just because the closest exit from the space-time continuum enclosing the Enclaves was in the Metroparks on the edge of town. Magic created a lovely tingling, energizing and yet paradoxically soothing background atmosphere here. He had used Neighborlee as a doorway into the Human realms for nearly seventy years before realizing someone in this quiet little college town was the source of the magic that had seeped into the air and soil. It had taken him another ten years of haphazard investigation before he tracked down the source.

Divine's Emporium sat like a lynchpin holding the controlling knot of the magical net that protected Neighborlee -- or in another metaphor, sat at the headwaters of the streams of power that spread through the town. He had been delighted to bring Phill here and share his discovery with her. They had spent many happy weeks here, getting to know Angela.

They had brought Angela artifacts that needed to stay in the Human realms, and yet Humans weren't quite ready to handle. Some things slept in the Human atmosphere. If exposed to the condensed power and magical atmosphere of the Fae realms, they might explode into life and alert sentience. *Explode* being the operative and much-to-be-avoided word. Divine's grew stronger with the slowly growing presence of magical, slumbering items.

Will and Phill loved to spend the holidays every few years in Neighborlee. They had discovered many children with a touch of magic in their blood. They had fun thinking up amazing gifts for the children, and hiding little treasures all through their houses, or at school. It amazed and amused them that Humans could pick up $10 bills all over town in the space of a few weeks, and not realize they were hundreds of dollars richer. Mostly this was because the treasures came in small increments and were spent almost immediately on needed items, a treat for the family, or to pay off a debt to a friend.

However, with several years between each visit, there were too many changes in the friends they had made last time. Unless they were touched with magic themselves, like the special ones Angela called the guardians, most people didn't remember them. Will and
~~~~~

Phill couldn't figure out how to get around the time differential between the Fae realms and the Human realms, other than settling in Neighborlee and actually living there, year-round.

"Wouldn't that horrify the matchmaking uncles and aunties?" Will muttered. He paced in front of the cave where Phill would emerge soon, and studied the landscape of the Metroparks in winter. A quick check told him it was December fifth. Only nineteen more shopping days until Christmas. He knew what he wanted for Christmas this year, but the problem was convincing Phill that her favorite playmate was someone she wanted to grow ancient with.

"Maybe I should just stay in the Human realms and find a nice girl with a touch of Fae blood," he mused aloud. "Yeah, that'd work. Lots of Halflings around. Settle down here. If she's stable enough, if the magic is strong enough, make her a Changeling and build a bond. Who really needs Need, anyway? I'm all for freedom of choice." His voice shook a little as he tried to lie to himself. He winced as it grew loud enough to echo softly, breaking the snowy hush of the twilight before dawn.

Who am I trying to kid? He stared out into the white and stark black of the trees in winter. *Phill's the only one for me. I have to trust in the magic of Neighborlee -- and get some really good advice from Angela -- and figure out how to state my case. I'll watch the Humans. See how they manage courtship. I'll use the next three weeks for my campaign. I'll keep Phill here in Neighborlee, and I'll win her heart. And if I don't get a kiss under the mistletoe on Christmas Eve... I have to get a kiss under the mistletoe on Christmas Eve. That's all there is to it. I'm not leaving Neighborlee until Phill and I have crossed the line. Either she's with me forever, or we're apart forever.*

He felt as if an enormous weight had fallen off his shoulders with that decision. And the next moment, he felt as if that weight had bounced back and crushed him.

Forever, without Phill?

~~~~~

Phill sank back against the cave wall, feeling like she had been punched just below her ribs. She needed to learn how to breathe again. She had been hoping to talk to Will about them, about making a commitment and hopefully triggering Need.

What she overheard made it very clear to her he hated Need,
~~~~~

hated the whole bonding concept.

What's wrong with me? Why can't he see that we're best friends, we've been together all our lives, and we should stay together all our lives? We're perfect for each other. She sighed, muffling the sound just as she had muffled her magic when she emerged through the doorway through the space-time continuum. *Obviously Will doesn't think we're perfect for each other. So what am I going to do? I want him. I need him, even if Need refuses to kick in.*

Some of her interfering aunties believed Need would never kick in *because* she spent so much time with Will. His presence prevented her from taking that final step to maturity. The nudge of deep magic that forcibly brought two partners together into soul and mind and physical wedlock, according to the aunties, refused to activate in his presence. That meant Need did not approve of Will as her eternal partner.

Phill decided right then: deep magic sucked. Who was the idiot who'd woven something so uncontrollable and nearly impossible to decipher into the blood and bone of all Fae from the beginning of time? If she could get hold of one of the ancient time travel spells, she would go back to the idiot and smack his head against a wall for a couple of years until he straightened out his thinking.

It occurred to her that such vicious thinking was totally out of character. Could it be a twinge of Need trying to awaken? Was that a good sign, or a bad one?

Enough tangling your head and your heart into knots. She took a deep breath, straightened her shoulders, and pasted a smile on her face. She used a spatter of magic to put some color back into her cheeks and a sparkle of excitement in her eyes. After all, she was in Neighborlee, the most magical spot in the entire northern hemisphere. Disneyland wasn't even a close second. Then she stepped out of the cave.

"Hey, what'd you come up with?"

The sound of her voice made Will leap five feet into the air. She projected a rosy haze into the air when she was flustered -- Will shot off purple sparks. An entire cloud surrounded him, whizzing in orbit as he slowly settled back down to the ground.

"Neighborlee at Christmas." He spread his arms, gesturing to indicate the entire town lying before them, just visible through the snowy trees of the parklands.

"Yeah. What about it?"

"It's Lori's answer. Bring her here to Neighborlee. It's busy enough to take her mind off things. All that magic spinning around. It'll cloud her trail, at the very least. If anyone tries to follow her and drag her back, they'll get lost here. We're such a part of Neighborlee, if anybody shows up, we'll sense it and we'll have time to get Lori out of town before anybody finds her. Brilliant, huh?"

"And it gives us a good excuse to spend the entire season here."

Phill envisioned all the fun they had at previous Christmases, all the magical, secret giving and spying and frolicking she and Will enjoyed so much. While they were busy helping spread Christmas joy, she could campaign to impress on Will just how much they belonged together.

At the very least, she would enjoy one more magical, giving Christmas season with Will before their lives changed forever.

"Absolutely," she said. "Lori needs this. It's perfect." She turned and let her Fae instincts point her in the direction of Divine's. She felt the warm, gentle pulses of magic emanating from the shop all the way out here. "Neighborlee, and Divine's Emporium, at Christmas. What could be more magical?"

If she had to, she'd sit Angela down for an all-night, girls-only gabfest and get some advice, or maybe a Human love potion, and ambush Will. He was hers and she was his, but getting him to open his eyes and realize the truth -- and enjoy it -- would be the hardest thing she would ever do.

Chapter Three

Thursday, December 6

"She's got magic," Harry whispered. He studied Bethany through the curtains while the emcee warmed up the audience for Alexi and Megan's last show of the night.

"You might be right." Megan adjusted her top hat. "There is something about her that makes my fingertips tingle. I just can't figure out what. If there's Fae blood, it's mixed with something that muddies the waters." She patted his back. "You're starting to fade."

"Oh? Sorry." Harry concentrated on his anti-invisibility spell and turned back to watching Bethany Miller in her shadowy corner table. That big, floppy hat and garish muumuu couldn't hide her, yet dressing in loud, obnoxious clothes did trick people into ignoring her. Somewhat.

Harry turned his vision sideways, looking into the 'tweening spaces, those half-step areas between dimensions. His long-term invisibility made it easy to slip halfway into the next dimension.

A soft, rainbow-streaked corona shimmered around Bethany, marking her as someone who had been touched by magic for so long, it had become embedded in her essence. The colors didn't quite clash with her outfit, but it was enough to make his eyes ache after a while. Still, he kept watching. She fascinated him. He loved puzzles, and Bethany had just presented him with one.

"So, she wants to be invisible?"

"She wants to spend the holidays with her father without being mobbed every time she steps outside," Megan said. "She's a nice girl who doesn't enjoy the rat-race of stardom. She refuses to change and act like a star, and that makes her even more popular. Kind of like a girl who isn't in Need is a whole lot more attractive."

Harry blushed, and his concentration slipped so he felt himself fading out. Which was actually a good thing. He wasn't about to admit to anyone he wished he knew the terror of being the target of a woman in Need. None of the girls he had grown up with had targeted him. It was humiliating. Hera-Jane maintained that if he socialized more, so people realized he had grown up into something of a stud, he would be hunted. Harry was too busy with his experiments to find out. Although, this adventure would be an experiment, wouldn't it?

"She doesn't mind having a stranger around?"

"Funny, that's the same thing she said about you." Megan gave her top hat one more tiny adjustment.

"We're on, sweetheart." Alexi caught up with them, wrapped an arm around Megan's waist, and kissed her for luck as he did every night. A kiss that packed enough heat into a two-second liplock, Harry burst out in sweat. They stepped out onto the stage.

He gulped, locked down his counter-spell so he wouldn't fade out at an inopportune moment, and headed for the side entrance. Time to meet his assignment.

He stepped into the supper club seating area and meandered around the perimeter to the booth where Bethany waited. On stage, Alexi kept up the patter while Megan searched the audience for the first volunteer assistant. All the women watched Alexi, all the men watched Megan. Harry felt slightly nauseous from the rising pheromones. Didn't these Humans have any self-control? Especially when it came to two entertainers who made it very clear they were married to each other?

He didn't see anything wrong with window-shopping, as it were, and appreciating what was on display. But Harry drew the line at plotting how to break the glass and steal what was inside.

"Bethany?" he murmured when he reached her table. Harry admired her self-control, so she didn't even flinch or look his way, betraying her disguise. He held up the half of Alexi's business card that served as his identification.

Bethany peered from under her floppy hat and slid her half of the card across the table toward him. She didn't take her fingertips off the card until he matched up his half to hers.

"Harry Morton," he said, and held out his hand. Bethany's slim, strong little hand slid into his. Something sparked, almost a buzz, between their fingers.

"Static electricity." She offered a crooked little smile and a whisper of laughter as she jerked her hand away.

"Uh. Yeah." Harry slid into the booth facing her while he gathered his thoughts. She had felt that? She had soaked up more magic than he had first guessed.

Fascinating.

"I think Alexi insisted on all this cloak and dagger just for the fun of it," she said, as the audience applauded the first illusion of the evening. She grinned, which made an inexplicable world of difference for Harry. If she had scowled or showed reluctance in any way, he didn't know what he would have thought of her.

"Yep, that's my favorite cousin."

"You look like him." Bethany offered an awkward little smile.

"You think so?" He glanced at Alexi, who stepped back and held up the silk purse on a pole, so Megan could demonstrate there was nothing in it. Real magic made things so much easier for magicians, Harry mused, but Alexi and Megan insisted on practicing sleight of hand, doing it the way full Humans did. He supposed it was all in the challenge.

"He has more glitz, but there's a strong resemblance. Of course, combing your hair back like that and dressing so casual, that makes people kind of pass over you. So, you're really good at this invisibility thing?"

"Umm... What exactly did they tell you about me?"

"Oh, I figured out the whole not-quite-Human thing a while ago. I just never confronted them with it." Bethany blushed and looked at her hands clasped on the table in front of her.

Something dropped inside his chest and warmth stole over him. He wanted to protect her. He wanted to take the paparazzi and the other bozos stealing her privacy, and send them to the Dungeon Dimensions for a couple hundred years. Nobody he knew blushed. The simple little reaction made her seem small and delicate and vulnerable.

Which she was anything but. He had seen her first movie, the tough chick who turned her world upside down to save it, who devised bombs and weapons from nothing to protect innocents. Even with that blush fading from her cheeks, he sensed a lot of similarities between the Bethany sitting before him now and the girl on the screen. It made no sense, but Harry didn't care.

"So, say something." Her smile went crooked.

"You're pretty calm about it. A lot of people would probably be freaking out, faced with the fact of a lot of other dimensions of reality, side-by-side with the one they know. I've always wondered what the CIA and FBI and all those foreign intelligence agencies and governments would do, if they knew about the Fae realms. If they'd maybe try to bomb us out of existence, or prosecute us as illegal aliens or whatever."

"So, who was here first? Fae or Humans?"

Harry sat for five seconds with his mouth hanging open, stumped by that question. That was definitely something for the Ether Lexicon. For all he knew, that was part of the no-need-to-know information the Lexicon sometimes stubbornly refused to divulge. Then he laughed. Bethany blushed again, but she grinned.

How come girls like her don't exist in the Enclaves?

~~~~~

"So, what do you think?" Megan said as she stepped into the lounging part of her and Alexi's dressing room backstage.

Alexi and Harry had gone to get their car and bring it to the backstage entrance, for a quick getaway. Megan had confided in Bethany that she thought Harry was cute, so excited about riding in a real, Human-made car.

"I like him. How does his wife feel about him spending the holidays with me and my Dad?" Bethany said.

"No wife." Megan shrugged and slipped into her clogs before sitting down on the other end of the couch. "Which is a total injustice. Alexi says the girls can't see past his science experiments and his research, to the really great guy under the brainy persona."

"What kind of science experiments?" Bethany imagined Harry doing a Nutty Professor routine, his lab coat smeared with stains, maybe scorched in places. It fit. How long since she had let herself feel anything but mild social friendship with a man?

Maybe the fact that he didn't ask for her autograph, didn't ogle her figure, had a lot to do with the attraction. Because yes, she admitted to a strong attraction between them, from the moment that zap of static electricity sent a lovely, hot shiver down her back.

It was great to realize she was a normal woman after all, not a frightened, frigid little teasing twit, as that last studio-arranged date accused her of being.

This was going to be a great Christmas.

A knock on the door, then it opened and her heart did a funny little skip when she saw Harry, and the way his gaze zeroed in on her all the way across the room.
~~~~~

"Ready?" He stepped into the room and held out a hand. "This might tingle a little."

"Kind of like a force field or tractor beam or something wrapping around a ship?" she offered.

Harry's eyes widened and his mouth dropped open a little, and that funny feeling in her stomach turned squirmy. Had she turned him off already?

Then he grinned. That lovely zing climbed her arm when their hands touched. A buzzing sensation raced across her bare skin. It tickled and massaged somewhere between her skin and her bones.

"Wow." She flinched when her voice sounded a little off, not quite hollow.

"Good job," Megan said. "I have to concentrate to get past the deflection."

"Deflection?"

"I've done some testing. It's not quite invisibility, when other people are inside the field with me. The more people I gather up, the more it stretches and loses its strength," Harry explained as they headed out the door. "I've run some experiments, and electronics seem less affected by the magic than eyes and other senses."

"So the security cameras can see us, and the guys in the control room, but people walking down the hall can't?" Bethany giggled. "What about when we talk?"

"Same with sounds. What I've found interesting is that digital cameras pick me up with minimal blurring, but old-fashioned cameras, with film to expose, don't see anything at all."

"It's like they postulated in some...oh, I can't remember the titles, but there were some books I read that claimed science and magic couldn't co-exist. Technology works against magic."

"Something like that," Megan said.

"How come you can hear us?" Bethany asked, as they stepped out the back entrance of the casino. She scanned the parking lot for paparazzi and assorted lunatics. The latest one claimed they had been lovers in four previous lives, so she had to marry him or else bring about the end of the world.

"Harry wants me to hear him."

"And she's family. When Megan broke the family curse on Alexi, it created a bond..." Harry sighed, offering her a lopsided grin that made him seem so very young. "It's a long story."

"We'll have plenty of time for talking later." Megan gestured at a dark silver Lexus pulling up to the door. Alexi rolled down the window to wave at them. They got into the car without anyone reacting or even noticing them.

"How are you going to include my Dad in the invisibility field?" she asked, when they were heading for the house Alexi had rented for her on the edge of the city. "He's not going to be too good about holding hands all the time."

"Oh. Yeah." Harry blushed as he let go of her hand. Bethany almost grabbed hold of it again. "A lot of it is control and proximity. Once I've got the field anchored on both of you, we can be five yards apart before the protection is threatened."

"The stretching thing you mentioned, right?" She nodded, and was delighted with the pleased light in Harry's eyes, like her favorite teacher when she learned her lessons well. Bethany hoped there was a lot Harry could teach her in the three weeks they were together.

Friday, December 7

"We've got a date." Maurice perched on the information desk in the center of the Neighborlee Library. He watched Holly climb to the top of the ladder and hang her fourth bunch of mistletoe and holly from the track lighting. "You and me, Christmas Eve, under the mistletoe. Got that, Holly Berry?"

In his imagination, he heard Holly laugh and promise him. He would get a promise from her tonight, when he visited her dreams.

Dream kisses were great, but he wanted real ones, flesh and blood kisses. Holly would remember that kind of kiss the next day. All the things they said to each other, all the adventures they had in her dreams: where did those dreamtime memories go, when she woke up? Into smoke and thin air?

"Miss Holly?" A gaggle of boys, all in that missing-tooth-and-tangled-hair stage, gathered around the base of the ladder. They watched her adjust the clump of mistletoe, ribbons, tiny gold balls, and holly. "Whatcha doing?"

"Hanging the mistletoe, of course." She smiled down at them. "You troublemakers aren't trying to look up my skirts, are you?"

"Ewwww!" they chorused, almost in unison.

Maurice took comfort from the soprano tones of the chorus. They were too young for their voices to crack and change, or to be interested in anatomy lessons -- and young enough to think such foolery was gross.

Besides, she wore slacks and a bulky sweater. His Holly was way too smart to give those future juvenile delinquents even a chance of an accidental glimpse.

She half-slid down the ladder. "How does it look?" Holly laughed when the boys shrugged and gave each other confused looks. They were obviously too young to care about the finer points of interior decorations or holiday traditions, as well.

"What's it for?" the first speaker asked. He had obviously been dubbed the spokesman for the entire group. Maurice had long suspected that boys at that age had something of a hive mind, moving like swarms of dirty, noisy, constantly eating insects. They became ravenous wild dog packs when adolescence worked its warped chemical magic on them.

"Oh, mistletoe and holly are good luck. They ward off the evil spirits that will try to invade during the dark and shorter days of winter, and they help bring light and warmth, and longer days, and eventually spring. The Druids considered mistletoe a sacred plant and used it in magical potions. Harvesting mistletoe was a sacred ritual and crucial to their magic and the protection and health and life of the tribes of Britannia."

"What's Britannia?" one boy asked from the edge of the swarm.

"That's those big books that all look alike over in the corner," another boy said, jerking his thumb toward the reference section.

"Britannia is the old name for England." Holly's face turned rosy as she muffled laughter. She gestured for the boys to move aside, and they obeyed with only minimal hesitation. Proof of just how much the boys adored Miss Holly and generally obeyed her without question. At least, the boys under the age of ten.

They formed an aisle to allow her to fold up the stepladder and drag it over to the arched doorway that led into another room in the massive old house-turned-library. The leader of the group dashed over to the table where Holly had left the last few clumps of mistletoe. He picked up the tray and brought it over before she finished steadying and positioning her ladder.

Maurice decided he wanted to keep an eye on such an alert child. The ones who could put faint clues together and figure out what people were doing, what they needed, and how to get in good with them, ended up as the ringleaders and mischief-makers.

"Thank you, Tony." Her eyes sparkled as she picked up a clump and held it over his head. "Is there a special girl you're hoping to catch under the mistletoe this year?"

"What would I do with her when I catch her?" young Tony asked, his mouth and his voice curling up in a sneer.

Maurice breathed a sigh of relief. These boys were too young to realize how great those differences were between boys and girls.

"You kiss her, of course." Holly burst out laughing when the boys made sounds of disgust and their faces wrinkled up in various levels of nausea and revulsion. "It's for good luck. It makes sure the coming year is healthy and wealthy and full of success." She bent down and whispered loudly enough for the entire swarm to hear. "And it makes sure that the other girls leave you alone."

"Can I kiss you, then, Miss Holly?" an until-then silent little boy asked from the edge of the group.

"Why would you want to kiss me?"

"You ain't got cooties like the girls do."

"I'm a girl." Her face nearly glowed from the effort of holding back laughter. Wisely, Holly picked up another clump of mistletoe and beat a strategic retreat up the ladder to hang it.

"Yeah, but you're a good kind of girl. You're almost as good as being a mom. You're not gross and you don't squeal and you don't get mad at guys 'cause we forgot to give you a Valentine and all that dumb stuff."

"You're even better than a mom," Tony said. "You don't make us eat gross stuff like salad and you let us eat cookies in the reading room and you don't yell at us to wipe our feet."

"That's because Miss Myrtle catches you at the door." She concentrated on the twisty that fastened the clump of decoration to the nail pounded into the woodwork at the top of the archway.

Maurice flew over and kept watch over her, just in case she lost her balance, caught up in this very interesting and slightly disturbing conversation. He had a vision of Holly tumbling off the top of the ladder and the boys scattering like roaches when the light came on -- or all of them clumping together to try to catch her. He knew Holly, and she would rather break a leg than risk hurting one of her children by landing on them.

"And you know what kinds of books we like, and you know great stories, and you belong to us because you ain't got a boyfriend," another boy offered.

"I belong to you, huh?" She still smiled, but the laughter had left her eyes and her blush faded to her normal indoor coloring.

"You belong to me, Holly. I'm your boyfriend," Maurice said, as loudly as he could. After all, if other people who got soaked in magic could finally see and hear him, maybe after a year of hanging around together, she might soak up enough magic to sense his presence. It was Christmas, right? A time of magic and hope. Right?

Yeah, but what good did it do him to be her boyfriend when she didn't remember him in the light of day?

"Yep, you belong to us. So nobody's allowed to kiss you but us. Right, guys?" Tony said, nodding so hard Maurice's neck ached in sympathy.

"You make a very convincing argument." Holly climbed down the ladder. "But what if I already have a boyfriend, and you just don't see him?"

"What kind of a boyfriend doesn't come see you at work or bring you flowers or candy or nothing?" His bottom lip stuck out in pique. "My sister's boyfriend is bothering her all the time. She says she likes it. She says that shows he's jealous enough to want to check on her, and that means he's really serious." He nodded for emphasis. "Mo's an okay guy. He doesn't get all gooshy in front of us. Know what I mean? But he told me the important stuff guys need to do to show their girls they like them a whole lot. So if you got a boyfriend and he ain't bringing you things and checking up on you... Well, he ain't good enough for you."

"I figure, if you got a loser boyfriend like that, you got no boyfriend at all," another boy stated, earning nods and murmurs of agreement from the rest of the swarm.

"Hey, that's not fair. I'd bring you stuff all the time, Holly Berry. If I could." Maurice's heart dropped somewhere beyond his toes. "We have lots of fun, don't we? I take you places you never thought of. I'd take you through paintings into other worlds and I'd bring you jewels and cover you in flowers every night. If I could." He sank down to the nearest shelf and his wings drooped. "You know what?

The kids are right. You really don't have a boyfriend, do you?"

"What do I need a boyfriend for, when I have all of you?" Holly summoned a smile.

The grandfather clock in the next room solemnly bonged five times. The boys looked at each other in dismay. Time to go home and get ready for dinner. And those who had wasted their study time at the library were doomed to study after dinner, instead of watching TV or sledding on the hill into the Metroparks. The one the police department kept lit and monitored, and stocked with hot chocolate and carefully tended fires in metal barrels.

"Time to scoot." Holly gestured at the door and all the hats and coats on pegs on the wall, hanging over a long row of little boots standing or leaning or lying on the plastic mats. She let out a yelp when Tony flung his arms around her. "What's that for?"

"Gotta kiss you for good luck." The boy blushed bright red, wide-eyed with terror and embarrassment for a moment. Then he flashed a smile that was missing two teeth on the bottom.

Holly laughed, and the tone of it made Maurice relax, assuring him her pain had fled. The next moment, his stomach tied in knots again and he gripped the edge of the shelf to keep from flying off it or hurling sparks of magic. The boys gathered around, tugging on the hem of her sweater, demanding their kisses, too.

She obligingly bent down and pursed her lips. Before she could do anything more, Tony lunged forward, smashing his lips against her cheek, and darted away. In moments, all of the boys had made their pecking little attack kisses and ran for the wall with their coats. Holly sank down on the second step of the ladder, pressing her fingertips against her cheeks that, fortunately, didn't glisten from all those little boy kisses. She watched the boys clamber over each other, rushing a little more than usual to flee the library.

A smile crept across her lips. Then a sigh escaped her, turning into weary laughter. She rested her chin in her cupped hands and her elbows on her knees, and didn't move until every last boy had vanished through the doors, outside into the growing twilight.

"They're good kids, huh?" Maurice fluttered over from his shelf and landed on her shoulder. "But you and me... We're gonna have the real thing for Christmas. I just wish you could remember me, Holly Berry."

A moment later, Holly stood and folded up her ladder and

moved it to the next site for hanging decorations. Maurice stayed close, prepared to use up all his day's ration of magic to steady her ladder and keep her safe. Several times, she turned to look at the door, as if she could still see and hear the slightly embarrassed, excited boys who had taken a large step toward adulthood without even knowing it.

Maurice wondered with a sinking heart if it would only cause Holly more pain if she could remember him and their dreamtime adventures during the day. The boys were right. What kind of a boyfriend was he, if he couldn't do anything for her, give her anything, visit her during the day?

He had realized something as he watched her interact with the boys. It wasn't really the ability to do things for her and give her things that bothered him. Her treasures were in her books and the adventures of the mind that they shared. What mattered to Maurice, and what he couldn't give Holly, was the pleasure of letting the town of Neighborlee know someone found her interesting. Someone cared about her and wanted to romance her and work to make sure no one else could claim her heart. He was invisible to most of the town, so how could anyone see how much Holly had come to mean to him in the last year?

"And another year to go," he muttered. "All I want for Christmas..." He sighed. "Sometimes I think I'd willingly give up magic for the rest of my life, if I could be visible to you, and full size, and get rid of these wings right now, and stay that way." Another sigh. "You're worth it, Holly Berry, and I wish the whole world could know."

Chapter Four

Saturday, December 8

"Sorry, but I'm not that big on shopping, and that seems to be the major sport among Humans at this time of the year." Lori let out a yelp when Will and Phill each linked an arm through hers and sped her into the dimensional slit. Two steps took them from the Waldorf Astoria, into a snowy morning in woods outside a small town. It faintly rang with undertones of magic. Maybe this self-induced exile would turn out to be interesting?

"There's more to Christmas than presents," Will said.

"More than getting them, he means," Phill said.

"There's giving. And that's enough to keep you busy for a whole year."

"Umm, isn't giving presents to Humans someone else's job?" Lori looked around, as much as blinding brilliant sunlight on dazzling snow allowed.

"Humans give to Humans. It's great. It's like their own kind of magic," Will said. "Now, you are absolutely sworn to secrecy, understand?"

He slowed to a stop. Fortunately, so did Phill, or else Lori would have been dragged sideways for a few steps. They both waited until she nodded agreement.

"A bunch of us sneak out on the Human holidays to help out. It's fun, pretending to be magic-less like them and doing things the hard way. So now, we're letting you in on the fun. Get it?"

"Got it." Lori felt suddenly breathless with anticipation.

"Good!" they chorused, and started up again at double-speed.

Half an hour later, she was still breathless, both from the speed with which her friends deposited her in the middle of Eden, the community center, and from the spectacle of masculine perfection in front of her.

He stood on a tall metal ladder in the lobby, hanging tinsel icicles on the tallest, greenest, prickliest pine tree Lori had ever seen. By virtue of stretching and bending to reach every branch possible, his Willis-Brooks College sweatshirt hiked up constantly, revealing a six-pack guaranteed to induce any woman to join a gym. He moved with that innate, thoughtless grace that only came from good physical condition.

"Hey."

Lori adjusted her gaze and found Mr. Decorating Committee grinning down at her. On top of everything else, he had green-blue eyes and thick, curly lashes and a dimple in the corner of his mouth. Her face warmed as she realized that he had probably caught her checking him out. Then she realized Will and Phill had pulled a vanishing act. She sensed their physical presence in the room, but they were as invisible as freeloaders when the waiter brought the check at the restaurant.

"I could use an extra pair of hands." He nodded at the plastic crates sitting between the legs of the ladder. "Toss some things up to me, so I don't have to keep climbing up and down?"

"Uh ... sure." She bent to pick up the first box of softball-sized crimson ornaments.

Lori wasn't flustered enough to interfere with her survival instincts. There was no way on the planet she wanted to look like a fumble-fingered dimwit. Especially since the ornaments felt like glass instead of the usual cheapo plastic reproductions. Using a couple flickers of magic, she lightly levitated each one up to his outstretched, gorgeous, muscular hands.

"Hey."

"Hey, yourself." Lori matched his grin, delighted when he paused while she dropped the empty box and picked up another.

"You're a good thrower. Natural athlete?"

"Just lucky, I guess."

"What's your name?"

"Angeloria." That was quite enough to reveal at this moment. She didn't need to freak out the guy with her ten layers of pedigree names. It was a royal pain, and then some, to be an aristocrat.

"Short for Christmas Angel?" That dimple just got deeper when he grinned.

"What's your name?"

"Brick. As in 'dumb as a.'" He held out a hand and she lobbed the next ornament up at him.

"I don't think your parents --"

"Cursed me with the family name, Brickley Ashton James Willis."

Lori gestured at his impressive chest, covered with the local college's sweatshirt. "As in?" She tossed, just to have something to concentrate on. Will and Phill had left the building, she sensed. Maybe she wouldn't be angry with them for abandoning her. They knew the people in this town, so they wouldn't leave her at the mercy of a brawny beauty who would turn into a beast without warning. Why not relax and have some Human-style fun?

"Yep, great-grandpappy built it." He caught the next ornament and moved up one step, to stretch higher and reach one last undecorated branch.

"Be careful!" She grabbed the sides of the ladder with both hands when it swayed a little too far off center. When that didn't seem to help, she zapped the ridged rubber grips on the feet of the ladder and anchored them to the tile floor.

"Oh, yeah, that about does it for this side." Brick flashed that crooked movie-star grin at her and headed down the ladder. Fortunately, she hadn't grabbed onto the side with the steps, because she didn't think to let go until he was on the floor. "Thanks. You're a lot stronger than you look. And a good pitcher. Play baseball much?" He kicked aside the empty decoration boxes and stepped around to stand inside the legs of the ladder.

"Uh, no, not really." She finally let go and skipped back a few steps to watch Brick move the ladder about four feet around the perimeter of the tree. "You're not going up there again, are you?"

"Someone's gotta decorate this puppy." He rubbed his palms on the sides of his thighs, checked them, then flashed her another grin. "Since I'm the guilty party, I'm responsible."

"Guilty party?"

"I bought the tree." Nodding, he gestured up to the unadorned side of the tree. "Can I bribe you to stick around and keep tossing to me until it's finished?"

"Hmm, maybe." She stepped back and peeled off her ski jacket to be more comfortable.

"Please? The faeries aren't going to come overnight and decorate, I guarantee."

"We prefer to be called the Fae, not faeries," she snapped, without thinking.

"Yeah, that's what Angela says." He grinned and headed up the ladder again.

"Angela?" Lori decided to be grateful his attention hadn't snagged on her slip when she said *we*.

"The owner of Divine's Emporium. She knows more weird things..." Brick chuckled and held out his hands, gesturing for the next ornament. She complied without thinking. "I'll take you over there after we're done and bribe you with some fancy coffee, okay?"

"Maybe."

She decided, just from that sparkle in his eyes, she could be bribed with a lot less. The coffee, as far as she was concerned, was just an excuse to spend more time in his company.

Will and Phill were right, she realized, as she emptied out the second box for this side of the tree and reached for the third. She just needed a distraction. She actually picked up three ornaments that had mistletoe and holly and didn't even sneeze.

When Brick climbed down and the last box of ornaments was empty, Lori felt a funny little twinge of disappointment. It couldn't be over so soon, could it?

"It's over," he said with a gusting sigh.

He didn't have to sound so mightily relieved, did he?

"Don't know how I would have done it without your help." He gestured with his chin as he folded the ladder and maneuvered it down so it didn't hit any of the passersby as they passed through the main room. "Give me about five minutes to put this away, and then we can fly, okay?"

"Sounds good." Lori felt that funny little jolt in her middle when they were on even footing and she still had to tip her head back to look into his eyes.

She packed up the empty ornament boxes and stowed them in the big plastic storage bin they had come out of before Brick returned. He grinned, heaved the bulky box up on his shoulder, and trundled it across the room to the front desk.

"Out for the day, Aunt Gracie," he announced, and dropped the storage bin, giving it a hard shove with his boot so it slid into a big empty spot under the counter.

"You can't possibly be done," the tiny gravel-voiced, orange-haired woman behind the counter snapped. She turned around on her stool, and kept turning, until she nearly fell off. Her mouth dropped open, and then she burst out laughing. "How did you get that monstrosity decorated so fast?"

"My Christmas angel, that's how." He slung a dark brown sheepskin jacket around his shoulders, his arms into the sleeves, and then one arm around Lori. "We'll catch up with you later."

"Watch out for the mistletoe, girlie," Gracie chortled.

"What did --" Lori began. Then she thought better of it. Why frighten him away? "Is she your aunt?"

"Everybody's aunt." He led her through the double doors and out into the frosty air, lightly dusted with snow.

Lori sighed in delight. She loved that particular kind of snowfall, soft and slow, putting a haze in the air and muffling all sound. Not that there was much in the way of noise or traffic going through this section of Neighborlee, anyway. Still, the sense of isolation or a curtain falling down to separate them from the rest of the world gave her a peaceful feeling.

"Gorgeous, isn't it?" Brick took a deep, loud breath. She felt his ribcage expand, he held her so close against him. The movement did funny things to her pulse.

"Yeah." She swallowed hard. Since when did a hunk of beefcake make her speechless? She had been around long enough that mere Human physique didn't impress her that much, so what was going on here?

"Look at that." He stopped them and pointed with his other hand.

She looked beyond the pointing finger and saw four brown smudges among the slowly drifting powder in the air. Her eyes adjusted to make out details, and the smudges turned into deer, just standing there, on the edge of the forest where the town ended and land sloped down into the park. For a heartbeat, she almost called out to them, then reminded herself that they weren't Enclave deer, able to sing and offer wild rides on their backs. These were wild deer. It said something for the town that the deer could come so close without being frightened away. It said something about Brick that he noticed them, through the snow filling the air.

"Prettiest thing I've seen all... Well, one of the prettiest things I've seen all day," Brick amended, and gave her a crooked grin that had her blushing.

How many decades had it been since she had blushed at a

simple compliment?

Brick led her to his truck. On the drive through the center of town, he pointed out businesses and then homes that were known for their decorations each year, and speculated on what they would do to top last year's. Far too soon, the ride ended on a dead-end street, in front of a big gold and olive Victorian house that looked down over the slope into the snowy park, like a guardian. Oil lanterns glowed in a dozen windows. The huge wraparound porch was hung with garlands of ribbons, gold beads, and white-berried sprigs of mistletoe and holly. The wrought iron fence surrounding the house displayed matching decorations. Lori itched at the mere volume of the unfriendly greenery so close to her. And getting closer every minute.

"Umm, so what is this place?" she asked once they were both out of the truck and walking up the sidewalk.

"Magic." He winked at her, looped his arm through hers, and led her straight to all that mistletoe and holly.

Before she knew it, Lori was through the gate -- and not a hive appeared. She was sure she'd get a big, ugly red one on the end of her nose, at the very least. Maybe Brick was magic and protected her from the malign influence in the air? Stranger things had happened.

She blinked, and he had her up the steps and onto the porch. Still no itching, no watering eyes, no shortness of breath. Maybe the cold slowed down the malicious effects?

Brick let go of her to reach ahead and open the big, stained glass door with the sign above it that welcomed them to Divine's Emporium.

Lori felt a prickle on the end of her nose and on the palms of her hands the minute Brick let go of her. She gasped and almost stopped short. Survival instincts kicked in and she hurried through the door, hunching her shoulders to keep as far away from the garland of mistletoe and holly framing the doorway.

"Here we are." Brick gestured for her to look around the store. He took hold of her hand. The itching vanished.

Just my luck -- he's the cure. What am I supposed to do? Hold his hand for the rest of my life? Lori looked up at Brick, who smiled as if he shared a treasure with her. Maybe that wasn't such a bad idea.

"Welcome." The woman who appeared through a momentary

dimensional slit in the air wore a long, loose gown of emerald velvet with heavy gold braid on her high collar, the cuffs of her wide sleeves, and the hem of her full skirts. More braid wove through her long hair in a dozen shades of gold, holding it in place. Her crystal blue eyes widened a little when her gaze met Lori's.

She knows, Lori decided, as Brick greeted her.

Indeed, I do. Be welcome. This is a safe haven. She winked and turned to Brick. "Done so soon?"

"I had help. Angela, this is Lori. I drafted her to help me with the tree at Eden, and hopefully with the rest of the trees."

"How many are you going to decorate today?" Lori blurted, blushing and laughing with Angela a moment later.

"Not decorate. Just deliver."

"Just deliver." Angela shook her head. "Let me see your hands. And roll up your sleeves, while you're at it." She glared, barely managing to conceal the mischief sparkling in her eyes, when Brick hesitated to comply.

He sighed, tugged back his coat sleeves and rolled up his sweatshirt sleeves. Red spots dotted the palms of his hands, on the webbing of his fingers, and ringed his wrists like bracelets. Lori couldn't decide if the itching across her palms was because Brick no longer touched her, or if it was sympathy pains. He hadn't gotten those killer hives from her, had he?

Could he be allergic to her?

No, wait a minute. Angela expected to see those hives.

"What are you allergic to?" Lori asked, when Angela just shook her head and Brick grinned like a boy caught with his hand in the cookie jar.

"Pine trees." Angela beckoned with a jerk of her head. "Come with me. Now," she added, tone implacable, when he hesitated.

He shrugged, gave Lori a "What can you do?" look, and followed Angela further into the shop. In moments, she was alone in the main room, looking at old-fashioned toys and penny candy in big glass jars on the shelves behind the front counter, an old-fashioned brass cash register, and the enormous tree decked with silver garland and rainbow-hued metallic balls.

A shimmer of magic in the air made the hair stand up at the nape of her neck. Lori turned around. Her mouth dropped open when her cousin Maurice swooped down to land on the counter in front of her. Albeit, Maurice dressed in G.I. Joe camouflage fatigues and five inches tall. With glittery, unreasonable wings. Fae hadn't had wings in centuries.

"How's it going, Lori?" Maurice snapped his fingers and a miniature black leather recliner appeared on the counter behind him. He sank into it and crossed his legs. "How'd you escape the Dreadfuls?"

"Maurice, what are you doing here? And -- like that?" She couldn't say "shrunk". The word stuck in her throat.

"The Council finally caught up with me like you always said. Exiled me here last year."

"Here?" Her voice broke.

"Hey, Divine's is a great place. I'm actually going to miss it when my gig is up in a year."

"Oh, no, I didn't mean this place. I meant -- well, who was stupid enough to exile you to the Human world when it was Human things that got you in trouble?" She seriously considered temporarily shrinking herself and sitting down. But would she have time to change before Brick came back and saw her?

"That's the beauty of it. I can't do much of anything. My magic got shrunk along with my size. I have to ration it, decide what's worth spending it on. Makes a guy really think about what's important, y'know?" He hooked a thumb in the direction Brick had gone with Angela. "So, how'd you hook up with Brick?"

"You know him?"

"Heck, I know almost everybody in Neighborlee. Anybody who's got a brain, who's worth anything, comes into Divine's at least once a month. I like him."

"So is he for real?" she asked, her voice dropping to a whisper. Now was the perfect time for Brick to come upon her and catch her talking about him.

"He's a great guy. Richer than the entire town all put together, but he keeps forgetting he has money. Oops!" He leaped up from his recliner, which vanished with a loud *pop*. Maurice kept moving, zipping up through the air until he came to rest on the topmost branch of the tree.

Angela and Brick came from the back. He had his sleeves rolled up and a pinkish-brown swath of drying calamine lotion circling his wrists and the backs of his hands and dabbed between his fingers. Lori's fingers twitched and she itched in sympathy. She opened her mouth to make some suggestions of remedies she used when her holiday allergies kicked in, but was stopped when she felt the sizzle of magic at work.

One corner of the front room, almost hidden behind the Christmas tree, held some wrought iron bistro tables and chairs. A coffee machine that sat halfway in another fold of reality suddenly hummed into life. Steaming water appeared in its reservoir and ingredients for frothy, rich, creamy coffee drinks appeared in the containers set up all around it. Lori was impressed. She met Angela's gaze and the woman gave her a little nod, one corner of her mouth twitching up in a smug little smile.

The three of them sat in a cozy little corner, drinking frothy, creamy cappuccinos, waiting for the calamine lotion to dry, and talking about all the holiday activities in Neighborlee. Lori thought it rather sweet that Brick didn't like to talk about the things he had done. She almost dropped her half-full mug in her lap when she realized what she had just thought. Was she falling for a Human, after less than three hours in his company?

Lori watched Brick as he and Angela debated the merits of opening up the shallow duck pond in the park as a skating rink before Christmas vacation started. He cared about things that affected other people. How many of the Fae men her aunts wanted her to consider as a husband thought about someone else when it didn't benefit them? Lori could count them with a closed fist.

Maybe something in the cappuccino affected her mind? She wasn't a bigot, but honestly, falling for a Human she had just met?

"Ready to go?" Brick laughed when she jumped, yanked out of her drifting thoughts.

"Did you even ask if she wanted to help you?" Angela asked. "You don't know a single thing about this poor girl, except that she wandered into Eden and you shanghaied her to help you out. For all you know, she could have a family waiting for her to get back home to them."

His eyes widened in undeniable panic, and all Lori could do was sputter and try unsuccessfully to muffle her giggles. That didn't seem to encourage him.

"Uh -- sorry. Honestly. I just didn't think --"

She killed her giggles with some effort. "To be honest, yes, I was looking for something worthwhile to do today. I just didn't expect to find it so fast."

"Then you'll come with me?"

"What else will you bribe me with? A girl can only drink so much cappuccino, after all." She fluttered her eyelashes at him, something she normally never did. Maybe it was the caffeine mixed with the dark chocolate Angela had grated into the coffee, but Lori felt more alive than she had in years.

"Give me time. I'll make sure this is a day you'll never forget."

"Oh, that sounds ominous," Angela muttered, which earned laughter from all three.

Half an hour later, they ended up in the municipal parking lot behind City Hall. There, Lori discovered an entire lot's worth of Christmas trees had been delivered and left leaning against every available upright surface. Four men Brick had called before he left Divine's were already busy tossing the trees into five pickup trucks.

Brick introduced her to his team, and she blushed all over again at their nods and grins and nudges. It wasn't their appreciation for her looks that affected her so intensely, but their very evident approval of her for Brick's sake. What kind of man was he that people cared? Lori intended to find out. She already had the feeling she would like what she learned.

She tried to help load the trees, and laughed when he scowled at her, teasing, and ordered her to get into the truck and out of the snow. The cold never bothered her.

The sight of Brick handling those trees when she knew he was allergic -- that bothered her. Where were Will and Phill with their bottles of calamine lotion and allergy medicine? Not that she really needed them, of course, since she conjured up the medicine with a snap of her fingers. No, it wasn't that she needed their help, but she wanted their input, their approval, and their opinion of Brick. Why subject himself to the discomfort? He knew he was allergic, yet the trees were the exact things he insisted on handling.

Maybe this Human-type magic had more to it than she thought.

Finally, every last tree was loaded in the trucks. Brick handed out long sheets of paper to his team. She strolled close enough to look over his shoulder and see the papers held maps of Neighborlee and the surrounding farmlands, and names and addresses. Wasn't he Mr. Efficiency? She laughed.

"What's so funny, Mrs. Frosty?" He tugged on her hair, dislodging a coating of fluffy dry snowflakes when she just gave him a confused look.

A flick of magic showed her what she looked like, coated in snow, her cheeks pink and eyes sparkling. That look in Brick's eyes drove away what little chill had gathered around her.

"Aren't you cold?"

"Toasty." She shook like a puppy, shedding all the snow and making him laugh. Then the laughter caught in her chest when he stepped up close so she caught his warm, spicy-clean scent and put his arms around her, just long enough to feel a jolt like electricity and Midsummer's Eve wine zapping through her from nose to toes.

"Wow, you are warm. I should take you home with me to keep me warm."

Oh please oh please oh please, something inside her begged, which shocked her to no end.

Brick laughed, not hearing any of her inner dialogue, and gestured at the truck. "Come on. We have one stop to make before we head out and play milkman."

"Is that anything like mailman?" she muttered. Her face suddenly hot, Lori snapped her fingers to cast up a very necessary illusion. When she blushed hot and hard, she turned neon pink and shot off rainbow sparks from her eyelashes and the ends of her hair. That was the last thing she wanted Brick to see. Not now. Not when she was still having fun and getting to know him!

"Milkman makes deliveries without anyone seeing him." Brick grinned. "And I think you're referring to playing Post Office. Big difference." He held open the door of the truck for her.

Lori slipped and fell, halfway into the truck. He caught her and that lovely, intoxicated jolt shot through her again.

Why did he have to be Human? She knew she could experience this sensation for the next 200 or 300 years before it got commonplace, but Humans simply didn't last that long.

Wouldn't the Dreadful Aunts have coronaries if they knew she considered any kind of long-term relationship with a Human? Well, as long-term as a Human could have with a Fae.

She was ready by the time Brick had walked around the truck and climbed in on the driver's side. Mutely, she held out the bottle of calamine lotion she had summoned. He sighed, grinned, and shook his head.

"Did Angela give that to you?"

"I have my own resources, I'll have you know."

"Yeah, you just conjured it out of thin air. Well, that's a Christmas angel for you." He tugged off his gloves and yanked up the cuffs of his sweatshirt, revealing new welts popping up. Sweat and friction had rubbed away the previous coating, and new brushes with pine branches had inflicted more damage. "Florence Nightingale, you're hired."

Lori smiled, taking his words as a compliment, and kept her questions to herself. She waited until Brick was busy driving, then turned sideways and called up the Ether Lexicon to explain the reference. The source of all Fae information appeared in her hands, the interface the size of a tiny day-planner. Sometimes it appeared the size of a Human phone book, whatever the need demanded. A quick request and a glance at the first page revealed that Florence Nightingale was a healer of some common sense and inspiration.

Definitely, he had been complimenting her.

Lori settled in and decided that was something she wouldn't mind doing in the long term: taking care of people, helping out, healing hurts and discomforts. Especially if Brick was her first and primary patient. She silently sent thanks to Will and Phill, wherever they were. The two were a little odd, preferring time in the Human world, following Human pursuits, doing things the hard, complicated, Human way. But right now, they seemed wiser than all the heads of all the Fae committees and guiding councils.

Brick didn't need help carrying the trees, at the fifteen stops they made, but Lori was glad to do little things like open fence gates and put an envelope in each door or mail slot. The envelopes held invitations to Eden, where each family could come for an evening of snacks and movies and make decorations for the trees.

"Stands to reason," Brick said, when she asked him about the envelopes' contents. "If these folks can't afford a tree, maybe they don't have decorations or money for decorations. This lets them get together with other folks who might be having just as rough a time as they are, so they can see they're not alone."

"And nobody knows you're doing it?"

"Hey, didn't you notice? A lot of people are doing this today."

"Yeah, but there's only one Santa Claus."

And Santa, you have definitely improved, she added, muffling a giggle.

~~~~~

"Hey, I got an idea," Brick said, after they had deposited the last tree and invitation. "Do you have any plans for tomorrow night?"

"I'm not thinking any further than dry clothes and hot chocolate." Lori demonstrated by shaking her head, shedding more snowflakes on the bench seat between them.

"Besides that." He took hold of her hand. That lovely jolting sensation was diminished by the gloves they wore.

"I don't really know that much about the holidays, so I imagine there are hundreds of things to do to get ready for Christmas, and I'm flattered that you want me to help you, but I've always heard this was a family time of the year, so shouldn't your family--"

His gloved hand over her mouth stopped her before she embarrassed herself by fishing for information about his personal life. Such as whether he was married. No, someone as sweet as Brick couldn't be married. Not after the way he made her feel. He was too good-hearted, too nice, too honest and giving to be a cheating worm with a wife waiting at home while he flirted with girls and called them his Christmas angels.

"My folks and my cousins are all out of town until Christmas Eve. So I'm all by my lonesome. I have two tickets for the play tomorrow night, and nobody to go with me. At least, nobody until you dropped down my chimney." He grinned, showing off a dimple in one cheek. "So to speak."

"Chimney?" She muffled a giggle at the memory of one time she nearly did go down a chimney, just to see what it was like. "What play?" she asked, instead of telling him the story. It really was funny, but required so much explanation, it would kill the joke.

"Over at the college. They've got a new drama professor who likes to rewrite the classics. He wants to make it a comedy, says it plays better. The tickets have been sold out for weeks, because nobody thinks he can do it and they want to witness whatever weirdness he pulls off."

"What play?"

"Well, *A Christmas Carole*, of course. What other play is there at
~~~~~

Christmas?"

Lori closed her eyes and shuddered as waves of prickles ran up her back, down her arms and across the palms of her hands and the soles of her feet.

Chapter Five

Sunday, December 9

"I am losing my mind." Lori stared into the mirror of the tiny bathroom of her room at the Neighborlee Arms, an old-style hotel smack dab in the middle of the town.

It was a nice little room, cozy with old-fashioned furniture and not a speck of mistletoe. Moving in was easy enough. She just opened up a transport globe and brought some of her favorite clothes and a small overnight bag instantaneously from the storage room she had "borrowed" at the Waldorf Astoria. Fortunately, there were only two other guests, so she didn't have a problem getting a room when she signed in very late yesterday.

"Going out on a date with a Human, after spending half a day in his company, just because he makes you all warm and gooey inside. That's insane." She checked her makeup in the mirror. "Going to see *that* play -- well, that's just plain suicidal."

"Yeah, but what a way to go," Phill said as she faded into sight.

"Just how long have you been spying on me?" Lori asked, caught between the urge to laugh, fall into her friend's arms in tears, or throttle her.

"I just got here." She sank down on the end of the bed and looked her over, head to foot. "Very nice. I can't remember you ever making such an effort back home."

"I didn't want to attract --" Lori shivered and took a deep breath. "I never wanted to attract anyone's interest before."

"Believe me, honey, you're long past the interest stage. So, what do you think of good old Brick?"

"Why do I have the feeling this was a setup? Are you and Will matchmaking? That isn't exactly the territory you're licensed for."

"We're not old enough to have a license to interfere with the Human world, remember?" Phill grinned and stood up, gesturing for Lori to turn around so she could button up her long, dark blue silk shirt dress. "We like Brick a lot. That's part of why we vanished so fast, once you took a good look at him. We didn't want him thinking we were setting him up. Too many people have done that. And a lot of nasty twitches have laid traps for him, too. All that Human money."

"He doesn't dress or act rich."

"Yeah, isn't it great? Except, when you think about it, the richest guys among the Humans are the ones who are more concerned about giving it away, making other people happy."

"When did you turn into a philosopher?"

"Better that than jealousy." She gave a little tug to the wide collar so it exposed Lori's collarbone and the sapphire necklace.

"Umm, I don't know if this is the time --"

"Please tell me you're about to give me some advice with my love life."

"I always thought you and Will..." Lori shrugged and snatched up the matching earrings to put them in her ears, while watching Phill in the mirror.

"Yeah? I just figured it out. The problem is... Well... Will he ever figure it out?" She shook her head and stepped back to look Lori over once more. "You look splendiferous. Go out there and wow the guy. Let him know there are some nice girls out there in the world who couldn't care less that he could buy the town twice over."

"Who'd want to?" Lori stopped and laughed. "No, actually, this is one town I would love to say I owned. I like the feeling here. There's magic. And I don't think it's just Christmas, either."

"Have you been out to Divine's Emporium yet?"

"Angela knows what we are. Knows us on sight." She tucked her hair back behind her delicately pointed ears and studied them in the mirror. What would Brick think or say or do if he saw them? They weren't ostentatious and obvious, like some Fae, who did magico-plastic surgery to enhance their points. Maybe Brick wouldn't notice?

"She didn't start out magical, but she's been inside magic for so long, it's part of her. At least, that's our theory." Phill shrugged and headed for the door.

"Why didn't you tell me Maurice ended up here when the Fae Council exiled him?" She laughed when her friend stopped short, almost stumbling, and turned to give her a wide-eyed look of astonishment.

"Where is he?"

"At Divine's, shrunk, with the most gaudy, cotton-candy-scented wings slapped on his back."

Total silence filled the room for five heartbeats, then both burst out laughing, so hard that Lori sat down on the bed and Phill just sank to the floor right where she was standing, holding her arms around her stomach to brace herself.

Lori was still grinning, feeling laughter bubbling up from deep inside when Brick walked into the tiny, Victorian-style hotel lobby to pick her up. The laughter died in a breathless sensation when he stopped short and looked her over, head to foot, and his eyes got wide. He swallowed audibly. She seconded that emotion when she looked him over.

Brick wore her favorite shade of dark chocolate: calf-length leather duster, dressy cords, and Western boots, with a *café au lait*-colored cashmere turtleneck sweater.

"Wow," he muttered, and flushed dark red. "Sorry. Couldn't tell I took speech class and attended Toastmasters for five years, could you?"

"I think it's a lovely compliment." Lori reached for her coat and lost her breath again when he snatched it up and held it for her to slip into. "And let me throw it back to you, doubled."

"Please tell me you're real and not a ghost or something come to teach me the error of my ways." Mischief sparkled in his eyes when he said it, killing the heavy sensation in her throat that threatened to choke her for a few moments.

"Why? What errors have you made?"

"Can't think of a one, right now." He glanced past her, and she was horrified to see the desk clerk, a boy in his early twenties, watching them with a wide grin. "Maybe we better get out of here before we get in any more trouble." He bowed, hooked his arm through hers, and headed for the door.

"Let me guess," she said, after they had exited the lobby and stepped out into the lightly falling snow. "Matchmakers hound your heels, too?"

"Too?" His grin went crooked. "So, you heard about me?"

"I was on my own all morning. Plenty of time to ask around. Poor little rich boy, trying to outdo the incredible reputation of his ancestors, making the world a better place, and terrified that every girl who smiles at him might be after his money and not his -- Not his personality," she amended quickly.

He laughed and hugged her arm a little tighter against his side. "That's pretty close, but not close enough. So, are you a poor little rich girl, slumming it and hiding from boyfriends who only want your trust fund instead of you? Idiots, that's what they are," he added, his voice taking on a rasp that made her heart pound.

"Umm, something like that. So, what made your family the local royalty?"

"Not royalty. Just a lot of responsibility. And yeah, lots to live up to." He let go of her arm to open the door of his truck and waited until she had climbed in to shut the door for her. He got in on his side before he continued speaking. "You probably won't believe this... Well, a long time ago, my great-great-whatever grandmother ended up here, pregnant and widowed and sick and tired of people telling her what to do and what was real and what wasn't real and... Let's just say she had more books in her covered wagon than any other supplies. She believed in things you can't see every day, know what I mean?"

"Like magic. Like the things you sense but you don't exactly see at Divine's?"

"Yeah." Brick stared at her a long moment before shaking his head, like coming out of a daze. He started up his truck and pulled away from the curb. "Anyway, she came out here and brought some folks who felt the same way, cared about what's between your ears more than what's in your hands. And one winter night, just before Christmas, she was out walking alone, listening to the magic she heard in the night, and she found this girl ... said she was a Fae, after Granny fished her out of the river, where she fell through the ice. She put a spell on Granny, that as long as she believed in magic and did what she could to help other folks, she'd always have what she needed, and more than she could ever use up." He shrugged and cleared his throat and finally looked at her. "Kind of a cute faery tale, huh?"

"I believe in the Fae," Lori murmured.

"Anyway, lots of weird, neat things happen here in Neighborlee. Granny wanted a school here, so her sons built the college. And she made it part of the family tradition to keep the story remembered, and to keep doing for people. So here we are."

He laughed. "And here we are." He turned the truck into a parking lot and Lori looked around, stunned to see they had driven all the way across town already and sat in front of the college theater building.

"Part of magic is just believing," she offered, when he had hurried around the truck to open the door for her.

"I've spent a lot of time wanting to believe." He offered her a crooked, wistful grin. Then someone called his name and a foursome hurried across the parking lot to catch up with them. Lori didn't have a private moment with him before the play started.

She laughed, which she supposed was the whole point of this new interpretation of *A Christmas Carole*. Thinking of Dickens, of the conversations she and her cousins had had with the man, she thought maybe he would appreciate the ability to turn his ghost story into a comedy and make people laugh. Especially at Christmas. He might not have understood some of the humor, the sight gags, but he still would have approved.

Lori didn't even notice that mistletoe and holly hung all over the auditorium, and sprigs of it decorated the end of every aisle, until she walked out with Brick, her hands sore from clapping. When she realized, she looked at her hands, ran her fingertips over her throat, touched around her eyes. No itching, no swelling, no hives, no redness. It was a Christmas miracle.

Or maybe some of that magic that had surrounded Brick all his life and soaked into him had rubbed off on her.

Either way, she didn't care. She had finally been able to listen to the line about "a stake of holly through the heart," without instantly needing to scratch. Was she cured?

Deliberately, she stopped under a huge bundle of mistletoe and holly in the reception room, where non-alcoholic rum punch and other pseudo-Dickens-era refreshments waited for the audience. Brick only took three steps before he turned around and hurried back to her. He glanced up once, to see what she was looking at.

Then he kissed her. Soft and lingering, with a humming sensation that went down to her toes and shot sparks off the ends of her hair and eyelashes. Brick kept his eyes closed for a good five heartbeats after he lifted his lips from hers, so it didn't matter what special effects she gave off.

Oh, yeah, Lori knew she was cured.

They didn't say much to each other after that. She appreciated the quiet, so she could let the moment sink in, and savor it. He led her back to the coatroom after only a few sips of the punch, and she let him. After a few steps, she moved out ahead, pulling on his arm.

"You know, today is the first time in years I didn't mind keeping up the family tradition," Brick said, as they walked down the theater building steps. "Sometimes I think I got allergic to the trees because of the pressure. Silly, huh?"

"No, not at all. Remind me to tell you about some of my stupid allergies, sometime." She sighed as he tucked her arm through his again.

"You're magic. You make the bad go away," he continued, before she could do more than inhale sharply at his words. Had Brick guessed? "We're good for each other, aren't we? I know it's kind of fast, only knowing each other a day, but when it feels this right--" He shrugged.

"I've always believed in magic," she offered softly, and lifted her gaze to the sky to look for the wishing star. Even Fae were allowed to have wishes come true, once in a while.

Monday, December 10

"Psst. Maurice?" Phill crept into the book room of Divine's Emporium and looked in all directions, using magical senses as well as physical. "Hey, Cuz, where are you?"

"Man, what is this? Grand Central Station?" Maurice glided into the room. "Hey, Philio, up here." He turned a somersault and came in for a landing on top of the rack holding videotapes and DVDs. "First Lori shows up, now you. If Asmondius shows up and acts like nothing happened, I'm gonna check myself in for some head-shrinking." He staggered sideways, nearly falling off the uneven footing on top of the video boxes. "No, wait, that already happened. Along with the rest of me."

"Very funny." She snapped her fingers and shrank herself down to his size, to land on the tapes next to him. "How are you doing?"

"Hunky dory. Which happens to be a great sandwich shop."

"Yeah, I know. I spend a lot of time in Neighborlee." She sat down so she could hang her legs over the edge of the rack. "How come nobody told us you were exiled here? I mean, we heard you were exiled, but --"

"Hello? Time's different between the Human realms and back home. I bet only a month or two have gone by. It's been a year for me. Man, for someone who spends so much time out here, you'd think you'd keep the time differentials straight." He tapped her on the top of her head and grinned.

"Yeah, well, I'm not so good at keeping anything straight lately." Phill managed to grin at his teasing, and gladly scooted over so he could settle next to her. She watched, fascinated, as his wings folded up and then turned sideways so they wouldn't get in the way. "Why in the world did they stick wings on you, anyway?"

"You know Asmondius. Always trying to teach a lesson. It's not so bad. I mean, how else could a guy my size get around when his magic is as small as he is? And you're not here to get flying lessons, are you, Cuz?" He nudged her with his elbow. "What's up? Looking for a great Christmas gift for Will?"

"I want Will to be my Christmas present, but how do I tell him?"

"You could just come out and -- no, you'd probably kill him, wouldn't you? I was there when Sephrinia did her dive bomb routine on his brother, Erasmus." He winced. "Poor guy -- and lucky guy. He got everything settled in one swell foop."

"That's fell swoop." She managed to grin, grateful for his teasing.

"Yeah? You ever seen this guy try leaf-gliding? Definitely a foop." Maurice demonstrated, gesturing with one hand, sweeping up in the air, then taking a dive-bomb downwards. "But Erasmus is a swell guy, so it works out. He and Sephrinia, they're expecting their third by now, right? Lucky guy."

Something penetrated Phill's gloom and desperation. She focused on the wistful look in Maurice's eyes, the twist of his mouth, the sigh hovering at the back of his voice.

"You aren't -- is there some girl back home --"

"Somebody I want to stumble over me when Need sends her on a rampage? Are you nuts?" He shrugged elaborately, which made his wings unfold and snap out, spreading behind them. They fluttered, nudging her, but not enough to knock her off the rack.

"Uh, from that reaction ..." She dropped her attempt at kidding. "Something in the romance department has got you depressed. Join the club."

"You and Will haven't figured out yet that you're perfect for each other, have you?"

"I figured it out, but how do you tell your best friend you want it to be a 38/10 proposition -- or 24/7, if we decide to settle in the Human realms. Can you believe, it never occurred to me that Will was a boy and I was a girl until about three years ago -- Fae realms time, not Human time."

"Ouch. That's a lot of waiting." He folded up his wings and patted her shoulder.

"I don't even want to calculate how many decades that translates into, in Human time. The thing is, how do I wake him up to the fact that we're like two halves of the same whole and we need to pair up, short of slapping him with a biology book?"

"Pair up as in ..." Maurice shook his head and whistled. He tried to smile, but the expression fell off his face. "Well, at least you don't have to worry about the whole mis-matched species thing."

"Mis-matched?" Phill leaned back and took a long look at him. All the pieces fell together in her head. Her stomach dropped with guilt and pity. "There's some girl here, isn't there? A Human girl." She caught hold of Maurice's hand in both of hers, trying to convey her sympathy with the tightness of her grip. "Let me guess. She doesn't even know you're alive, because she doesn't have enough magic to see you."

"Worse."

"How could it be any worse? You don't have a chance, under the terms of your exile."

"Wanna bet? Angela managed to get me four days of parole every year. So far I've only managed to hook up with Holly twice when I'm full-size and able to talk to her, with no magic whatsoever. The other two times, things got in the way."

"That's no way to carry on a courtship. You can't cram months of dating into a single day. The poor girl's going to think you're a stalker." Phill sighed. "Wait a minute. Holly? The librarian?"

"That's her."

"Maurice, Holly is a Lost Kid. She doesn't have a lot of magic, but I know she does have some. That means there's hope."

"Not enough magic for her to see me or hear me."

"Oh." She swallowed hard, feeling sick from the sudden leap of hope and even more sudden drop of despair and pity. "Sorry. At least you get a few days to show her what she means to you."

"Ever hear of Tantalus?" Maurice's smile twisted, looking wry and sickly and bitter, all at the same time.

"Yeah. The Fae clan that masqueraded as gods to the Greeks. Tantalus got in bigger trouble than you and spent a couple centuries locked up where he could see food and drink and books and other things he loved, but never touch or drink or eat or read or anything." She shuddered. "I know exactly what the poor guy went through. What's that got to do with you?"

"I visit Holly's dreams. We're... Well, as far as I can tell, she loves me, but the thing is, she's sure that's all it is, dreams."

"But when you show up --"

"She doesn't remember her dreams in the daytime. And she can't see me when I'm like this."

"Oh, Maurice, that's awful." Phill flung her arms around him. She silently wept a few tears, pity for both of them in their hopeless love problems.

That was how Will found them, before she found her voice. One minute Maurice was rubbing her back. The next he gasped and jerked back and nearly pulled her sideways off the videotape rack.

"Hey, Will, how's it shaking?" Maurice called, his voice just a little too loud and a little too cheerful.

Phill wondered what in the world was wrong with Will. He just stood there, his eyes wide, his mouth half-open like he was about to say something. He swallowed loud and hard and shook his head. She knew she had mentioned to him yesterday that Maurice was here in town and anchored to Divine's Emporium for his term of punishment. She was pretty sure she had said Maurice was shrunk and had wings, so what could be so shocking to him?

"What's up? Where did you leave Lori?"

"She's going ice skating with Brick and they want us to come along." Will's voice cracked a little. He lifted a hand, showing the ice skates hanging by their laces. "I checked with Angela, and she has some in back you can borrow."

"Oh. Great." She glanced at Maurice, wanting to continue their conversation, but how could she ask for advice about Will and getting through to him when he was standing right there?

"It's okay, kiddo, I'm here for the duration. You know where to find me." Maurice winked and gestured as if he would shove her off the edge of the rack. "Go have some fun."

"Oh. Okay." Phill pushed herself forward, falling a few inches before she shifted back to full size, landing with a soft thump on the floor.

"You guys planning on sticking around for the whole Christmas season?" he asked, as she took a step toward the arched doorway out of the book room.

"Maybe." Will sounded somewhat sullen, making Phill stop and look over her shoulder at him. What was his problem?

"My next day at full size is Christmas Eve day. Lots of parties and stuff going on. It'd be great to hang with some folks from home when I'm not stuck looking like a sugar overdose bad dream." He tugged on one of his wings, making a shower of sparks dance around him, along with the scent of cotton candy.

Phill surprised herself with a giggle escaping from her throat. "Sounds like fun. I wouldn't miss it. Will, you want to stay?"

"Christmas in Neighborlee, after we missed the last three or four? You better believe it." Will sounded more like his normal self.

"Great! We'll grab Lori and Brick, and I know a girl you gotta meet, and we'll do the whole old-fashioned couples thingy. Sound good?" Maurice winked at her.

"I wouldn't miss it for the world. Remember that dance class we took when we were little?" Phill leaned against the doorway, feeling laughter catching in her throat as memories surged up to her thoughts.

"Which dance class? Waltzing in Austria? Or something in this century?" He made a shooing motion. "Go check out your skates. I wanna catch up with Wilfred here, and we don't need any dizzy girls interfering."

Phill stuck her tongue out at him and scurried off in search of Angela.

~~~~~

"Yeah, but what a girl," Maurice added, a moment after Phill disappeared from sight. "So, how's it going, Will? For real, I mean."

"I didn't know you and Phill ..." Will felt a moment of
~~~~~

disorientation. He knew he stood nearly six feet tall, but for a few seconds there he felt as if he was shorter than Maurice.

No wonder he wasn't getting anywhere with Phill. She was stuck on Maurice, and he was always out and about, spending more time in the Human realms in the last fifty or sixty Human years than in the Fae realms. It was hard for Need to kick in when Phill's perfect match wasn't around to latch onto.

Will firmly believed in the theory that Need didn't kick in until the right male and female were in close and prolonged proximity with each other. That was why Need so often seemed to be a surprise to both partners--the Fae were so busy traveling between Enclaves and other dimensions, enjoying their long lives.

Which just confirmed that he and Phill were never going to get jolted and shackled by Need. If it was ever going to kick in, it should have a long time ago. They spent more time together than they did with their own families, combined.

"Me and Phill, what?" Maurice fluttered up until he hovered in the air about eight inches in front of Will's nose. "You do know we're distant cousins, don't you?"

"How distant?" Will realized just how desperate he sounded.

"Distant enough that I'm not immune if Need ever hits her. But the thing is, I think she's already got her eye on this guy, and he doesn't seem to realize she's... Well, he doesn't seem to think she's a girl, know what I mean? Poor sap doesn't realize what a treasure is right under his nose." Maurice darted in and slapped the tip of Will's nose, adding a couple sparks so the tap stung a little.

"Who does she have her eye on? What kind of an idiot wouldn't notice her?"

"You'd be surprised. If you're smart, you'll find that guy and slap him upside the head, and tell him not to waste any more time. A girl like that, you make her wait long enough, she'll get her heart broken. The way I hear it, a girl gets hurt enough, heart and spirit, Need never happens. And some stupid mopes, they think they have to wait for Need, instead of making the first move."

He settled down on the videotape rack where Will had first seen him and Phill, hugging. "You know what's really interesting? Human girls, they're independent and smart and they don't need guys to figure out much of anything for them. But Human girls still like being chased. They want a guy to feel like he has to work to catch them, and work to keep them. Keeps things fresh and fun, know what I mean? Maybe Humans are smarter than we are. Guys need to be the hunters again, instead of sitting on their sorry butts, waiting for Need to throw a net over them. Know what I mean?"

"Hunters, huh?" Will glanced over his shoulder, into the shop. He couldn't see the back room where Phill was looking through all the skates Angela had found, but he could sense her. "Hunters. Yeah. You think Phill..." He knew yellow and blue sparks buzzed around his ears -- his usual embarrassing telltales when he blushed.

"I bet she'd love it. But be subtle. Play it slow. Ease into it. The best hunters don't let the prey know they're being tracked until it's way too late to escape." Maurice fluttered up and landed on Will's shoulder. "I happen to know where there's just gobs of mistletoe available, to help give her a nudge in the right direction. After about ten days of it just hanging there, scooping up all that emotional energy, and all the Christmas spirits filling up this town, you catch Phill under a bunch of mistletoe, she's yours. Who gives a flying fig about Need by then?"

"Sounds great." He would have flung his arms around Maurice in gratitude, but he would have had to shrink to do that. He thought about Maurice and Phill clinging to each other, sitting on that videotape rack, when he walked into the room just a few moments ago.

He gave himself a mental shake. So what if Phill felt some emotional tie to Maurice? She belonged to him, and he was going to let her know. Somehow.

Chapter Six

Tuesday, December 11

Harry had enough control over the invisibility spell, he and Bethany could go out in public and interact with people, and she would remain unrecognized.

"It's along the lines of a 'Don't look at me' spell, mixed with a 'Don't remember me' spell," he explained. He gave her a sheepish look when she knew her confusion showed. "Standard spells every Fae child learns when they're old enough to go out into the Human world. Little kids' ear points are more pronounced until they hit adolescence, and they don't have the knack for covering their ears with their hair. Leads to trouble. Especially when people are prone to believing elves and leprechauns are half their size. Something about Human brains lets them ignore oddities in adults."

"To a point," she offered with a giggle, and was delighted when he laughed with her.

Harry wanted to test the control he had over the invisibility before they picked up her father at the airport. Ostensibly, Mr. Miller's visit to Vegas was a test run, to see how closely the paparazzi were monitoring his activity. If he could travel without being trailed in the hopes he would lead the media to Bethany, then phase two of the plan would be implemented. Bethany would get on a plane for Europe, step into Harry's invisibility field, then get off the plane and take another one for Cleveland.

They visited two casinos, and got thrown out of the second when Harry calculated a system for betting and told Bethany what he was doing. She was too delighted at the proof that people could hear and see them without recognizing her to be indignant at the abrupt treatment. And really, it wasn't fair. Harry wasn't cheating. He was just using math, in his head, without any gizmos or electronics to influence the machines.

"You weren't using any magic in there, were you?" she asked, as they strolled down the strip. She was getting used to people bumping into her without recognizing her, so she didn't flinch anymore when someone looked her in the face.

"What's the fun in that?" Harry looked so confused by the suggestion of cheating, Bethany's heart turned a couple somersaults. How could anybody be so smart and so innocent, and such a hunk? She hooked her arm through his and shook her head.

"Stupid question. You don't need to cheat. It's the game, not the money, right?" She envied him. Somewhere along the line, the fun had gone out of her acting. She had gotten through a few miserable roles by focusing on the money, putting enough aside that she could start to get picky. Now, all her roles felt like more work and less fun. While she had a tidy sum tucked away that she could certainly live on for the rest of her life back in Neighborlee, it wouldn't last her long in LA. Not if she wanted to keep visible, so she could get more jobs.

Vicious cycle, she decided with a jolt. Did she really want to leave it all behind and go home, get her college degree, maybe become a theater teacher or acting coach, and live comfortably as a has-been? Maybe, despite all her complaining and misery, she was addicted to the bright lights?

"Hey, it's okay," Harry murmured, leaning close enough his warm breath brushed her cheek.

She turned to him, and their noses almost touched. What would he do, she wondered, if she wrapped her free arm around his neck and pulled him close for a kiss?

Harry turned red and swallowed so hard she could hear it, and his eyes got wide. Could he hear what she was thinking? Or maybe it was more a matter of picking up the images in her mind?

"Uh, Bethany --"

"Hey, you two." A man coming up behind them laughed. "Get a room!"

"We're not -- we don't --" Harry turned even redder. The pleasant tickling buzz of the invisibility field flared and died.

"Hey," the man said, his eyes widening with shock and amazement. "You're Bethany --"

"Run!" Harry grabbed hold of her hand, nearly pulling her off her feet before she could get them moving.

He was faster than the best sprinter on her high school track team, and Bethany was grateful.

~~~~~
~~~~~

"It was just like when I knocked myself out with that explosion," Harry mused. He sat on the balcony of their hotel suite. He ignored the multicolored light show of Vegas spread out before him. His thoughts kept spinning back to that afternoon, when he thought, hoped, Bethany wanted him to kiss her.

That tickling buzz all through his body hadn't been terror, like he had felt the three -- count them, only three -- times a desperate woman in Need seemed to be looking right at him. Every time, she dashed right past him, to ambush some poor unsuspecting guy whose bachelorhood had suddenly come under attack, like the Plains Indians who woke up one day to find themselves in the way of the railroad.

No, that feeling had been anticipation, touched with hunger. All his senses were swamped with Bethany.

So he hadn't realized it when the background whisper, like wind constantly brushing against his bare back, vanished. He had lived so long with the feeling of the magic that wrapped around him and kept him invisible, he should have been shocked when it abruptly cut off like that. But no, everything had been focused on Bethany. He had even let go of his concentration on blurring their images so they could interact with people and not be recognized.

Running was the stupidest reaction he had ever had. Common sense said if he had re-established the blurring around them, they could have convinced the passerby he was mistaken. Running only confirmed the man's glimpse of Bethany's face.

"What explosion?" Bethany's quiet question yanked him out of his musing.

That was the problem, he decided with a grin. That funny, warm, hollow feeling jolted through his chest when she settled down next to him on the lounge chair. Bethany distracted him. The haze of magic or power surrounding her interfered with the invisibility spell, canceling it, and all his discipline and control over his magic.

She still sat there, watching him, waiting for an explanation with that soft, optimistic smile on her face. Bethany still expected the world to be nice, even with all the nasty surprises that dogged her steps since she had shot to stardom. He had never felt old, at the age of 237, but she made him feel worn out and cynical, and it wasn't just because she was a sweet young thing in her twenties.

"Alexi explained about my invisibility spell, didn't he?"

"It malfunctioned, so it sticks to you all the time, and you have to consciously make yourself visible." She nodded. "That's about it. What explosion?"

Haltingly he explained some of his experiments, his inventions to do things the Human, non-magical way. Bethany leaned closer, eyes widening, sometimes forgetting to breathe, all physical evidence his story fascinated her. When had a woman ever been fascinated by *him*? She wasn't amazed or turned off or freaked out by the fact that he was Fae and he had to use a separate blurring spell for his ears. So it wasn't the alien factor that caused this interest. Could Bethany be interested in him, Hargrove, the man?

That was almost as fascinating a concept as Bethany herself. The mystery of the magic that soaked into her flesh and bones and yet wasn't at her disposal or command.

"Okay, you were unconscious, all your control over counteracting the spell turned off, but you were visible." She frowned, nodding slowly, and her gaze seemed to turn inward. "I wish Daddy was here. He loves puzzles like this."

"Umm, maybe you shouldn't tell him about me. Being Fae," Harry hurried to add, when she gave him a confused little frown.

"My dad's the original philosopher, or quantum physicist," she said with a chuckle. "It's not hard to believe at all in Fae and magic and other dimensions of reality all pressed together into one space, living side-by-side, because of Daddy and the things he taught me. Just because he owns a diner doesn't mean he's --"

"I'd never say dumb or ignorant or anything like that." He pressed two fingers over her lips, to stop her before the words came out. Both of them froze for several frantic heartbeats as that zing jolted through them. Harry didn't want to lose contact with her, but he knew it would look pretty silly to keep sitting there with his finger against her lips.

Bethany solved the problem by taking hold of his hand in hers and keeping hold of it. She swallowed hard and a ragged little giggle escaped her.

"Daddy reads everything. He's a genius, but he never had a chance to get past junior college, that's all. He'll accept what you are, but I have to warn you, he'll bury you with a thousand questions within the first day of you two meeting. Think you're up for it?"

"Sure," Harry managed to say, vitally aware of her pulse in the little hand that held his. "Why not? It'll be fun. At least we'll have something to talk about."

Bethany's laughter was the most beautiful thing he had ever heard.

Wednesday, December 12

Brick pulled up in front of the Neighborlee Arms and put his truck into park. The stately old brick building at one point in the town's history had been his family's home. Among other activities, depending on the economy and the growth of the town. He hadn't cared much when it was turned into a hotel, but now he liked the idea of guests and visitors staying there. Because of Lori. He hadn't really paid attention to the flow of strangers through the hotel and the town, until now. Because of Lori.

He'd never been attracted to a woman as strongly as he was toward her. Maybe because she wasn't throwing herself at him in the mistaken belief that he was wealthier than Midas and owned half the town. Great-Granny had been smart, handing over businesses, chunks of land and responsibility to people who could take care of them properly. She had always maintained the best way to hold onto influence and power was to earn respect. That meant service. And serving meant --

His train of thought totally derailed when Lori stepped out the front door and looked around. She and Brick hadn't made any plans for today. However, the friends who had come to town with her had her company for two entire days while he worked like a good little boy. It was his turn to indulge in some fun and show Neighborlee's most beautiful visitor what the town had to offer. Besides, she was his Christmas angel. Family tradition said Christmas angels only stayed on Earth until Christmas Eve. That meant Brick only had twelve more days to convince her to shed her wings and stay earthbound and be his angel all year round.

That thought came out of nowhere, stunning him so much he nearly forgot to flag her down before she headed down the street, most likely to Hunky & Dory's for breakfast.

Convince Lori to stay? What did he really know about her, besides the fact that she dressed with understated elegance, she didn't seem to care about money, and she treated Christmas like it was a totally new experience? Oh yeah, and he wanted to drop everything that meant anything to him to spend all his time with her and see her eyes light up with wonder and admiration for him.

Lori started down the steps of the hotel and the movement jarred Brick's brain out of neutral. He fumbled with the latch of his door and managed to fling it open before she came even with his truck. For a moment, he had a vision of opening the door right into her midsection and knocking her flat. Not his idea of sweeping a girl off her feet.

"Where do you think you're going this fine morning?" He leaped out and nearly lost his footing on some ice hidden under last night's dusting of snow. Fortunately, he still had one hand on his door and saved his balance without looking like a total idiot.

"Breakfast. I'm dying of starvation." Lori's eyes sparkled, cold kissed her cheeks, and she tucked her hands into the deep pockets of her simple black coat.

"Can't have that. How would that make Neighborlee look, if our visitors were strewn all over the streets, passing out from starvation?" He slammed the door of his truck. Then checked that he had the keys in his pocket, along with his wallet. Fortunately, both were where they belonged. He bowed and offered Lori his bent arm. She tucked her hand into the crook of his arm and they strolled down the sidewalk together.

"So, have you thought about where you want to go today? Or maybe I should ask what you did yesterday, so we don't repeat it," he said.

"I'm sorry. I completely forgot we had plans for today." Lori blushed delightfully.

"We didn't, but I'm shanghaiing you, so you can tell your friends they're out of luck."

"How about we make it a foursome?" Will said, appearing seemingly from nowhere. Brick nearly lost his footing on another patch of ice. He could have sworn the very air split apart, letting Will and Phill catch up with them.

"Do you know Lori?" Brick asked.

"They're the ones who brought me here," Lori said. "Since I was kind of down and blue with nothing to do, they decided to finally share their favorite place with me." She hooked her arm with Phill's without loosening her grip on Brick's.

"Ah... That's good." Brick flashed onto the warning he had carried in the back of his mind since the day he started school: *Coincidences usually aren't, and people who seem too good to be true definitely are.* Just the fact that Lori had never mentioned she was with Will and Phill made him suspicious.

And that hurt.

"Something wrong?" Will said, falling into step on the other side of Phill, so they strolled down the sidewalk boy-girl-girl-boy.

"No. Just wondering how come nobody mentioned you knew each other. How good of friends are you, anyway? Are you, like, staying together?" He wanted to cut out his tongue the moment those idiot words left his lips. He knew it was none of his business. Though if his plans for him and Lori moved any further down the road, it most definitely would be his business.

"Phill and I are sharing a room. Will is down the hall," Lori said. "It'd be okay if Will and I shared a suite -- although he's such a slob, who would want to? -- because we're distant cousins. But Phill definitely isn't his cousin, although she is one of mine, on another side. It's all complicated. I never paid attention during the family tree and genealogy discussions in school."

"Cousins." Brick's sigh of relief caught in his throat. Somehow, knowing they were related didn't make the situation any better. Calming one worry just raised more. "How come you two never mentioned Lori to me?" he asked as they reached the doorway of Hunky & Dory's and paused to let a group of early diners walk out. Christmas music poured out through the open door.

"The same reason we never mentioned Neighborlee to her. We're kind of rebels, where we come from," Phill said with a shrug. "People say we're feckless, always gallivanting all over the world. So we kind of keep quiet about things when we're home, so nobody accuses us of tempting and corrupting the young."

"You're ridiculous," Lori said with a sigh and a grin.

"And we don't talk about things and people back home while we're out roaming free because we just don't want to remember. Kind of ruins the buzz." Will whimpered as the door slowly swung shut. "I'm starving. Can we please go in? Or are we going to have snowballs for breakfast?"

"Definitely going in." Since Brick had a free arm, he reached out and caught the handle of the door and pulled it open. Lori laughed when he bowed, refusing to let go of her arm, which forced her to semi-bow with him.

Will grinned evilly, hooked his arm through Phill's, and stepped through the door, pulling her along with him. They were all four laughing as Phill pulled Lori, who pulled Brick, who pulled the door shut. The people in the small restaurant looked up as the four headed to the ordering counter along the left-hand wall of the deep storefront. Most of them smiled. A few stared, eyes wide.

Brick caught frowns from several girls who had tried to catch him recently. He knew that because of a sure-fire test of a hopeful girlfriend's sincerity that his grandfather had taught him. He would carelessly drop a falsified bank statement, showing he was broke, teetering on the edge of bankruptcy, somewhere in her vicinity. No matter how the statement was folded up, it always came open by the time she stood up and handed it to him. Each time, the relationship cooled down like nuclear winter within a day or two.

Brick thought about pulling that test on Lori, and it settled something heavy, cold, and pointy in the pit of his stomach.

They took a booth in the back. Brick and Will went up to the counter to order, leaving Phill and Lori to hold the booth for them. It was still early enough in the morning for the breakfast rush, meaning that at any moment, a gang might come in and use up all the open tables and booths. Usually on weekdays, seating wasn't a problem, even during the breakfast rush at Hunky & Dory's. However, this was the Christmas season, and all bets were off.

"So, the two of you seem to be getting along pretty well," Will said, as they got into the line at the counter. There were five people ahead of them. The couple directly in front of Will and Brick looked undecided as they studied the extensive breakfast menu.

"Yeah. She's fun. I didn't know you three knew each other."

"We brought Lori here to get away from it all." He jammed his hands in his back pockets and leaned back as he studied the menu.

"Get away from what?" Brick's antenna for trouble quivered. He hated that feeling.

"Lori's trying to avoid being railroaded into a commitment that won't ... fit her, I guess you'd say. Back where we come from, powerful people tend to try to breed for power." He glanced away from the board and waggled his eyebrows, as if that would make things perfectly clear to Brick.

Unfortunately, it did.

"Yep. Matchmaking relatives who think the bottom line is about property and wealth and social status and nothing else."

"Got it in one. All sorts of matchmaking cousins and uncles and aunties have been pressuring her. They don't believe in love at first sight." He snorted. "Okay, more accurately, infatuation at first stare. They don't believe in it, didn't wait for it, or squandered their one chance at it. Since they think they turned out all right, they don't have to give anyone else a chance to find it, either. So Lori's been under a lot of pressure. We figure nobody would ever think to look for her here. And it gives Phill and me a chance to get away from it all, too. Two birds with one stone."

"If you say so." Brick hated the awful feeling he was being set up, primed for a scam or a trick of some kind. The thing was, he thought he knew Will and Phill well enough not to expect such a trick from them.

"So give her some breathing space, okay?" Will said, as the couple in front of them stepped up to the counter and stumbled through their order. "Let her just have fun. Show her she can spend time with a guy without him shoving prenuptial contracts in her face before she decides if she even likes dancing with him."

"We haven't gone dancing." Brick grinned despite the warning queasies running through him. "Is she any good?"

"*Fly Me to the Moon* takes on a whole different dimension when Lori is your partner." Will shook his head, grinning. Then that grin faded, and Brick glimpsed something dark and implacable in his eyes. "But be warned. You might be my friend, but blood is important. Do anything to hurt her, make her cry one tear ..."

"Or what?"

"Nightmares will come true." He nodded as the couple in front of them stepped away from the counter. "So, everything clear? Not that I don't trust you to be good to her. You're a good guy, Brick. But I learned a long time ago, it's better to be warned and not need it, than to assume someone won't be stupid, and then be disappointed." He clapped him on the shoulder and stepped up to the counter. "I'm starved. We got a lot of things to do today."

"Yeah. Starved." Brick fought down a shudder that tried to turn his insides into knots. There was no doubt in his mind that Will meant every word he said.

So did that mean Lori was totally innocent, no ulterior motives for coming to town?

But just like Will had said, better to be warned than to assume and be disappointed.

~~~~~

"You haven't been shopping yet? How long have you been here?" Brick said, stunned and a little apprehensive when Lori made the admission. What had she been doing all this time?

"We've been giving her some culture," Phill said. "The Cleveland Natural History Museum --"

"Depends on what you consider 'natural,' you know," Lori said, holding her hand up to the side of her mouth, as if she was making an aside. Will snickered.

"The Cleveland Museum of Art. Severance Hall--"

"The Cleveland Orchestra hasn't started its concert season yet," Brick objected.

"A tour," Phill said, glaring at him. "Stan Hywet Hall. Holden Arboretum. Great Lakes Science Center."

"What?" he said, feigning dismay. "Not the Rock Hall?"

"Bleah. Not my type of music at all," Lori said. Mischief sparkled in her eyes. "Today, I want to be lazy and just go shopping. Window shopping, even. Just walk this lovely town from one end to the other and see how ... things are done in this part of the country." Her gaze flicked away from Brick's for a moment, sending that heavy, suspicious feeling back into the pit of his stomach.

He could have sworn for a moment she was about to say something like "how the other half lives," but that made no sense.

"Shopping it is. Until after lunch. Then I intend to take you sledding. Is it a deal?" He held out one hand to shake hers.

"Deal. I guess. Why wait until after lunch?"

"The kids go back to school after their lunch break. The snow that fell overnight is packed down, and we can see from the tracks in the snow where the danger spots are, the deep spots, and where to go for the best, fastest run."

"You sound like a man who takes his sledding seriously." She let him shake her hand, and laughed.
~~~~~

"Very seriously." Brick blinked and nearly shook his head. For a moment, he could have sworn actual sparks shot off their hands where their skin touched, and a pink haze filled the air around Lori's face. Just for a moment.

~~~~~

Brick dropped the falsified bank statement while he and Lori waited for Will and Phill to come out of the Papyrus People shop. The sidewalk was clear of snow and actually dry from the warm morning sunshine, and he heard the folded paper hit the cement. He concentrated on the display window, watching Lori's reflection.

She glanced around, but didn't bend over, didn't turn, and didn't say anything.

He waited, braced for that first gust of wind to rise up and blow his paper away and ruin the test. Will and Phill came out of the shop with an assortment of funny Christmas cards. When the group turned to go, Brick turned to look for the paper, but it wasn't where he was sure it had landed.

"Something wrong?" Lori turned, walking backward a few steps, watching him when Brick didn't immediately turn to leave with them.

"No. Nothing." He hunched his shoulders, and heard the distinct rustle of paper tucked in the inside pocket of his jacket. He should have nothing in there, now that he had dropped the paper. He forced a smile and got his feet moving. Lori turned around and followed Will and Phill, who were caught up in comparing their funny cards.

Brick tugged his jacket open and felt in the pocket. He caught the paper between two fingers and pulled it out. He nearly dropped it, when he realized it was indeed the false bank statement. Had he just imagined dropping it? Maybe he had dropped something else and it blew away?

He shrugged it off and hurried to catch up with the others, after securely tucking the paper away again.

The next attempt came outside Jane's spa, as the four of them were leaving. Jane had seemed to know the four of them were coming. She greeted them with smiles and soon she and Lori and Phill were chatting like old friends, while Will and Brick hung back and wandered the shop, sniffing the tester bottles of sprays and creams and oils. Brick was so relieved to leave, he almost forgot to
~~~~~

slip his hand inside his coat and pull out the paper.

This time he dropped it on Lori's foot. He heard the dry snap-smack sound the paper made when the short end hit the top of her boot and it went flying. Lori hesitated, then held out the bag with her purchases, putting it up to within six inches of Brick's nose.

"Doesn't that just smell heavenly?"

"Uh --" He choked when clashing aromas converged and assaulted his nose.

"Oops. Sorry." She giggled, took the bag away and pulled out one candle. "This." She held it out to him.

"Yeah, I suppose." The spicy yet subtle fragrance reminded him of a freshly mown lawn on a hot summer afternoon, with hints of spearmint and cinnamon. Warm and green and bursting with moisture. It drove away the dry cold that bit at his nose in this weather. "That's incredible. What do they call that?"

"Booby-trap," Will muttered, and pretended great pain when Phill elbowed him.

"Only the truly perceptive and talented and sensitive could smell something like this," Lori said, arching an eyebrow and tucking the candle away again. Brick didn't know what amused him more -- her pretend disdain, the lofty tone, or the pleased gleam in her eyes.

They were ten steps away before he realized she hadn't picked up the paper. He excused himself and hurried back to the doorstep of the spa. No paper anywhere in sight. He bent to look around the corner, down the alley between the two old buildings, and heard the distinct, crisp rustle of paper in his jacket pocket. A shiver that had nothing to do with the cold crept up his back when he reached into his jacket and pulled out the paper.

What was truly odd was that it had a couple wet spots on it. But if he hadn't taken it out of his pocket, and if he hadn't dropped it and Lori hadn't kicked it... How did the paper get wet?

He tried three more times. He even took the precaution of bending one corner before he tossed it in front of Lori when her head was turned. The corner was still bent, freshly creased, when he found it in his pocket. The final attempt came at lunchtime, when he made a show of emptying his pockets to look for his wallet, and set the paper nearly on top of Lori's plate, then got up and excused himself to look for the bathroom. When he returned to the table, the paper was nowhere to be seen. He felt a mixture of triumph and disappointment, and the sense he had been very stupid. Lori had pocketed the paper, obviously, and simply waited for the proper time to confront him.

Or so he thought, until they got up to leave. He swung his coat off the chair, slid one arm in, and heard the distinct rustle of paper in his inside pocket. Brick nearly dropped his coat.

Lori stood, shrugging into her own jacket, and looked around the sandwich shop. "Looks like we beat the rush," she said with a smile, as a party of eight came through the door.

"Yeah, beat the rush." Brick took a deep breath, finished buttoning his coat, then bowed and offered her his arm. That pinkish haze filled the air around her face when she blushed.

Definitely, he was having hallucinations. What was wrong with him?

Lori had probably put the paper back in his coat for him while he was away, but what about all the other times he thought he had dropped the paper, and found it back in his pocket?

"I'm ready for either sledding or a nap, after that huge lunch," Lori said, as they stepped outside and a gentle, refreshingly chill breeze caressed their faces. "I wish Will and Phill could join us."

"Where did they say they were going?" He guided her down the street to his truck, with a vague idea of stopping to get better clothes for sledding. Definitely she needed sturdier boots.

"They didn't. Oh, Angela did say if I planned on any outdoor sports while I was here, she'd loan me better clothes." Lori gestured at her down vest and matching slacks, sweater, hat, and gloves. "Something better suited for snow, rather than sitting around the fire, drinking hot chocolate, you think?"

"Your wish is my command, my lady." He reluctantly let go of her arm as they parted to go to different sides of his truck. Lori laughed, the sound chiming like bells coming from a long distance over the snow.

~~~~~

An hour later, they had found more appropriate clothes for sledding at Divine's Emporium, rented a sled at the rental shack inside the park, and managed to take two test runs down the medium-sized slope. They stopped for hot chocolate at the snack hut that normally rented out roller skates and skateboards during
~~~~~

the rest of the year.

"How you holding up?" Brick asked Lori, as she perched on the edge of a bench and looked down the slope. They had the place nearly to themselves, except for a cluster of homeschooled kids, and some daycare children with their teachers.

"I'm just fine. I could do this all day. And all night. I notice there are some spotlights, so that does mean sledding at night, right?" She gestured up at the spotlights at the top and bottom of the slope.

"Most definitely. That's when the real daredevils come out. See that patch over to the left?" He gestured and waited until she turned to look.

"Doesn't look like anybody has sledded there yet."

"The school kids don't dare. They call it Headless Hill, because supposedly some kid took a bad bump, got tossed in the air, and the runners on his sled took his head right off."

"Oh, puh-lease." She wrinkled up her nose in disgust.

"Of course, that was like a hundred years ago, when sleds meant business and you kept the runners sharp to fight off Indian attacks and wolves."

"A century ago? I'm sure Neighborlee was very civilized a century ago. Maybe you mean two?"

"Hmm, maybe." Brick tipped his hot chocolate cup back and drained the last drops. It wasn't any good when it got cooler than lukewarm, so it was wise to drink it while it was still near-scalding hot. "The thing is, that side of the slope has some pretty steep drops, and they get hidden under fresh snowfalls. Nobody takes that side of the sledding hill until the more experienced ones break the snow for them, so they can see what's underneath." He got up to toss their cups away and deliberately struck a heroic pose, with his chest out and his fists jammed into his hips.

"I suppose you're one of them?" she said, laughing.

"One of my many inherited responsibilities, passed down from my Great-granny." He held out his hand and gestured with the other at the slope. "Brave enough to join me?"

"I wouldn't miss it for the world." She let him pull her to her feet, and then ran for their sled twenty feet away, still holding onto his hand.

Brick laughed and stumbled after her, and felt his heart racing faster than he could account for. He was still laughing as they dragged the sled over to the proper starting point for the run and got into position on it. He guided Lori's hands around his waist and made sure her boots were firmly wedged into the gap between the frame and the wooden seat of the sled. Then he took tight hold of the ropes tied to the steering part of the frame, wrapped them twice around his gloves, and leaned forward, tipping the sled down that first, steep drop.

"The key is the first drop," he said, ending with an *ooph* as the sled hit hard and zoomed down the slope. Lori answered with a delighted shriek. Her arms wrapped so tightly around him, they threatened a couple ribs.

They plowed into the first hollow in the slope, sending snow flying everywhere. Brick got snow in his mouth and ended up blinded by white gobs plastering his face. He shook his head and tried to feel his location on the slope. The sled jolted and careened downward so fast, he had no idea where he was. Wherever it lay ahead of them, the bottom was coming up on them too fast. He couldn't let go of the ropes to clear his eyes, or they definitely would crash. It was a law of nature that the moment a sledder stopped steering, the sled became magnetically attracted to the nearest, biggest, hardest immovable object.

Brick did the only thing he knew to do: he jerked himself bodily sideways, tipping them off the sled. A vision filled his head of hitting one of the light poles or a bench or even going off the course altogether and into the river.

Lori shrieked, this time not in delight, and lost her grip on him. Brick let go of the steering ropes and tried not to stiffen up as he tumbled head over heels. He rolled like a fallen log, until he jolted up against something and came to an abrupt stop.

"Lori?" He spit out snow. He cleared his eyes and found he had lost one of his gloves somehow. Probably pulled off by the rope before he fully let go. His hat was gone, and his scarf. From the icy wet enclosing his feet, he wouldn't be surprised if he had lost one or both boots.

"Here." She laughed and slid down the slope a few feet on her bottom. A fast shake sent snow flying from her hair and jacket. She raked her gloved fingers through her hair, getting it out of her face. Melting snow made her face glisten. "Look at you. I swear, I've spent the whole day picking up after you!" Laughing, she dug into a nearby pile of overturned snow and pulled out his hat and scarf.

How had she known those were there under all that snow? His mouth dropped open when another plunge into a pile of snow on the other side of him revealed his missing glove.

Her words jolted into his consciousness. Picking up after him? Had she been picking up his papers all day and putting them back into his pocket?

But how could she have put them in his pocket without him noticing? Unless she was a pickpocket, or a magician?

"You, Mr. Willis, need a keeper." She leaned forward, and just when he thought she might kiss him, she wiped snow off his face.

Brick laughed and pushed his questions aside for later. If he let them occupy his mind, he would sit here all day, slowly freezing and becoming one with the hill. He wondered if it was any consolation that he might not be going crazy after all.

But that brought up new questions: Why had Lori gone to such trouble to keep putting his paper back in his pocket without him knowing? Did she have time to look over the paper? And if she did, why hadn't she said anything about what she had read?

Then he had a more horrid thought that wiped out all the others. From what Will had said at breakfast, Lori was in something of the same position as Brick, with people coming after her for her money and family connections and social standing. If she thought he was broke, did she think he was only being nice for the sake of her money and connections?

Was she going to dump him because he was seemingly penniless, but for the entirely wrong reasons?

Sometimes, he scolded himself as they dragged the sled back up the slope, *you are just so smart you're stupid.*

Something ached to the point of distraction that evening, when Brick made his slow, limping way into a Christmas party committee meeting for the Chamber of Commerce. Part of it came from being unable to go to the movie with Lori, Will and Phill tonight. Part of it came from his aches and bruises from sledding that afternoon. And part of it was the horrid fear he had made the worst mistake of his life, and anything he did would only make things worse. He would lose Lori before he even had a real chance of winning her.

Chapter Seven

Thursday, December 13

"What is your problem?" Phill planted her hand flat in the middle of Will's chest and stopped him on the steps of Divine's Emporium.

With her other hand, she snapped her fingers and flung a shield around them, sliding them into a parallel dimension. They were effectively invisible and silent to anyone who might come to the doorway of the shop, and even walk through them. Phill was determined to get some things out in the open, even if they had to stand there all day.

"Problem?" Will looked down at her hand and shuddered, ever so slightly. Then he summoned up a cocky grin. "What makes you think I have a problem?"

"Besides running around like a madman, always wanting to do something, see something. You're all fun-fun-fun since we dropped Lori practically on Brick's head. What's the rush? We're not under a deadline. Or are we? Something you're hiding from me?"

She held her breath and stared him straight in the eyes and waited. For good measure, she crossed her fingers, two sets on each hand, as well as managing to cross her big toes over the ones next to them, despite the tight quarters inside her boots.

"No deadline." His voice cracked on the second word.

"What is going on with you? Why can't we have fun like we always do when we remember to get here for Christmas?"

"We're not having fun?" Will settled on the railing of the porch. Because they were in a parallel dimension, he didn't disturb the snow that had piled up overnight. Phill wished he could feel the cold of the snow, or even have it melt into his clothes.

If she had to, she would lift the dimensional warping shield and knock Will onto his back, sit on his chest, and wash his face with snow until he confessed. Or drowned. Whichever came first.

"Aren't we having fun? We're doing everything we always do. Caroling and playing Secret Santa with half the town and helping the kids with their Christmas pageant rehearsals, unseen, as always. And isn't it even more fun than usual, since we can hang with Maurice? And going sightseeing. That's a blast, playing tour guide for Lori. Right?"

"All that, and more. It's like you have to cram ten Christmases into just a few days. It's like you think we'll never have another Christmas again." Phill gasped and nearly lost her grip on the shield. Then a gaggle of children, escorted by a dozen adults, ran right through her, and she almost did lose her grip.

She watched the children go through the door of the shop. What were they doing out of school? Had she lost track of time? Wasn't it still morning, barely 10?

"Christmas story time," Will said, leaning to one side to look around her and watch the children scurry into the shop. He flinched when the door slammed shut. "Don't you wish you were a kid, a Human kid, believing that magic is real even without much evidence? And then coming to a place like Divine's where you get just enough proof to keep believing, even when adults tell you magic isn't real. Sometimes I envy Humans. Life is so much more of an adventure, when you don't know, when you don't see and--" His eyes widened and his eyebrows raised up almost past his hairline when Phill slapped her hand over his mouth.

"Are you sick?" She glared when he didn't answer. Then she realized she still had her hand over his mouth. "Is that the problem? You're sick and you think you're dying, so you're cramming everything in?" She took her hand away and stepped back.

Maybe that was the problem with them both. Need wasn't turning on because Will was dying. How could she bond with her best friend, her partner in crime-and-adventure, if he was dying? It was kind of like a protective reflex, according to some Fae physicians and philosophers. The first two or three decades after Need bonded a couple together were the most dangerous, because if something deadly hit one partner, the other could die just from the snapping of the bond.

Please, no. I can't lose him now, just when I'm getting up the courage to do something about how I feel. I don't care if we're not officially bonded, he's mine!

"Not me," Will said slowly, shaking his head, his eyes big and dark with sorrow. The light around them actually dimmed, and it had nothing to do with the dimensional shield. "I'm scared it's you."

"Me? I'm perfectly healthy." She would have laughed, even accused him of making a very bad joke to distract her, but the sorrow clear in his eyes was too real. "Will, I'm fine. I promise. I even went to visit Great-Uncle Throckmorton before we came here. What? Don't give me that terrified, the-sky-is-falling look."

"You're worried about it too, aren't you?" he whispered, sounding like he choked.

"About what?"

"About not --" His face got red.

On second thought, if he wasn't choking, she might just do it for him.

"Not what?" She realized her hands were going up, aiming for his throat. She tucked them behind her back and strategically stepped backward, out of the danger zone. "I'm not what?"

"No, you are. You're dying. You're sick, at the very least. Because you aren't... You know."

"No, I don't!" To her shock and amusement, her voice was loud enough to penetrate the dimensional shield and make three icicles fall from Angela's porch. "Spit it out!"

"Need," Will whispered, and turned even brighter red.

"What about it?"

"You aren't -- you haven't -- you won't -- you know." Now he went pale and stood up tall, straightening his shoulders like he braced himself for bad news.

"Idiot!" Fury made an entire asteroid belt of sparks burst out of her and swirl in crazy orbit around her head, penetrating the side of the house, through the door and coming back out the other side.

At the same time, Phill wanted to burst out laughing. Was that what people were saying about her? She was dying and that's why she hadn't hit Need? Privately, she thought all the time she spent in the Human realms had knocked her cycles out of whack, but she couldn't get Throckmorton or the half-dozen other Fae physicians to listen to her theory, let alone consider it. They always brought up handfuls of cases of other Fae women who went into Need right on time, despite spending their entire lives among Humans. That just proved Phill's point, as far as she was concerned: her life was unstable, so why shouldn't her body clock be as well?

"Aren't you worried about it?" Will braced himself against the porch support post, as if the volume of her voice threatened to knock him off his feet.

"Yes, I'm worried. Any sane woman would be. But honestly..." All her roiling emotions suddenly fled, gone, as if a trap door had opened up and they just plummeted out of her. She felt empty, exhausted. "Maybe it's all for the better."

"That's crazy." He shook his head as if a swarm of bees had decided to pester him. Which was ridiculous. Since it was winter, bees were hibernating, and even if some kamikaze bee braved the cold, it couldn't get through the dimensional shield anyway.

"The last thing I want is for Need to kick in and shackle me to someone who won't be any fun, who will come between us. Or worse, someone who wants to take over. And still come between us, instead of making me stay home in the Fae realms all the time. I'd rather go the rest of my life like this than break up the team."

"Yeah?" Incredibly, the big goofball grinned.

And that got her angry again.

"You blithering coward!" Phill wished she had a pair of wings, even something as frilly and glittery and stupid as Maurice's. She wanted to rise up in the air, beating them furiously, battering Will with the hurricane-force winds she felt inside her. "That'd be just fine and dandy for you, wouldn't it? No risk. No fear of getting ambushed. That's been your problem all the time, hasn't it? That's what's been killing our fun. You're keeping us busy because you're afraid Need is going to hit me at any minute. You think if you run me ragged, I won't feel it, won't let it take over -- and won't trap you."

"Trap?" he squeaked, and slid off the railing, stumbling away from her.

"I don't know what made me think I was in love with you, when --" Phill inhaled so hard and fast, she nearly swallowed her tongue. She slapped her hands over her mouth and wished she knew a time reversal spell, so she could take back those words.

Especially when Will stared at her, so pale the sparkling white diamond blanket of snow looked dirty by comparison.

The only four-letter word capable of striking more terror into a Fae male than *Need* was *Love*.

"You're hopeless. We're both hopeless." Phill let out a shriek and propelled herself up, through the roof of the porch, into the chilly morning sunshine. She popped the bubble of the dimensional shield, raining snow down on Will as he stumbled down the steps and looked around, searching the sky for her.

Who needed wings when she had embarrassment and fury to propel her?

She needed to get away. Far away. Somewhere quiet and calm and isolated, so she could think things through.

"Phill, listen, you've got it all wrong." Will propelled himself up into the sky.

"Stay away from me, you sniveling coward!" she shrieked, and tore open a slit into whatever available dimension she could find. She hung around on the other side just long enough to seal it closed and keep Will from following her, then she took off.

Friday, December 14

"It's the Mr. Spock effect, Daddy."

Bethany sat perfectly still, staring at her father across the kitchen table, unable to believe what had spilled out of her mouth. Sure, Harry's ears fascinated her, but had she subconsciously been comparing him to Spock? Was she turning into the *Bimbo of the Week*, who fell in love with the alien and then either got amnesia or died or had to give him up for the good of her planet?

Ben Miller sat down at the little bistro table next to the door and laughed hard enough to make his comb-over slip down over his eyebrows. "Honey, all I said was that you two seemed pretty friendly after such a short time together, and you're more relaxed with him than I've ever seen you with anybody. And then you got defensive." He fought the grin by narrowing his eyes and pursing his mouth into his deep-thinking expression.

"Yeah, defensive. And there's no reason to be. Harry is a great guy. I liked him from the minute we met." She sank into the chair opposite him and rested her elbows on the table, her chin in her fists. "Weird, huh?"

"'Some enchanted evening,'" he half-sang under his breath.

"Daddy!"

"That's how I felt about your mother, first time I saw her. Why shouldn't it happen to you?"

Bethany forgot how to breathe. Was her father, her best pal and defender, the man who taught her to never settle for second best, actually giving his stamp of approval to Harry? After only a two-hour ride from the airport to the hotel? What had they talked about, besides sightseeing and last-minute Christmas shopping?

"Men. You're an entirely different species," she sighed. "What went on between you two that I missed?"

"It's not what happened between us, honey, but what I see between the two of you. You're the focus for him. And it's not a job to him, either."

"Oh." She pressed her hands to her face. Her cheeks were definitely as hot as she imagined.

"Don't push it, Bethy. Let whatever happens, happen. But don't let any worries about what I'll think get in the way, okay?"

A new thought cut through the swirling images and giddiness trying to take her breath away. She tipped her head to one side and studied him, eyes narrowing as her insides calmed. "It isn't the Spock factor with you, is it, Daddy?" She laughed when Ben sat back, eyes widening, and his mouth opened and shut a few times. "The alienness. I bet you can't wait to put him through the inquisition and learn everything you can about the Fae."

"Well -- yes -- I suppose --"

"Everybody set?" Harry walked into the kitchenette. "Alexi and Megan are meeting us for dinner between their third and fourth shows. I warned them you'd be full of questions, so don't worry, ask away."

Bethany burst out laughing, with her father not far behind. Harry's confused little frown, as he looked back and forth between them, only made them laugh harder.

~~~~~

Holly sighed as she attached the last bundle of silk daisies to the overhead lights in the small gym at Eden. Relief, the pain in her arms from holding them up for hours, or jealousy? She couldn't decide which was the stronger root to her sigh. Rubbing the back of her neck, she held onto the ladder with the other hand and leaned back a little, to get a better view of her handiwork.

Streamers of variegated blue and white swooped from the tops of the walls to the lights and between the lights, creating an illusion of puffy clouds in a bright blue sky. Blue gels borrowed from the
~~~~~

theater department at WB covered the lights, which were surrounded by bundles of daisies.

"If you can't wait until summer to get married," Holly muttered as she climbed down the ladder, "this is the next best thing."

"Perfect." Diane paused in the doorway of the little gym and gazed up at the ceiling.

"Not quite, but getting there." Holly decided her aching muscles were well paid for by her friend's delight. Then she laughed when a flicker of guilt rippled through the delight on Diane's face. "You thought it'd be a disaster, didn't you?"

"I didn't know how you were going to pull it off, and I couldn't visualize it." She stepped farther into the gym. "This is a thousand times better than I imagined. Tomorrow is going to be ..." She nodded for punctuation. "Perfect."

"That is incredible," Troy said, as he stepped into the gym at the end of Diane's words. "Holly, forget about the library. You should go into decorating and become a wedding planner or something like that. You're a genius."

"Inspired." Holly bit her tongue to keep from confessing that she had dreamed several times of turning the small gym into a sunny meadow under a blue sky, when she agreed to be in charge of decorating for Diane and Troy's wedding. Somehow, she had written notes to herself of how to pull off the decorations while she was half-asleep, or maybe even fully asleep. Was there such a thing as sleep-writing? All she knew was that she had awakened one morning with a notepad clutched in her fingers, pages of scribbled notes, and the answer to her dilemma clearly spelled out. Reading her notes, she remembered dreaming the plan.

How many months had it been since she became unable to remember a single detail of her dreams when she woke up? It used to be a single dream could carry her through an entire otherwise unbearable day. Now she had nothing when she woke, except a sense that she had thoroughly enjoyed herself. Sometimes she woke up with the strangest sensation of a kiss on her lips, and phantom warmth on her arms, as if she had embraced someone.

Holly mentally gave herself a shake and sternly, silently scolded herself to get back to the matters at hand. Diane and Troy were getting married tomorrow. The hard part was done, filling the sky with clouds and daisies and sunshine. Now to bring in the tables and cover the walls with blue and green plastic tablecloths to simulate more sky and a meadow. It was nearly 8pm, and she wanted to have a good night's sleep, after a long soak in her tub, so she would look her best as a bridesmaid tomorrow. Thank goodness she wasn't maid of honor and didn't have all those chores Troy had saddled his sister, Meggie with. Decorating was much easier than all the social obligations, coordinating the groomsmen, and picking up Diane's many relatives at the airport all afternoon.

"Dang." Holly stopped short, two steps out into the hall, just as she was about to open her mouth and call for the second wave to start hauling in the next cartloads of supplies.

"What's wrong?" Diane grasped Holly's arm.

"I forgot all about the rehearsal dinner. Why'd you have to schedule it so late, anyway?"

"Because of everybody's schedule. We can't rehearse without the best man, and he's arriving about..." Troy looked at his watch. "Ten minutes ago." His cell phone growled at him. "Right on time. Sorta," he muttered as he dug in his pocket.

"What's next?" Diane hooked her arm through Holly's, and they set off down the hall. Gina had let them have a storage room to stash all their supplies over the last two weeks of preparations.

"Got it!" Lanie called, wheeling out of the storage room with a plastic bin full of tablecloths precariously balanced on her lap, and her two brothers pushing the carts that held the tables.

"I swear, you read my mind lately," Holly said on a sigh.

"Nope, you're just such a good organizer, we can predict down to the minute when you'll be ready for the next wave." Lanie glanced at her shoulder, and for a moment Holly glimpsed a flicker of some kind, a sparkle, like an errant ray of sunshine. She definitely needed to get home and soak in a hot tub with the herbal bath salts from Jane's spa. Holly could have sworn she heard a tiny voice laughing and telling Lanie to "Mush!"

The glimpses of sparkles got worse as the evening progressed, and she wondered if she had pushed herself too hard. Three times, Holly dropped the container of poster putty she was using to attach the plastic tablecloths to the walls. Three times, she started down the ladder to get it. Three times she saw the container sitting on the shelf of the ladder as soon as she got eye-level with it.

"Who's Maurice?" she asked, when the entire gym was draped

in blue and green up to the ceiling. Nothing could be done about the speckled linoleum without creating a safety hazard. At least it was a shade of green, even if in her personal opinion it looked more like dark puke than grass.

"Maurice?" Diane and Lanie gave her wide-eyed, innocent looks that were nearly convincing. "What are you talking about?"

"I know I heard both of you talking with someone named Maurice, but I don't see any strangers here at all." Holly arched her back as she crossed over to where they sorted through the golden crackle-glass vases Angela had donated from some deep dark corner of her cellar.

"No, we were talking *about* Maurice. You remember him, don't you?" Diane said slowly, glancing sideways at Lanie. "Angela's distant cousin, who was here in September?"

"Oh. Yeah." Holly rubbed the back of her neck. How could she have forgotten Maurice? It was a little frightening how he had seemed to know so much about her, how intent he had been on spending time with her, just showing up at the library when she got off work. Yet nice, too. He'd walked her home and said he was dying to go to that art movie she wanted to see at the Cedar Lee. Holly was only going to the art theater because a friend from college had a small part in it.

"That Maurice. That's right." She remembered how insistent he had been that she had to take the entire day off from work, Christmas Eve, so they could spend time together when he came back to town. "Is he here already? I thought he wasn't coming for another week or two."

"That's right," Lanie said. "We were just talking about that time he was ..." She glanced at Diane.

"When he was walking Meggie around town and the Keystone Kops attacked him, thinking he was trying to kidnap her or something," Diane filled in, her words stopping and starting as if someone was feeding her the words.

"Angela said Maurice contacted her a few days ago, to remind her to remind you that you and he have a date for Christmas Eve." Lanie glanced at her shoulder, and there was that sparkle again.

"A date?" Holly snorted. She knew she shouldn't be so cynical, but she was tired and her head hurt and she was having delusions. "I'm the incredible invisible woman, when it comes to dates."

"That's just because the right guy hasn't shown up yet. Or often enough," Diane added. A flash of light bounced off her nose and she flinched, then muffled laughter.

"Okay, I definitely need to see a doctor or get my eyes checked or something," Holly said, rubbing her eyes. "I am seeing things and hearing things and... Sorry." She offered an apologetic grin when Diane and Lanie exchanged concerned looks. "I'm just tired, that's all. I think I'm more nervous about your wedding than you are."

"That's because the half of my family that would try to turn my wedding into the event of the century is the half that isn't talking to me," she said with a sigh of laughter. "My fun relatives, the ones who like me just the way I am, are the ones coming into town. They're sensible enough to get into their hotel rooms tonight and leave me alone until after the ceremony."

"Lucky," Holly sighed.

"Double that," Lanie offered with a smirk. "My Mum is the last person I'd expect to care about all the fussy details, but she gets this look in her eye when she's helping Di and Jeri with wedding things. If I ever get married, I'd want to elope. But Mum would probably kill me for depriving her of a big, fussy, white wedding."

Lanie's adopted parents were only slightly reformed Hippies. Holly tried to imagine Charlie Zephyr in a tux and his trademark battered sandals, with his long gray ponytail halfway down his back, or Rainbow Zephyr, her hair dyed neon green, wearing a demure mother-of-the-bride dress.

At least Lanie had parents to drive her crazy, and Daniel Sheridan certainly seemed to show all the signs of wanting to get a lot more serious. All Holly had were friends who were as close as family could get. Wait a minute, how could she say that was *all* she had?

And Maurice, Angela's distant cousin who showed up a couple times in the year, for just a day at a time, and seemed to know all about her.

"Everybody ready?" Meggie scurried into the gym, dragging a tall East Indian stranger by the hand. "The best man and the maid of honor are here, so let's get this party started!"

"Thank goodness Meggie is thrilled to have you as a sister," Troy said, coming over to the table to join them. He wrapped an arm around Diane's waist. "Imagine how impossible she'd be if she didn't like you."

"Yeah, she's a good kid, our Meggie," that tiny voice said, off to Holly's left. From the corner of her eye, Holly could have sworn she saw a tiny man, surrounded by a corona of sparkling light, but when she turned her head, he was gone.

She excused herself and ran to the pop machine in the lobby. A dose of caffeine and sugar and a double dose of ibuprofen would get her through the evening.

Saturday, December 15

Maurice rode over to Eden on Angela's shoulder, rather than flying over from Divine's for the wedding. He wanted to save all his magic and strength to ward off any unforeseen disasters. Diane had admitted, in a rare spurt of nerves, that some of her nastier relatives might just show up and try to sabotage the wedding. It would either be in retaliation for the trouble Troy had caused a family-owned company when he worked with the EPA, or to punish Diane for not letting them use her in their dynastic plans. She had taken warning from centuries of faerie tales and political disasters, and invited every member of her family, no matter how distantly related they were, along with their various hangers-on and sycophants. If everyone was invited, no one could claim offense. Evil faeries who *were* invited to the christening didn't show up. The ones who *weren't* invited showed up with curses.

Chances were very good most of her relatives were too busy or wouldn't even remember who she was. A best-case scenario had an avalanche of presents, from people paying tribute to the Rittenhouse family megalith of power, and lots of RSVPs with regrets. A worst-case scenario had people showing up for the wedding who hadn't spoken to or seen each other in decades, turning the wedding into an armed camp of backbiting and murderous looks.

So far, more than half the people who had been sent invitations had sent regrets and money. Diane had calculated that half of those who hadn't responded just wouldn't show up or send anything. Those who she wanted to come had responded. But there was still that quarter of the invited guests who were still in limbo. That was where the problem would come from.

"Look at it this way, kid," Maurice had offered. "They'll all figure you're on the other guy's side, and write you off their lists forever. You won't have to invite them to baby showers or birthday parties or graduation parties or Christmas, for the rest of your life."

He had decided it was better to take precautions and be prepared for the worst thing to happen. So he hoarded all the energy and magic he could. He stayed on Angela's shoulder until it was time for her to go into the dressing room set aside for the bride and her attendants. Maurice hovered near the doorway until he made sure Holly had arrived all right. For just a moment, he feasted his eyes on her, relieved to see she looked well rested, with a flush of excitement in her cheeks, her eyes sparkling.

"Next year, Holly Berry." Maurice flew off in search of Troy. He wasn't a groomsman, but he could still offer some advice, or at the very least tell a few jokes to help Troy get through any last-minute attacks of nerves and cold feet.

"Don't tell me how she looked, whatever you do," Troy said, when Maurice caught up with him. He was checking the silvery blue runner that led from the doorway of the small gym to the raised platform in the middle of the room.

"Ahh, it's not bad luck to hear about the bride before the wedding," Maurice offered.

"No, but I might just break down and try to sneak a peek." He grinned and gave a testing kick to the platform, which had been covered in green outdoor carpet, to simulate a hillside.

Maurice felt particularly proud of the decorations, because he and Holly had worked on them in her dreams for what felt like months. He had looked into Diane and Troy's memories of that fateful night when they had fallen through a painting in Divine's Emporium and had an adventure in another world. Then he had shared those memories with Holly, repeatedly, hoping that somehow, something would sneak through from her dreams to her waking mind, to help her recreate the setting Diane and Troy remembered with such fondness.

"I swear, I haven't peeked. She could be wearing a blue dress for all I know. Do you mind? Wanna save my strength." He gestured at Troy's tuxedo-clad shoulder.

"Be my guest." Troy waited until he came in for a landing

before striding out of the room.

They couldn't talk anymore after that, because Troy was surrounded by people until it was time for him and his two attendants to take their place on the platform with Pastor Rocky.

Maurice folded his wings back and played with the idea of giving himself antennae and changing his wings, to look like a psychedelic butterfly. Troy wouldn't see him, but Diane would, coming down the aisle. He liked the idea of making her burst out laughing as she approached the platform. Angela might even laugh, although Maurice suspected she would consider it her duty to frown and scold him for the wrong type of levity.

He dropped the idea after playing with it for a few minutes. There was nothing else to do but listen to Troy talk to guests and watch out for Diane's relatives, just in case the nose-in-the-air troublemakers decided to show up after all.

Maurice had one mission today: make sure Diane and Troy's wedding went off perfectly. That meant heading the troublemakers off at the pass. And that meant he couldn't be a troublemaker, even if it was innocent, fun trouble. Still, he saved the butterfly disguise for later, when it would be safe to generate some hysterical laughter. Maybe he could talk Angela into having a costume party the next time he was full-size and magic-less, and he could make a big, goofy butterfly his costume.

What would Holly think, seeing him in a goofy costume like that? She hardly knew him when she was awake. He didn't want to generate the wrong impression.

Wow, he thought, stunned, and was glad he was sitting down. *I guess maybe I'm finally growing up!*

As if his thoughts conjured her, Holly appeared in the doorway of the little gym. Maurice's heart jerked to a stop, and then took a couple hops and skips in his chest before settling back into place and its proper rhythm. Her eyes glowed and a happy flush put roses in her cheeks. She and Meggie and Angela wore white wreaths of daisies and baby carnations, and simple, calf-length dresses of pale green and yellow.

He remembered how pleased Holly had been with the style of the dress, and the fact she could wear it again. She especially liked how it flattered her figure without looking like a sack on Meggie and Angela. Maurice had been confused for a few minutes, wondering what was wrong with her figure. Then he had flashed back to his first sight of her, and how he had groaned and begged Angela not to make Holly his first assignment, because he didn't think he could find anyone who would want her.

"I'm an idiot." He promised himself, when he got back to Divine's, he would beat his head against the wall in recompense for being such a stereotyped testosterone-driven guy, judging Holly by how well she fit into a bikini.

"All guys are idiots," Troy murmured. "That's why we need women to help us figure things out. Thank God I found Diane when I did."

"You tripped over her, pal," Maurice offered, earning a snort of laughter from him.

Then he wisely shut up, because Angela had started up the runner behind Holly and Meggie was right behind her, and Diane stood in the doorway, a vision in flowing white, with a cascade of ivy and daisies clutched in her hands.

"Showtime," Maurice murmured. He patted Troy's shoulder and launched himself into the air. "Good luck, pal. I got your back." He would have preferred to keep his ringside seat on Troy's shoulder, but Maurice decided a bird's eye view would let him spot potential problems before they struck.

Chapter Eight

Sunday, December 16

Harry felt a buzz and tingle soon after the plane crossed the Indiana/Ohio border. The magic holding off his invisibility flickered, and he prayed the flight attendants wouldn't come through first class until he got everything back under control. He glanced across the aisle, where Bethany sat by the window and her father sat next to her. Both were asleep. That was a relief. He told himself not to be such a whiny baby. Of course, Bethany would want to spend as much time with her father as possible. Still, he felt like he had to sit by and watch someone else play with his favorite toy, just because he couldn't sit next to her during the flight from Vegas to Ohio. What was wrong with him?

It wasn't like they were an item.

Besides, they had first class all to themselves, so it wasn't like he had to worry about autograph hounds or sleazes hitting on Bethany. Her father could certainly keep slimes from drooling on her, if anyone recognized her -- and it certainly didn't look like anyone had. His invisibility field blurred her features just enough she was unrecognizable. That was what he was being paid for, and other than that aberration when they had nearly kissed, everything was working according to plan.

"Almost there," Ben said softly, glancing at Harry.

"Almost where?" Harry liked the man. The fact he trusted Harry with his daughter's safety almost from the start meant a lot. He didn't even mind answering the questions Ben threw at him at unexpected times. They were logical questions, showing he had a good grasp of the workings of magic and tried to separate the truth of the Fae and Fae culture from all the smokescreens and legends and fables started by the Ministry of Misinformation. Even discounting all that, Harry just liked the guy. He was a good example of the salt-of-the-earth type who had settled the wilderness that used to be America.

"Neighborlee." He raised up a little in his seat to see out

Bethany's window. "We're probably flying right over it, or close enough it doesn't matter."

"Flying over..." Harry realized the buzzing tingle of something at work felt stronger, had been growing while he had his pity party. "Something special about it?"

"As our local comedian says, Neighborlee is the weirdness capital of the United States."

"Is that on a bumper sticker or something? On the billboard as you leave town?"

"That's one of the things that makes us weird. Strange things happen, and outsiders don't seem to notice, or remember very long, while locals just shrug it off. It's normal for us to have odd things happen. It drives away the people who don't belong and kind of tests and strengthens those of us who choose to live there." He glanced at Bethany, who was still asleep, and met Harry's gaze again. "I think you'll have a good time there. Bethy will certainly enjoy being home. And able to run around outside of town without being mobbed."

"What about inside town?"

"That's the nice thing about Neighborlee. Folks will leave her alone if she wants to be. And folks who won't be polite have a hard time finding her."

"Convenient. I suppose you can't figure out what causes this and put it in a bottle, maybe something Bethany can inoculate herself with, to protect her when she isn't home?"

"I wish." He sighed. "She's been gone too long. She needs to recharge badly. Just wander up and down the streets and hang around with her friends. You'll help her do that. She needs that more than she needs anything else."

"Gottcha."

Harry mulled what Ben said while the plane made its approach to Cleveland Hopkins Airport. Maybe this was the answer to how Bethany had an air of magic that clung to her, and yet had no inherent magic born into her. She had absorbed magic from the land and air.

So that hypothetical answer led to another question: what was the source of magic in Neighborlee? It had to be strong, well-grounded, if the magic it emanated seeped into the air and ground and water, so people could soak it up.

So did that mean everybody in Neighborlee had magic?

No. He shoved that idea away immediately. Ben didn't have magic seeping out of him. If the magic in Bethany came from living in Neighborlee, her father should have even more magic. So that brought Harry back to square one. There was something special about Bethany that made her soak up magic.

That answered the question of what he had felt when they flew over Neighborlee. Whatever was there was the source of Bethany's magic. Maybe.

Harry closed his eyes as the plane descended and muffled a groan. Every time he thought he had some answers, he got more questions, or found something that contradicted his theory. He was as close to answering the question of Bethany's magic as he was to turning off the wonky invisibility spell that had plagued him for so long.

"I should have listened to Mother," he muttered, as the plane gently touched down on the runway. Then he gasped as insight slammed into him with near-blinding brilliance.

Since her father didn't seem to have any inherent magic, maybe Bethany got her magic from her mother, who had died when she was nine.

~~~~~

"What's wrong?" Bethany whispered, as her father turned down the main drag running through Neighborlee. She had taken the back seat, insisting Harry had to take the front seat and get the ten cent tour of her hometown. She rested her arms on the back of his seat and leaned close enough she could smell the clean scent of his soap.

Or maybe that was Harry himself. She sighed quietly, not at all amazed that everything about him was nice.

"There's...strong magic in this town, that's all. It's kind of like going home, without all the hassle of relatives asking what I've been doing, how long I'm staying home, and if I... Ah, never mind."

Bethany muffled a giggle when she saw how the tips of his ears got deep red. Too bad he would be wearing a stocking cap when they went outside, to hide his pointed ears. Then again, so many odd things got overlooked in Neighborlee, Harry probably could go around bareheaded, and blushing so hard his ears glowed, and nobody would notice.
~~~~~

"Are you sure you won't stay with us?" her father asked. "There's plenty of room."

"You don't really need me to shield Bethany, now that she's home. After what you told me about the town. From what I just felt, driving over the border … there's a spell to keep the creeps away. I'll be more effective if I'm able to move around and get a feel for the town, who belongs and who doesn't." Harry looked over his shoulder, meeting her gaze. Bethany loved his crooked, half-shy grin. "I can imagine a bunch of the real die-hards coming here to try to track you down once they realize you're not in Hollywood, and coming up zippo. Even if they know your address. Easy enough to learn from the Internet." Again that grin. "It's easier to find out what's what with that, than if I used the Ether Lexicon."

"What's that?" Ben asked, his tone so eager Bethany sank back in the seat, muffling her giggles with both hands over her mouth.

"It's a book that's as large or as small as you need it to be. It contains answers to everything, but you have to know what the right questions are."

"So if some of the loonies who won't let me have a minute of privacy got hold of the Ether Lexicon, they'd know where I am right this moment?" Bethany shuddered, not sure she liked this glimpse into how things were run among the Fae.

"If the Lexicon thinks it's worthwhile to follow what you're doing. It might just decide the person asking is being rude, and refuse to answer."

"It sounds like this thing is alive," her father said.

"Kind of. It can make connections and sometimes even figure out what you want before you do. It's that old, it's that full of knowledge. And it gets bigger all the time, as more things are learned and Fae do more things."

"Cool." Bethany sighed as her father came to the stop sign in front of the Neighborlee Arms. "Here we are. I'll be back in two hours, and we'll go on a walking tour, okay?"

"Sounds good." Harry turned and looked at the front door of the stately old building, his tone fading out a little and his expression growing distracted.

Bethany knew that look. She had grown up seeing it on her father's face, heard the same sound in his voice. Something had caught his attention and all his concentration was being drawn away from her. Having grown up in Neighborlee, she knew the possibilities were endlessly wonderful and weird.

Harry got out and her father popped the hatch so he could walk around to grab his duffle and suitcase. Bethany waved and watched him walk to the front steps of the old hotel. She turned, trying to keep Harry in sight as her father drove away -- home.

~~~~~

Harry felt his anti-invisibility spell wavering as he signed into the Neighborlee Arms. With all the theories bouncing around in his head and the sensations vibrating through the ground and air and ether, it was no wonder he had a hard time concentrating.

The strongest sensations told him there were several Fae nearby. If not physically present in the old hotel, they had spent enough time in the building recently to generate a resonance. It was similar to someone with a strong aroma leaving an impression of his presence behind after he exited a room.

Holding onto his patience -- and visibility -- Harry kept a pleasant expression on his face, a casual tone to his voice, and avoided thrumming his fingers on the counter as he waited for the chatty young man at the counter to finish signing him into his room and hand him the key. Harry knew many eyes would be watching him as he climbed the stairs. He was a stranger here. No doubt a number of people saw him get out of the Millers' car. Small towns being what they were, word was already spreading that not only was Bethany home for Christmas, but she had brought a young man who was not staying with her and her father.

"You think you know everything, but you don't know anything," Harry muttered, once he had his second floor room's door safely shut behind him. He raised a muffling spell so someone standing with a stethoscope or a glass pressed to the door wouldn't hear what he said or did, even if he played a bass drum.

Sighing with relief, he let go of the anti-invisibility spell. The faint tingling faded to nothing. His hand and arm went invisible, and the rest of him did so after a few moments. He felt as if a heavy blanket that swaddled all his senses had been pulled away.

"Now for the first big question." He took the power he no longer expended on being visible, and called for the Ether Lexicon.

It popped into his outstretched hands, appropriately shaped like the old-fashioned hotel register he had signed moments ago.
~~~~~

Three names flashed through a rainbow of colors among all the faded, muted, black ink smears of ordinary Humans signing the guest register.

"Wilfred and Philomena and Angeloria. Interesting. What are they doing in town?" Harry muttered.

The Lexicon wasn't forthcoming with that information, but it did tell him all three Fae were not currently in the hotel. None of them were together. Harry didn't know Will and Phill personally. They were explorers, making a good name for themselves and a good living exploring the Human world and finding explanations for things and practices that had been puzzling the more sheltered, isolationist Fae for centuries. As for Angeloria, the less time he had to spend in her presence, the happier he would be. They weren't enemies, but some painful childhood stupidity was better left forgotten, and she was a large part of it.

After getting more thoroughly settled in his room, Harry decided it was time to do some reconnoitering of his own, before Bethany came back for him. He set himself an internal timer so he could be back to the hotel before Bethany arrived. Then he sent out a locator, to pinpoint where each of the other three Fae were.

Phill was nowhere within a thousand miles. Lori was on the far side of the town. Will was closest. That suited Harry perfectly. He left the hotel and less than two minutes later found Will sitting in the Sipping Post, the coffee shop right next door to the Neighborlee Arms. Harry had always faintly loathed Fae men like Will, handsome, elegantly casual in jeans, a bulky black sweater, and a vest jacket, relaxed and assured.

Or maybe not so relaxed and assured. Something was distracting him, or Will would have sensed the locator that brought Harry to him, and reacted when he showed up.

He sat there, one elbow on the little table, gazing out at the street with a glum, almost forlorn expression. Interestingly, in the ten minutes Harry observed him, every time a woman with long black hair walked past, Will sat up and his eyes brightened. Then something about the woman disappointed him and he slumped over the table again.

Lose something? Harry asked as he approached the door of the coffee shop. He raised his gloved hand to catch Will's attention. Mental contact was a courteous warning. Nothing like sneaking up on another Fae and startling him into shooting off sparks or vanishing outright. He was doubly sensitive to such tricks. Someone or something had startled him while he was working his invisibility spell as a child, leading to his current condition.

Has Neighborlee suddenly become the place to be for Fae out on adventures? Will asked, offering a weary smile. He gestured at the chair next to him. Harry nodded thanks for the invitation and sat.

"Gorgeous day." He hated inane, useless conversation, especially when he wanted to know what Will and Phill were doing in Neighborlee. It made perfect sense that they were here investigating the power that pulsed through the whole town, but it was more polite to ask. And it was easier on him to use vocal communication when he maintained his anti-invisibility spell for the sake of all the people around them.

"Supposed to get even more gorgeous as Christmas approaches." Will came alert, sitting up straighter as yet another lithe figure topped with long, black, curly hair strolled past.

Harry nearly laughed aloud when he realized what Will was on the alert for: Phill. He had only studied their images in the Ether Lexicon to be able to identify them on sight. How could he be so oblivious, not to make the connection right away?

"So, where's Philomena?"

"She blew a couple dozen fuses at me the other day and split into a parallel dimension." Will snorted when Harry stiffened at the carelessness of his words. "You obviously don't know anything about Neighborlee, do you? You can have conversations like this all the time, and people mostly ignore you. I still haven't figured out if it's some sort of low-level masking and mild general amnesia spell, or if people are just so used to off-beat things happening, they ignore it. Or the fact they have a really, really active *Star Trek* club that plays with every known science fiction and fantasy universe. I've been here when they've had one of their spring rites parties, and people are walking around town in full costume. Doesn't faze anybody." He settled back in his chair, deliberately turning away from the window. "So, what does bring you here?"

"Work, actually. I'm guarding a local celebrity, helping her move through the crowds, semi-invisible. Give her some breathing room."

"Oh, yeah, that's right. Bethany." He nodded. "You treat her right, understand? I watched her grow up. Besides, she's under Angela's protection."

"Angela?"

"I suppose I should give you the fifty cent tour, warn you about the trouble spots, the hot spots." His grin grew a little wider, a little more secure. "Then there's Maurice." He shook his head.

"Maurice?" Harry wondered if somehow he had fallen into one of those role playing game books some Humans were fond of a few years ago, where there were choices to make on every page, and each choice took the reader or player in a new direction.

Maybe a questing spell had gone awry years ago, soaking into the air and soil and water of this town before there were even people, and that caused all the off-beat occurrences?

"Angela is the town's guardian. Along with a couple other people who have grown up here, kind of soaked up the energy, I guess you'd say."

"Ah ha. And Bethany is one of the town's guardians? I knew the minute I met her there was some sort of magic in her, but she doesn't exactly have magic, per se."

"Lots of that going around in a town like this." He tapped his cup of hot chocolate with a peppermint stick in it. It filled, and a second one appeared next to it.

"Thanks." Harry inhaled the rich scent of dark chocolate. He needed that more than some Humans needed aspirin and Prozac.

"My pleasure. The folks who run this place won't mind, which is why I don't normally do it, but..." He tipped his head toward the back of the coffee shop, where the two lines waiting for service were four people long, each. "So, how'd you get the gig helping Bethany do the 'Don't notice me' game?"

Harry sighed. Even worse than getting periodic lectures from relatives on his foolish carelessness so many years ago, was telling a total stranger his background. Especially one who definitely needed some cheering up and who struck Harry as a possible friend. Especially if he could explain certain things about Neighborlee that would make Harry's investigation a lot simpler and shorter. Taking a deep breath, Harry explained with as few words as possible about his accident, accompanied by images that went straight from his memory to Will's consciousness, to illustrate what words sometimes could not explain.

To his great relief, his new friend leaned back in his chair, whistled softly, and shook his head. There was no scorn, no amusement, but something akin to wonder, mixed with sympathy.

"Ouch. Nice that you've got friends and family on the outside who can help out, let you get around and actually put the short circuit to good use." Will nodded. "I've heard about Alexi and Megan. It seems to me her father is a distant relative, maybe by marriage. Phill and I don't spend that much time back home. Too stuffy and enclosed, know what I mean?" He grinned when Harry nodded. "So I don't really hear all the gossip, who's calling who out for rebellion and hauling others in front of the Fae Disciplinary Council for violations of the Invisibility to Mortals Act, or some such stupid political nonsense. Maybe I should head out to Vegas and give them a visit. Just to offer her some support from family."

"I hear, she wasn't really accepted until Alexi married her," Harry offered.

"Yeah, the old folks -- anybody over 600 -- can be pretty snobby and unreasonable. Why punish the Halflings for the philandering of their parents, anyway? It's not like they chose to be born."

"You don't know the half of it. Alexi and I have another cousin who spends all her time in the Human realms as a daycare teacher."

"Oooh, nice power source right there, all those kids." Will nodded appreciatively.

"She hooked up with a guy who has some Fae blood way far back, and he had to get free of a curse put on a distant, distant ancestor back when there were knights in dented armor running around. Sure, curse the bozo who tried to cut the points off your ears or force you to grant him three wishes, but don't punish his kids and their kids. That's just overkill."

"Fae have long, nasty memories." Will sighed.

"So do you mind my asking what Philomena blew circuits about?"

"I'd rather not talk about it. Still can't figure it out myself. I should probably go talk to Angela, but you know how women stick together. She'll probably tell me it was something I should have seen and done fifty years ago."

"Yeah, typical. But I'd still like to talk to her about my problem."

"Don't know if she can cure a wonky invisibility spell," Will offered with a grin.

"No, more like figuring out how Bethany is magic, but doesn't really have magic. It shorted out my anti-invisibility spell and my invisibility spell at the same time, in a public place. How am I supposed to keep her safe from the lunatic fans and give her a nice, quiet, family Christmas, if I can't depend on things to stay the way they are and where I put them?"

"Good point." He got up, snapped his fingers, and several dollar bills landed on the table. "Let me give you the tour, then."

Will gave Harry a running monologue on the various shops and current events in Neighborlee as they walked down several streets and made a few strategic turns. He sometimes slowed his words, looking around as yet another woman only distantly similar to Phill crossed their path. Harry swallowed a grin. Whatever was wrong with Will and Phill, it was clear his new friend was smitten with her, as the old-timers said. Couldn't he see that?

Or was that the problem?

"Will?" A shiny black pickup extended cab pulled up next to them as they approached a stoplight intersection. A pretty blonde leaned out the window. "Have you seen Phill?"

"Not for a couple days." Will stepped up to the truck. "Something wrong?"

"No, I just haven't seen her or you and ..." The young woman's gaze strayed from Will to Harry. "Hargrove?"

"Hey, Lori." He sighed and silently asked if there was a convention of Fae descending on Neighborlee for the holidays.

"You look great. What are you doing here?"

"Business. In fact, I need to get back to the hotel to meet my client." He nodded to Will. "Thanks for the help. Bethany's taking me on the tour, so we'll probably end up at Divine's. Nice seeing you again, Lori."

"Hargrove, wait." A purplish-pink haze spilled through the air as Lori leaned further out the window of the truck cab. "Please, don't run off."

"Not running. I just have to be somewhere else soon. I'll catch up with you later." He continued down the street and consciously fought not to burst into a mad dash. Or worse, let go of his control over the anti-invisibility spell.

He had been spying on Lori and several of her best friends

when he had his accident with the invisibility spell. Her face would be forever linked with his accident and the problems that had plagued him ever since. It didn't help matters any that Lori had laughed at him for years when they were growing up. Nice laughter, mostly, but she had thought his dreams were silly, of becoming an explorer of the outer limit realms where few Fae had gone and survived to return.

She had apologized and blamed immaturity, but that had never really taken away the embarrassment and the lingering discomfort of memories. The less time Harry had to spend in Lori's presence, where she would remember and maybe make the mistake of telling others, such as Bethany, about his foolishness and his accident, the happier he would be. Harry had been able to give Bethany the gist of his difficulties, and she had been sensitive enough not to ask for details.

He couldn't bear it if she heard the full truth of his immaturity and stupidity. Starting with his tendency to spy on people when he should have had the courage and intelligence to confront them directly. The last thing Harry wanted was for Bethany to either feel sorry for him, or worse, be disgusted by him.

He had time to kill, so he stopped at a bakery on the same street as the hotel, where the very air tasted of chocolate and melt-in-your-mouth pastry. He saw enormous chocolate muffins displayed in the window and went in for one. Strictly for medical purposes, of course.

By the time he got to the front of the line in the very crowded little bakery, his order of one triple chocolate mega-muffin had grown. Chocolate chocolate-chip biscotti dipped in dark chocolate, three triple chocolate mega-muffins, and a chocolate lava cake that he told them to not even bother putting in a bag. He held the warm mini cake filled with steaming hot fudge in one gloveless hand and ate it as he wandered down the street.

Harry settled on a bench in front of the hotel to nibble blissfully at his treat and watch the traffic of the town. Children built snowmen by the gazebo. Various shopkeepers and city workers decorated the gazebo and other municipal buildings.

The glitz and living magic of Fae high celebrations couldn't hold a candle to the joy and fun and old-fashioned glitter of smalltown Americana at the holidays. He loved it. Maybe, if he could keep control of his invisibility spell affliction, he would just stay out here in the Human realms. Who needed to go home to the Fae realms where everybody knew about his problems? If the people of Neighborlee could overhear conversations like he had with Will, and go on about their business without blinking, maybe he had found the place to stay.

Or maybe the fact that this was Bethany's hometown made him love the place.

"I'm in paradise right now," he muttered as he licked the last of the cooling fudge off his fingertips.

For punctuation, a car pulled up to the curb in front of the hotel. The window rolled down on the passenger side and Bethany leaned over from the driver's seat.

"Hey, sailor, new in town?" She waggled her eyebrows at him. When Harry leaped to his feet, she burst out in that delightful, chiming laughter he loved.

He took two steps to the car and remembered he had forgotten his bag of bakery. He turned back, slipped on a patch of ice, twisted sideways, then jolted as his feet hit the un-iced sidewalk.

"Are you okay?" she called, as he carefully continued reaching for his bag. Harry had a horrified vision of hitting that ice again on the return trip and losing all that life-giving dark chocolate.

"Fine." His face radiated enough heat to melt all the ice in the skating rink on the town square. Harry yanked on the handle of the door, half-expecting to find it locked. It swung open and he slid into the car.

It occurred to him that in that moment of total confusion, he should have lost control of his anti-invisibility spell. Then again, according to what Will had told him a little while ago, no one would even notice that he had gone invisible for a few seconds.

"Please tell me you love chocolate as much as I do," Bethany said, as he tossed the bakery bags on the seat between them.

"Triple chocolate mega-muffins or chocolate on chocolate on chocolate biscotti?"

"Marry me," she groaned. "A man who finally understands that chocolate is one of the essential vitamins."

"You better be careful, Miss Bethany. I might just take you up on that." Harry's hands shook a little as he dug into a bakery bag and pulled out the first thing he found.

His heart jolted a little and a soft voice wailed in the back of his mind when he pulled out a mega-muffin. He consoled himself that he had bought three. The awed delight in Bethany's eyes and her brilliant smile more than repaid him when he handed it over.

"So, have you got your bearings enough? Do you have any idea where you want to start with the tour?"

"Well... I ran into this guy at the coffee shop. He said Divine's Emporium would be a good starting point."

"Yeah, definitely. I wonder what Angela'll make of you?"

~~~~~

"Hargrove?"

The voice that came out of nowhere when he followed Bethany into Divine's Emporium didn't shock Harry. It was the fact that when he saw the source, he recognized the face. Just not so small. He belatedly remembered Will had mentioned Maurice being at Divine's Emporium, but the name just hadn't clicked. Then again, how many Maurices did he know of, even in the Fae realms? Harry's face burned and he felt his anti-invisibility spell slipping as he stared at the other Fae man.

"What are you doing here?" he blurted, and was glad to look ahead and see Bethany had continued on into a room with a counter and a cash register just inside the doorway.

"Exile. Man, you must have really had your head buried in your research, not to hear that I got caught by the Disciplinary Council." Maurice fluttered his wings so fast they were a blur, and came in for a landing on a shelf almost on eye level with Harry. "What do you think?"

"What? You have to wear them during daylight hours?" Harry bit his tongue against asking if he had to shrink himself to try out the wings. If they weren't so frilly and glittery and extravagant, he might have felt a little jealous.

"Pal, these things are attached, permanent-like, until my exile is over." Maurice shrugged. "What are you doing in town, anyway?"

"Bethany." He gestured toward the main room. "Guard duty."

"Guard? Like... You're going into bodyguard work?"

"More like letting my invisibility spell wrap around her so she can avoid some loonies and have a semi-normal Christmas at home with her father."

107
~~~~~

"If she's from around here, I doubt there's any such thing as a 'normal' Christmas at home." He chortled and leaped up, turned a triple somersault and glided down to land on Harry's shoulder. "Be a pal and introduce me, would ya? If you can."

"What do you mean, if I can?" Harry obediently continued down the aisle to the main room.

"Part of my exile is that I'm pretty much invisible and un-hearable to most Humans. Except the ones with a lot of magic."

"Bethany's got something, but I'm still trying to figure out if it's real magic, or something else."

"Well, we're having an actual convention of Fae this year. I wonder why," the blonde woman behind the counter said with a bemused smile, as Harry stepped into the room. "Another old friend, or a cousin?"

"Old school pal," Maurice said. "Angie-baby, meet Hargrove. Hey, I didn't think of this before, but maybe there's a cure in Divine's for what ails him. And I just got an answer to my other question." He leaped up from Harry's shoulder and fluttered over to hover in front of Bethany, on a level with her wide, staring eyes. "How ya doing, babe?"

"Maurice," Angela said, shaking her head, fighting not to smile.

"Uh ... fine." Bethany swallowed hard and glanced sideways at Harry. "I'm not imagining things, am I?"

"Bethany, meet Maurice, an old friend from back home. Maurice, this is Bethany Miller, movie star and current object of adoration by hundreds of psychos who don't know the meaning of 'restraining order.'" Harry breathed another sigh of relief when his words earned a grin from Bethany. He didn't know what he would have done if she hadn't taken his words as the teasing he meant.

"Nice to meet ya, kiddo." Maurice came in for a landing on the counter. "I just love it when people show up who can actually talk to me and see me. It gets really hard for Angela here, being the only who can talk back most of the time. I might be easy on the eyes, but not the nerves, know what I mean?"

Bethany giggled, which was exactly the right response, both for her and Maurice's sake. Harry just wished he hadn't been close enough to see the admiring once-over look Maurice gave her. Bethany wasn't his, but he had come to a realization during his chocolate glut that he was more than interested in staking a claim.

As soon as he got some answers to the root of whatever magic ran through this town, and how it had soaked into Bethany so she *was* magic more than she *had* magic. And from the considering look Angela gave him, head tilted to one side, lips slightly pursed, Harry sensed he might just be able to get all his answers from her. At the very least, he wouldn't have to do much explaining, since she obviously was on good terms with Maurice.

"Did you say you were exiled here?" Harry shook his head. "I don't see how this could be a place of exile. It's fantastic. The energy, the magic running through this town --"

"I knew it." Bethany pulled over a tall stool and settled at the counter, elbows on the marble surface. "There's always been something special about this place. You're why I am the way I am, why I see things that shouldn't be there, and I can... Oh, I don't know, finagle things to get out of jams. Most of the time. Maybe why I managed to be in the right place at the right time. Like Harry said -- magic, right?"

"In a sense." Angela reached across the counter and caught hold of one of Bethany's hands. "But in a larger sense... Well, I guess the time has come to take off the blinders. Especially if you're hanging around with Fae now. The magic is in you. You inherited it from your mother."

"My ... mother?" Bethany's happy, rosy glow faded a few notches. She glanced at Harry. He moved over and rested a hand on her shoulder, ready to support her in whatever she needed. "What about my mother?"

"In the simplest terms, she was a guardian. Of otherness. You know about the lost and abandoned children found nearby, who end up at the children's home?" Angela waited until Bethany nodded. "Your mother was a lost child. Or as Lanie and her gang call themselves, the Lost Kids. Stephanie had some minor talents, including the ability to essentially slap a patch on the barrier between dimensions of reality, when cracks developed and nasty things tried to break through."

"So you're a guardian too," Harry said quietly. He didn't like the tiny frown lines gathering around Bethany's eyes and mouth. He wondered why this information was new to her. Why wasn't she taught about her heritage?

"Neighborlee is a gathering place for the odd and unusual and even visitors from other realms, other dimensions. That's how I became connected to some representatives of the Fae, and how I became Maurice's parole officer for two years."

"Parole officer." He rolled the words around in his mouth and mind. They certainly fit Maurice, with his tendency to go overboard with his pranks and ideas of justice, and to get into trouble with the powers that be.

"Mom died in an accident," Bethany said, her voice a strained semi-whisper. "Things Dad has said over the years, things I remember... He didn't know about her being a ... what did you call it? Guardian?" She waited until Angela shook her head. "But this guarding got her killed?"

"She gave her life protecting this town, and stopped something very nasty from opening a doorway that would have brought our reality into dangerous contact with something it should never touch." Angela reached up with one hand to cup Bethany's cheek, brush a few strands of hair back from her face. "Unfortunately, the battle is never-ending. Her sacrifice only slowed the process and blunted the enemy's power."

"Uh... This nastiness is coming through?" Harry wondered why he hadn't sensed the inimical elements when he flew overhead. Certainly he should have sensed the discord in the power that pulsed through Neighborlee.

"It tries to. The guardians are vigilant, and we have been making alliances with others who fight the darkness. We have survived some crucial encounters with inimical forces in this world who try to break down the barrier, and let the dimensional invaders enter." She closed her eyes a moment and shook her head. "I'm sorry, Bethany. I was pleased when your acting took you away. You had the potential to carry your mother's strength and gifts, and more, because of your father's heritage. But Stephanie didn't want you to be a guardian, so we ... we agreed, when she died, to block your memories and keep you from being aware. Last year, when Athena came to visit you, it was to make sure our enemies didn't track you down and try to use you while you were outside of Neighborlee's protection."

"Athena?" Bethany shook her head. "She's a guardian? But she's not a lost kid."

"No, but her grandfather is, and so is her father, and growing up in Neighborlee just infused her with the power, as Lanie would say."

"Lanie. My Miss Lanie? My teacher?"

"Lanie is a guardian. She was performing her duties as a guardian when she broke her back."

"I … I remember her babysitting me … but I didn't remember until just now …" The pallor had left Bethany's skin. She rested more of her weight on her arms on the counter. The frown lines had smoothed out in her forehead. Harry suspected deep concentration, maybe even a little angry fascination, had taken the place of her pain and sorrow.

"I'm sorry, sweetheart," Angela murmured, and rested her hand on Bethany's head. "You will remember more as the cloud is lifted. Don't be angry with Athena. She had her own shock last year, and she hated keeping secrets from you. I have to assume that the timing of you coming here, the revelation … perhaps you have a part to play in the next phase, despite your mother's wishes."

"It's like a lot of my favorite books becoming real," Bethany murmured. "But it can't all be real, can it? What's real now?" She glanced to Harry, and he caught hold of her hand and held it, wishing he could do much more for her.

Angela nodded to Harry. "Bethany obviously knows about the Fae, since she's with you. Could you explain to her the basics of dimensions and doorways and realms?"

"Be glad to." Harry fought the urge to salute, or maybe he should bow? Something about Angela, so relaxed and timeless, despite her sorrow, reminded him of the Fae Queen and her court of intensely brilliant, ferociously logical advisors and councilors. Not that he had done more than watch them at work in the Bureaucratic Transparency viewing globe available to all Fae.

"So, you'll be hanging around for a while?" Maurice asked.

"Oh, yeah, we're home for Christmas. Maybe until New Year's. Just depends on how long it takes until the loonies realize she came here instead of hiding out in LA, like she did last year."

Bethany snorted and her mouth twisted in a crooked, one-sided grin. She seemed to be coming out of the brief mental haze. "Daddy and I rented a place in the hills last year, guaranteed un-find-able. We had to move out in the middle of the night, Christmas Eve, because people were camping in front of my door." She sighed.

"Maybe I never should have left Neighborlee. I was happy doing commercials and community theater. Maybe I should quit Hollywood and come home. Start my own theater company. Does Neighborlee High need a new drama teacher?"

"Go get your lessons, enjoy Christmas with your father, and we'll worry about your career next year," Angela said, making a shooing motion toward the door. "Oh, and take this with you."

Harry saw the dimensional slit pop open and a bag of chocolate paradise wafers, from his favorite Fae confectionary, popped into her hand. He had time to read the label and see it was his favorite flavor, with raisins and cinnamon and peanut butter swirls, as he caught it with the hand not holding Bethany's.

"You two will need some fuel for your discussions," Angela said.

"Hey," Maurice said. "That's the good stuff. The really good stuff. How come you never conjured up any of that for me?"

"You never needed it." Angela smirked. "Besides, I'm Bethany's godmother."

"Okay, now we know who's really to blame." He winked at Harry and Bethany, who had paused in the doorway. "Nothing like having a not-quite-Fae godmother to mess up your life."

Bethany giggled. That was all the assurance Harry needed that she would be fine. She just needed time to think, and a good dose of Sarafina's Ambrosial Chocolates to soothe the soul and body.

"Where's the best place we can go for some privacy?" he asked as they walked out the front door of Divine's.

"I need to walk. Can you just let go of the spell holding back your invisibility and keep me in the field?"

"Sure, but we'll need to be pretty close to keep you inside the buffering field, so people don't run into us." Harry handed her the bag of chocolates. He was afraid he would squeeze it hard enough to pop it, maybe even melt it.

"That's fine by me. I... I really need someone to hold me for a while." Her lips trembled a little as she smiled. "And there's nobody I'd rather hold me than you."

Chapter Nine

Monday, December 17

Lori wondered if maybe she had outstayed her welcome. Brick was busy with all sorts of Christmas preparations. The last few days, he had seemed distant. There was a reticence about him, as if maybe he couldn't figure out why he spent time with her. Or maybe he expected her to put an evil spell on him. Which made no sense, because he certainly didn't believe in Fae magic -- only the magic that Humans could create at this time of year by believing and giving and doing for one another.

She hadn't seen Will or Phill in several days, except for running into Will in town, talking with Hargrove. And she had no idea if Brick was even going to show up today.

There was only so much sightseeing a Fae on her own in a strange, unfamiliar land could do, even if she did have unlimited credit, and taxis showed up whenever she needed them. How many museums and galleries and shopping malls could she explore all by herself? How many movies could she watch?

There was just so much shopping she could do before her hotel room got a little too full for comfort. Yes, she could put all her purchases into ether-space, but she might forget them once they were out of sight.

She had done that with a flock of sheep back when she was still a child. It wouldn't have been so bad with just the sheep, because they didn't care about time, but she had been playing with the shepherd boy tending those sheep, and accidentally put him in ether-space without thinking of the consequences. When she remembered more than two Fae years later, only a few minutes had passed for the boy and the sheep, but thirty years had passed in the Human realms. That poor boy hadn't been very happy. He had been sweet on the shepherdess in the next pasture, and now she was all grown up and married -- and fat and graying.

Besides, using ether-space to store all her purchases and souvenirs would send up a homing signal to anyone who might be looking for her. That was the last thing Lori wanted to do.

"Okay." She shuddered as new insight washed over her. She was by herself, taking an early morning walk in the Metroparks, so it was safe to talk to herself. No one could hear her and think something was strange. "I guess that means you don't want to go home any time soon." She sighed, the sound turning into laughter. "Well, duh. Going home means the Aunties will drag you out to parties and teas and dances, to meet all the totally boring, Enclave-bound prospective husbands they've chosen. Why can't they leave me alone and wait for Need to find the perfect match for me?"

"Probably because Need isn't fashionable anymore." The familiar female voice chimed off the ice coating the bushes and rocks all around Lori.

The air split apart and Epsibellah skipped out into the park. She gasped as icy air wrapped around her, snapped her fingers, and a navy mink coat enfolded her, with a matching poofy hat and gloves.

"That's better." She snuggled down into her new wraps, and looked around. "Interesting place you've come to hide out, Lori. Where are we?"

"The Human realm."

"The Human realm?" Epsi hunched down and dashed into the shadows of the nearest pine tree. It was covered with snow, and the moment she touched it, the entire sparkling load cascaded down on her. Her repulsion field kicked into effect, sending the snow sliding down around her without touching her, in a visible bubble effect.

Lori fought a giggle, remembering that Epsi was an Enclave baby, with an ingrained fear of anything remotely related to the Human realm. Something like agoraphobia among the Humans.

"What in the name of the Dungeon Dimensions are you doing here?" Epsi demanded, when Lori gave up her walk as a lost cause and crossed the snow to stand with her in the shadows.

"Hiding from the matchmaking Aunties, same as always."

"That's actually why I'm here. You have no idea how much magic and how many favors I used up, tracking you down. If Titomio hadn't seen you hanging with Will and Phill before you went missing, I never would have thought to check on their flight plans. That's how I found you."

"Then how could you not know where you ended up?"

"I didn't actually *read* the flight plans, just plugged in the coordinates and followed the trail of their exit." Epsi tipped her head back to look at the sun, which was about an hour away from emerging from the tops of the trees. "You certainly picked a gorgeous place to hide."

"And you're here because?"

"The Aunties. They've found somebody for you."

"Not again." She wanted to drop down and sit on something. Maybe kick her legs in a miniature tantrum. "What's he like?" she asked, opting for a heavy sigh.

"Boooooring, what else?" Epsi echoed her sigh. "One of those well-bred boys. You know the type. Emphasis on breeding. As in breeding out Need altogether."

"They know how I feel about letting Need do the choosing." She tried not to growl, but it was hard. She wanted to turn into something fanged, with big talons, every time her aunties lectured her on how antiquarian it was to depend on Need to find the perfect mate.

Her aunties, and quite a few of their generation, were of the opinion that the Fae race had outgrown the usefulness of Need. They believed that matches should be made for more intellectual reasons: family connections, politics, magical talent lines. A growing number of matchmakers and political movers and shakers tried to make matches and get "those young folks," meaning anyone under the age of 200, married and bound together before Need had any chance of awakening. Their intent was to someday "raise" the Fae race to the point where no one was caught in Need anymore.

The unfortunate fact was that their theory had too much reality and plausibility to it. Need matches usually resulted in children who themselves experienced Need. Conversely, those who married and procreated without Need produced children who were less likely to experience Need as the generations went on.

"Thanks for the warning." Lori needed somewhere to sit and think, no matter how long it took. She thought there was a bench around the next bend in the walking trail. "What do you think I should do? Go back and fight, or stay in hiding the rest of my life?"

"Sweetie, you know how I feel about being out among the Humans. Not that I'm a germophobe, but... Well, there has to be a reason why so many of us decide to settle in and stay among

Humans after long exposure to them, right?"

"Right. They like it better out here than back home."

"No! It's like an infection. Madness." Epsi looked around and wrapped her fur tighter around her. "The thing is, if you go back, you know they'll be waiting for you. They probably have all the access portals set with tripwires to sense you the moment you appear. They could have the groom waiting and the wedding planned and have your house constructed, right down to the baby rooms and the babies' names picked out. All they need is for you to show up, so they can wrap your wedding dress around you."

"Sounds like an execution." Would it be so bad, staying out here in the Human realms for the rest of her life? Will and Phill certainly seemed to like it better out here.

Of course, she couldn't honestly say she thought they were happy. She had seen so little of either of them the last few days.

The longer she stayed away from home, the more time her aunties would have to set up the ambush wedding. Then again, the longer she stayed out here among Humans, the less appealing she might be to whichever inbred Enclave groom they chose for her.

Would it be so bad, staying out here until she became so contaminated by Humans that no one would take her if she begged? She was very aware of how certain socially upright members of Will's and Phill's families disapproved of them and avoided socializing with them when they were home. The eccentrics, the weird cousins and explorers and experimenters, were delighted with Will and Phill. The eccentrics were the ones who were so much fun at parties, festivals, and assemblies.

That settled it. Lori would much prefer being considered eccentric and interesting rather than socially acceptable and predictable and boring. She would stay out here.

All right, so what was there to do besides shop, visit museums, learn about Human history, and celebrate Christmas? She would have to go to Divine's and check with Maurice.

"You've made up your mind, haven't you?" Epsi wore that smug little we're-in-so-much-trouble grin from when they were children and cutting out on various socially restricting lessons. Such as the proper spells to make sure their dresses stayed crisp and sparkly, and their hair held up to the strongest breezes. Or to ensure butterflies' wings changed colors on a set rhythm or in accord with the emotions of the people who wore them in their hair.

"I don't suppose I could talk you into staying with me? It'd be fun, at the very least."

"There's fun, and then there's fun." She shuddered hard enough to knock more snow off the branches overhead, which sent another umbrella-shaped shower of white cascading around them. "Thanks. Maybe in another fifty years or so, I'll build up the guts to venture out. Not right now. Maybe if there's a global-thermonuclear war to clear the land a little bit..."

"You're horrid. Humans are not bacteria."

"I know. But they're so savage."

"And so full of life!"

"Mmm hmm. And some kinds of life can just stay on their own grimy carcasses, thanks very much." Epsi snapped her fingers and made her blue fur shimmer and fade away. "I'm heading home before someone realizes I've gone. If they don't know I've been looking for you, they won't track me and find you. Be happy, sweetie." She smirked as they hugged. "Invite me to the wedding."

"There isn't going to be any wedding." Lori almost clutched her friend tight in a panicked reaction. Or maybe she just wanted to squeeze Epsi until she squeaked, to pay her back for that momentary scare.

"Hmm, you say that now, but something tells me there's a man involved. A Human male. It makes decisions so much easier when the reason *to* do something is stronger than the reason *not to* do something. Know what I mean?" She winked, stepped back, and the slit in the dimensional wall split open and wrapped around her. In another moment, before Lori could think of a suitable retort, strong enough to change her hair to green, she was gone.

"A man?" There was something delightfully scary in the idea.

She had needed a quiet day alone to think and get her bearings, but maybe she would have been happier if she had been somewhere crowded and noisy. At the very least, she wouldn't be able to think quite so hard right now. Where was a distraction when she really needed it?

~~~~~

Sometimes Brick suspected various members of the Chamber of Commerce resorted to extra-curricular help to survive some of the more mind-dulling boring meetings. Until about five minutes
~~~~~

ago, he had never suspected someone had shared those survival tactics. Especially without permission or asking if he wanted help.

It had to be drugs. Someone had slipped him something at the breakfast meeting in the Chamber offices. Put it in his coffee or sprinkled it on that bowl of blueberries while his back was turned.

He was positive Lori had been talking to a woman just a few minutes ago. Later he would worry about why they stood about eight feet off the path, hiding among the trees and snow. Or why the woman wore a blue fur coat.

While he stood there, trying to read their lips, wondering what they were doing there, the air seemed to split open and the stranger vanished. Just vanished, without a pop or a flash or a bang. How?

The only answer he could come up with was that the woman hadn't been there in the first place. He had just imagined her, maybe mistaking a movement in the shadows for a person.

One problem with that theory: he had heard voices. He couldn't make out the words, because both the woman and Lori kept their voices down, but he had distinctly heard two different voices. Unless Lori was a ventriloquist, either that woman talking to her knew how to vanish into thin air, or someone had drugged him at the Chamber meeting.

Brick chose the drugs. If he chose a woman in blue fur who had the ability to vanish into thin air, then he would have to choose to go quietly insane. Or maybe loudly. His immediate family didn't care that much about social standing or appearances, so if he wanted to go screaming, drooling, spinning nutso, he was free to do so without feeling his ancestors' disapproval.

He didn't want to go nuts. He wanted to spend Christmas with Lori. Hallucinating was the more benign explanation.

What if he had been hallucinating Lori, too?

"Lori?" he called, and flinched as his voice bounced off the ice-covered branches and the crust of the snow.

"Hi." She waved and plowed through the drifts to get back to the path, and then more drifts to where he had stood for the last twenty minutes or so, dithering and tying his brains into knots. "What are you doing out here?" Those sparks he had seen before seemed to swirl around her. "Please feed my ego and tell me you were looking for me."

"Oh, definitely." He crooked his arm and bent it out, offering it to her. She blushed delightfully, a pink haze filling the air around her cheeks, and slipped her hand into the crook of his elbow. "I can't go a day without seeing you."

"Now that you've made my day, what can I do for you?"

"Want to help me with some extremely important shopping?" Brick hadn't come looking for her, per se. He had been driving down the park road when he thought he saw her, so he had gotten out of the car and come closer. His errand came to his mind again, just as it occurred to him that he had waded through snow higher than the tops of his shoes, and his socks were getting wet and icy, crusty cold.

"Well, considering how few my talents are, it's a good thing that's what you need. I've become a whiz at shopping over the last few days. Shopping where, for who, and for what?"

~~~~~

Two hours later, Brick scooped half the contents of the shelf of cinnamon-scented candles into the shopping cart Lori pushed. He nodded to the list she consulted. "What else?"

"Containers." She waved the paper. "They're not on the list, but it makes sense that if you have candles, you should have something for them to sit in, to contain the wax when it melts."

"That's why I keep you around. Common sense." He turned, surveying the shelves in either direction along the aisle.

"Hardly." She laughed, fighting down the funny little quiver of pleasure from his half-teasing praise. No one had ever accused her of having common sense before. Usually, she was lectured for having ridiculous values, conflicting with the high social standards her blue-blood family felt duty-bound to uphold. "I just like candles. I even made candles as a hobby for a while, so I know all the disasters that happen when you don't control melting wax."

"Now see? That's something new I just learned about you. Must have been a lot of leisure time to have a hobby like that." Brick watched her from the side of his eye as he wandered down the aisle, leading the shopping cart with one hand.

"Too much leisure time, if you ask me. This is an adventure, doing something worthwhile for other people. So, when we get all the items on this humongous list of yours, what do we do with it all?" she continued, stopping him when he opened his mouth to ask yet another question. Or more likely, make another cryptic
~~~~~

comment about how little they knew about each other. Lori didn't want to be reminded of how little they knew each other. Only seven more days until Christmas Eve, and then what would happen, where would she go? Were Will and Phill going to take her somewhere else to hide from the matchmaking aunties, or was she on her own?

If she hooked up with Brick, she wouldn't be on her own, would she?

Spend the rest of her life in Neighborlee, helping Brick with his charitable deeds all year long? He would grow very tired of her Human-skills ineptitude very quickly.

"Tired of what?" Brick asked, laughing. He turned around to face her, his hands full of fancy glass containers to hold all the candles he had just put in the cart.

Lori's face burned. The scents of a dozen different candles grew stronger as the warmth she radiated softened the contents of the shelves next to her.

Had she spoken aloud?

"Okay, I'm used to weird things happening in this town, and usually it's fun, but this ..." Brick's eyes narrowed. "How do you do that?" He stepped closer and held his open palm maybe two inches away from her face. "That's a fever, for sure. But you look just fine. Other than a head-to-toe blush."

"I do not blush down to my toes. It only goes..." Lori sighed, closed her eyes, willed the pinkish-purplish haze away, and lowered her radiant temperature. She slapped a cooling wave at the candles and decided not to look too closely, to see if she had done any damage to them. They were wrapped in plastic, after all, so it wasn't like they would have been disfigured and melted across the shelf, right?

All the same, she wasn't going to look.

"The thing is, if this happened to someone who grew up here, I'd understand. But you're not from around here," Brick said.

"No ... but maybe I could belong here?" She tried to smile, even though her face felt sunburned, sensitive to the touch of his gaze.

"Yeah...maybe you could." He looked around and his quizzical look hardened into a frown. Lori looked past him and saw two women at the far end of the aisle, whispering to each other. She didn't like their sly smiles. "How about we finish this and then go sit somewhere and talk?"

All she could do was nod.

By the time they had the list taken care of, it was mid-afternoon. Brick made a call while they were on their way to Eden, and a pizza waited for them at their next-to-last stop. Lori appreciated his foresight and planning skills almost as much as she appreciated pizza.

They delivered all their shopping bags to the room where the Christmas baskets were being assembled. No one was there, but long rows of tables were set up with large, sturdy baskets sitting on big sheets of red and green and gold cellophane, with ribbons and bows waiting to tie everything together. She was impressed. Especially by the fleet of wheeled carts sitting by the door.

"Let me guess. You put the goodies on the carts and go up and down the rows, putting things in the baskets, saving people's backs from having to haul things all over the place."

"Gotta love a girl who figures things out. Unless mind-reading is among your hidden talents?" His grin said he was joking, but that spark of something wary in his eyes made her think he was worried about her answer.

"It doesn't run in my family," she replied honestly, "but you never know what might pop up to meet a need."

"Uh huh. You sound a lot like Lanie."

"Oh, is that Angela's friend?"

"She always says weird things. Part of it could be brain damage from being a high school teacher. Part of it could be from landing on her head when she broke her back." Amusement lit his eyes, so she knew he really was joking this time.

"Blows to the head have been known to awaken telepathic powers. Or at least prophetic gifts. Something about removing barriers to the ether beyond the space-time continuum."

"Are you a Trekker?" He stopped, turning to block her way down the hall.

"A what?"

"*Star Trek* fan. See, sometimes I go to the club meetings, and the really hard core ones talk that way."

"No. Sorry. But if they're having a meeting, maybe we could go." If there were people in this town who understood trans-dimensional travel and the rules of ether-related physics and could explain magic to Brick better than she could, Lori was all for making friends with them.

She nearly stumbled as they continued down the hall, at the realization she *wanted* Brick to understand. She wanted to be open with him about her big secret: she was a Fae. She wanted Brick to stop giving her those wary looks. The problem was that even if he didn't label her as insane and run away, he could still run away in fear and loathing *because* he believed her.

She pushed her worries away as Brick settled them in a small meeting room, currently unoccupied, and set out their lunch. She had eaten spaghetti and had spent a few years investigating the various world-famous restaurants in Italy, sampling the cuisine that each region was noted for. Why hadn't she discovered pizza while she was there?

"So, you're a world traveler, then?" Brick said, when she posed her question to him.

"Not as much as I would like. There's always something keeping me tied up at home. Until I need to run away." She contemplated taking a third piece. Brick had ordered a large deluxe with double toppings and triple cheese, and garlic dipping sauce on the side. There was plenty, even if she ate herself into a semi-coma, so she indulged.

"So who was that I saw you with before, out in the park?"

Lori barely stopped herself from choking. She finished her bite of pizza, and considered taking another, just to buy herself more time for answering. Then she decided it was time to stop being a wimp. She wanted to be honest with him? Maybe she should start with some smaller, easily digested bits of truth. If Brick accepted those, she could work her way up to the big, prickly, reality-bending ones.

"So you saw Epsi. That's interesting. She's usually so good about being ... stealthy. Unseen. She's kind of paranoid. Agoraphobic -- no, not agoraphobic." *Stupid,* she scolded herself. *How do you explain her meeting you outside in the woods, the great outdoors, if she's scared of the outdoors?* "Xenophobic. That's it. She's really shy, scared of strangers and strange places. Except when she has a really good reason for venturing away from home. And warning me, that's a very good reason."

So Brick had seen Epsi. That meant either her illusion shield, her don't-see-me spell was slipping, or he had enough magic in his blood to negate the basic shielding spell all Fae were required to activate the moment they emerged in the Human realms. The question now was determining how much magic Brick had in his blood.

"So a really good friend, then." He nodded and reached for his fourth slice of pizza.

"The best." She concentrated on her slice, consciously fighting not to inhale it.

For a few minutes they ate in silence, while she ran through her options and what she wanted, what she could and couldn't risk. If there was some Fae blood in Brick, not just Fae influence because of the spell cast on his ancestress, he could become a Changeling. If he could believe in the Fae as a reality. If he wanted to be bound to her for the rest of his life. Which would be centuries. And it wasn't like he would have to move away. Not with the general, half-blind acceptance of magical events and general weirdness, here in Neighborlee.

If he wanted to be with her for the rest of his life. If he accepted that she was Fae.

She didn't know him well enough to risk it.

What had happened to her? A few weeks ago, she had been frustrated with her aunties' matchmaking to the point of being allergic to the whole concept of marriage. Besides, wasn't she the throwback, the uncivilized one, holding out for Need to strike?

But couldn't Need strike when two people were drawn together? It happened often enough. Why couldn't it happen to her?

Could she make it happen with Brick? Could she make him acceptable to the matchmakers back home, so they wouldn't torment him and her for decades after the deed was done?

"Deep thoughts?" Brick asked.

Lori physically and mentally shrugged off the gloom and thoughts wrapped around her. She had been sitting and staring at the crust in her hand for who knew how long.

"Epsi came to warn me," she said, following through on her earlier resolution. "I'm basically hiding out from matchmakers, back home. Dynastic marriages. Power and social standing, that sort of thing. Will and Phill helped me get away. Well, Epsi came to warn me that the Aunties are on the verge of leg-shackling me to someone I've never even met. He's acceptable to them, and that's more important than me being happy."

"Ouch." Brick sat back in the cushioned chair and shook his head.

Lori wondered if she was just imagining it when some of that creeping tension that had grown over the last few days faded a bit.

"So power and money and the movers and shakers trying to keep it all in a few select families." He picked up his can of ginger ale and gestured with it as he talked. "I know the story too well. Fortunately, my close relatives in town won't push me, but it's the other social grand dames and the out-of-town relatives who want to finagle me into their plans for their own family lines. You'd think with a nice, small town like Neighborlee, you wouldn't have the whole royal family mentality, but... So, you're pretty rich, I'm guessing."

"Where I'm from, we don't really care about money. It's all power and social standing. Politics." She had said something that relieved Brick's wariness. She could almost feel and hear the loosening of those taut cords inside his mind and heart. "There are different kinds of power beyond military and economic. If I could find and stay in a place where things are simple and open and honest, where people care about others...maybe even where people have needs, so others can help fill them, I'd like that more than anything."

She choked for a moment as a new thought instantly corrected her. "Well, almost anything." Her face warmed, but she fought down the blush before it radiated and threw off different colors of light. "I like all this giving and doing for others and charity things."

"You like doing charity work, huh?" Brick rubbed his chin, only partially concealing the big grin that lit up his eyes. "Well, you're in luck. I've got a deal for you. I can keep you so busy for the next week, you'll get your charity quota in for the rest of the year."

"I'd like to see that."

~~~~~

Brick watched Lori when they took the first load of completed baskets and dropped them off at the various homes on this year's list of struggling families. The lists were carefully researched to make sure families that truly needed help got the goodies and the gift certificates to stores and restaurants in town. Those certificates
~~~~~

were geared toward their needs, such as toy stores and children's apparel for families with children; auto shops and hardware stores for older families who needed help keeping a car going to hold onto a job, or house repairs they could do themselves. Families known for wasting their resources, or who refused to correct problems, received smaller baskets, tokens to bolster their spirits. They also received visits from counselors or city officials, to give them firmer nudges back onto the road of rehabilitation.

"Great-Granny wouldn't have stood for calling drinking and gambling diseases," Brick explained to Lori. They had already visited a dozen homes where he knew no one would be at home to actually see the delivery of the gift baskets. "In her book, someone who knew he had a problem and didn't do anything about fixing it was just a lazy bum. Someone who tried to use his drinking habit as an excuse for not trying was worse than a lazy bum, and she usually ran such people out of her town. She didn't see any justice in making hard-working folks who took care of their own dig into their pockets to foot the bill for those who wouldn't even try to take care of themselves. Women who kept popping out babies and then held out their hands, expecting help, didn't deserve any sympathy, in her book. If you couldn't afford to feed and clothe your kids, you had no right to keep making more." He snorted laughter. "She was all for gelding the husbands of such women and putting the responsibility squarely on them."

"Brick." Lori's soft, warm hand on his wrist startled him into realizing he had been preaching. "You don't have to defend yourself or your granny. She sounds like a sensible woman. I'm sure it was a little easier back then to identify those who needed help and those who just wanted to live off other people's hard work. Nowadays... Well, it's easier to fake, to fool people and pretend to be something you aren't."

"Everybody wears a mask, of one kind or another."

"But not you." Her lips twitched like she tried to smile.

"Everybody." He looked down at her hand, still lightly grasping his wrist, then reluctantly tugged free so he could put his truck into reverse and get out of the Wilberforces' driveway before the children came home from school. That would ruin the surprise.

Not that it was that much of a surprise. Nearly everybody living in Neighborlee knew about the basket program, carried out at all major holidays. As long as the delivery people did the job unseen, and the recipients didn't meet up with them, didn't see anybody leaving the scene of the crime, there was still an element of mystery. The sense of freedom from admitting they had sunk low enough to need that kind of help was just as valuable as the gifts they received.

Besides, it was more fun imagining the Wilberforce kids digging through the basket before their widowed father got home from work, than actually seeing them do it. Brick thought about the model car and airplane kits for the twins, and the deluxe makeup kit for their sister, who was a sophomore this year. He thought about the dinner she would probably make for her family tonight, all the goodies that would be waiting for Gary when he dragged himself through the door. Brick was especially proud of the discrete little business card tucked into the box with the new tie, directing Gary to talk to Harcourt Bammerschol, who had confided to him just last week that four men were retiring after the New Year, and he didn't know where to find someone with their years of experience to replace them.

"You're much better at this than Santa Claus," Lori offered, when they had driven in silence for a few minutes.

"Oh yeah? And you know this from experience?" He glanced sideways as they reached a stop sign, to find her watching him, her expression somber.

"Just common sense. You do it over the course of a week or two, in daylight, when nobody is home. Far more sensible than trying to take care of half the planet in the space of a single night, employing magic to stretch and fold time and fit down chimneys and ... well, all those logistical problems." She turned to face forward again. Her lips twitched, fighting a smile.

"I'm really tempted to keep you here year 'round. I don't want to miss a minute of your incredible brain at work."

"Is that a good thing?" She blushed, and Brick swore there were overtones of violet to the blush, shading out from the rosy haze encircling her entire head.

"A very good thing."

"I could live here all the time. It's not like I expected at all. There's so much darkness, but that makes all the brightness and color so much more wonderful. When you're surrounded by beauty and color and light all the time, you get used to it. You take it for granted. You think the entire world is that way."

"And it's not?" He wanted to pull over to the side of the road and just watch the emotions playing over her face, the changing lights in her eyes. It was as if she were having an epiphany right there, seeing the world in a whole new way she had never considered before.

"Where I'm from, we don't have this. Poverty and struggling, hopelessness and illness. Yes, there are classes and power struggles, but maybe they're more prevalent because the basic needs are met. We don't think about people needing anything because nobody really needs the important things. And maybe we don't appreciate the non-tangible things that matter so much. That's why nobody wants to let you wait until you've found the one, the perfect match, the one you need, who needs you. It's all politics and plotting and warfare and..." She flung her hands up in the air, as far as the confines of the cab of the truck would allow, and let out a half-groaned snarl of frustration.

"So you're like the faerie tale princess who ran away from the castle and an arranged marriage with the idiot prince in the next kingdom. Is that basically where you're at?" He grinned as they headed down the street again.

"Close enough." Her smile looked tired.

"We need to find you a poor but honorable swineherd."

"No, thank you!"

"What have you got against poor but honorable swineherds?"

"I could tell you a thing or two about them. There's a reason why they land in jobs like that. The faerie tales you're referring to left out a lot of details." She wrapped her arms around herself, shuddering so violently, Brick knew she was joking.

"What about the prince who pretends to be a swineherd to win the princess after she's been humbled?"

"I've always wondered about the sanity of such princes. Why would you want to marry a girl who has to be humbled before she's worth anything? After she gets back into the castle, she'll just revert to her old ways. Swineherds are filthy and smelly, and they've been with the pigs so long their sense of smell is totally trashed, so you can never fully housebreak them." She shook her head, nose wrinkled in disgust. "Thanks, but no thanks. Give me a decent, middle class man with good hygiene and good manners. One who doesn't need to battle anyone or prove anything or fulfill some idiotic quest. He doesn't mess with things best left alone, and dangerous. But he stands up for others and he knows when to help and when to let people do it on their own." She frowned, staring at a far distant point that Brick suspected wasn't anywhere on the road ahead of him. "And he likes children. And even more important, children like him."

"That's a pretty tall order." He clamped his teeth together, to fight the urge to blurt that he loved kids, and he liked visiting his friend Jon-Tom, who planned to open a daycare center next summer.

Jon-Tom and Jeri's wedding was coming up. He would take Lori with him and position her where she could see him playing favorite uncle with all the children who had been invited. Maybe with enough hints, she would finally come to her senses.

He thought he had finally come to his.

Chapter Ten

Tuesday, December 18

"You know Holly, don't you?" Maurice said.

"The librarian? I've met her a couple times." Will settled back further into the lounging chair he had made out of a plush lamb. There was something to be said for shrinking himself down to five inches tall. It didn't make his problems go away, but it helped him put some things into perspective. He had decided instead of wandering around Neighborlee, trying to get into the Christmas spirit without Phill, and failing miserably, he would camp out with Maurice.

Maurice seemed pretty happy, despite his exile, limited magic, and size. Will had to admit it was kind of fun, being small and invisible to most of the world, sitting here on the shelf behind the counter at Divine's Emporium, watching the world go by. And it didn't hurt that a single can of diet cherry cola could last him all day, and a single piece of dark chocolate that would have melted in his mouth in under two minutes would take him hours to savor. Maurice didn't have it all bad.

Except for now, Will decided with a flash of insight that nearly blinded him. There was something in his voice, in his eyes. Not something noticeable, but rather the effort not to be noticeable. Maurice wasn't made for acting casual.

"What about Holly? She's a good kid, from everything I hear. She needs a... Oh, so that's it." Another flash of insight told him if he was so miserable over Phill, then Maurice had to be doubly unhappy, verging on agony. Not only was he unable to be seen and heard by his heartthrob, but she was a Human. That put up a lot of barriers between them. Sure, Fae had been romping through the Human realms for centuries, falling in love, taking Human mates, and producing enough half-blood children to prove the two races were not incompatible. The problem was that unless that true love had some Fae blood, she was going to age and fade and eventually die far too soon. The most powerful spell a Fae could find would only delay the inevitable, not change the dictates of biology.

"What's it?" Maurice snuggled down a little further into the embrace of the teddy bear dressed as Santa Claus that was his chair of choice for the day.

"You and Holly. Ouch."

"Is it as hopeless as I think it is?"

"Let me think about it. There's the year remaining to your exile, and the fact she's Human. Of course, she's a Lost Kid, but she's the kind who doesn't seem to have any magic. Otherwise she should have seen and heard you from the beginning. Especially with the influence of spending so much time here at Divine's."

"Thanks. That's exactly what I didn't need to hear."

"There's gotta be something in the Ether Lexicon to give you an answer." Will flinched as another flash of insight went off in his eyes. That wince from Maurice told him yet another detail of his exile. "You can't even access the Lexicon? That sucks harder than gravity. What do they think you'll do? Find a --" This time Will managed to close his eyes before the flash went off in front of his face, close enough he felt the sparks and heat.

"Find what?" Maurice demanded. He reached across the bright red furry arm of the teddy bear and tugged on Will's sleeve.

"Why would they deny you access to the Ether Lexicon unless there was something in there that could either help you, or there's a loophole out of your exile, or even something to break the exile? Like a bunch of tasks you have to complete."

"A Get out of Jail Free card," Maurice whispered. His mouth twitched like he either tried to smile and couldn't, or he fought not to smile because the hope was almost too much to be endured. "Would you --"

"I'd be glad to. Especially if we can finagle things to let you and Holly work things out. Man, how can you stand not even being able to talk to her? At least me and Phill, most of the time we're... Well, it's good most of the time. Except when we're wanting what we can't have."

"You mean you two haven't checked the Lexicon either?" A more normal smile touched Maurice's face now.

"Yeah, well, she's pissed at me and took off into another dimension, so what's the use if she never comes back? I'm concentrating on your problem. If Phill ever shows up, we'll work on us." Will snapped his fingers and held out his hands, calling for the Ether Lexicon.

It didn't show up. He didn't even feel that flickering in the air around his hands, meaning the book was trying to come but was too busy providing interfaces with too many other Fae right at that moment. That rarely happened, he knew, because Fae in general were a self-reliant breed. Meaning a good number of them managed to work their way into trouble of some kind because they *didn't* stop to ask for help from the Lexicon.

He tried again. Still nothing.

"Ah ... let me make a suggestion." Maurice tapped his chest. "I'm probably the problem. If I'm not allowed to look, there's probably a safeguard in there to keep me from reading over someone else's shoulder. It won't come to you if I'm within a certain distance."

"Those guys on the Disciplinary Council are hard core." He gestured, as if clearing a space around himself. "Do you mind?"

"Go ahead. I'm gonna flit on over to the book room and see what those kids are up to, so I'll be busy for a while. Don't forget to make notes -- maybe use ordinary paper and pen, just in case conjured notes fall under the same spell. If that's not too much trouble?"

"You got it." Will looked around the main room, cast a temporary shielding spell that included a misdirection charm in it, then took a flying leap off the shelf. He returned to full size halfway to the floor and landed, crouching, behind the counter. When he stood up and walked out from behind the counter and out into the main hallway, the shielding spell wore off slowly, so he didn't startle the customers moving through the shop right then.

Will tried to call up the Ether Lexicon four times, each time moving farther away from Maurice. He finally had to go outside and walk halfway to the corner before the book came to him. Knowing it was useless to fight or waste his time working around the spell, Will conjured himself back to his hotel room. Might as well be comfortable while he was doing his research.

~~~~~

Will had a few ideas by the time he had read through a third of the information the Ether Lexicon had pulled up for him. The information and the amount of pages kept growing, the further he
~~~~~

read and as more possible offshoots of research occurred to him. When he lifted his head from the book, after filling the second notebook he had conjured up, he realized it was nearly two in the afternoon. He thought about Maurice, waiting for an answer, and the idea of putting aside his studies to go report to him sounded good.

Will had never minded hours of study because the subjects he pursued were always interesting. However, he had never confined himself in one place and focused so hard on anything else before. Maurice was probably pacing by now. With the Ether Lexicon as the source of information, there should have been an answer by now. After all, it was a law of Fae physics that every spell and curse and sentence of punishment had a loophole, some way of shortening the term or short-circuiting the curse.

Will made a marker for himself, along with a running record of everything he had looked at, so he wouldn't have to go over old territory when he re-opened the Lexicon. Then he called up his coat and scarf, planning to walk over to Divine's Emporium and get some exercise after sitting all day.

His stomach growled. He laughed at himself. Yes, of course, he had worked through lunch. He thought about calling room service as he tucked his notebooks into a backpack, then decided not to waste all that time waiting. He could detour through a sandwich shop on his way to Divine's.

Someone knocked on his door just as he reached for the knob to pull it open. Will pulled, and found Phill standing there, her hand still up to knock. They stared at each other, frozen for a dozen heartbeats. Then he told the voice of caution to shut up and pulled her into his arms, yanked her into the room, and shoved the door closed with a thought.

"I'm sorry. I was stupid. You are never leaving me again," he blurted, and realized Phill was talking just as fast and desperately. "What?"

"You idiot." Phill laughed and punched him in the shoulder. To his relief, she didn't step out of his arms. "We're both idiots."

"I know. And I shouldn't have listened to my relatives, telling me I should let you go, that I'm making you sick by keeping Need from coming. We want to be together, right? You and me, we're a team forever, right?"

"Absolutely." She shuddered and multi-colored stars swirled around her head for a few seconds, reacting to her burst of anger. "I swear, my relatives must be in collusion with your relatives. They've been putting pressure on me, too, saying I'm hurting myself, holding back and fighting Need because of you. And I'm keeping your perfect mate from finding you. That we're working all sorts of unconscious magic. It's stupid!"

"I don't want to be with anybody but you, Philomena." He grasped her shoulders and held her still, lifting her a good five inches so they were eye-to-eye.

"Ditto. And if that means I never experience Need, that's fine, because I don't want to lose you."

"Ditto ditto." He *needed* to kiss her, but something kept his arms stiff, even though he wanted to pull her up tight against him. What was wrong now? Will had the horrid suspicion he was afraid of what would happen next. What if he kissed Phill and it was awful? Worse, what if he kissed her and she hated it so much she left permanently?

So, do we really need all the physical goop? We've gotten along just fine all these centuries without sex. We've lived without it so far, so we'll be just fine without it. Right?

It sounded fine when he put it that way, but Will suspected if he sat and thought about it, he would find some major holes in his reasoning. Or he might just drive himself crazy. He feared if he spoke his thoughts aloud to Phill, she would agree too quickly and easily, which would be painful. Or she would get angry again. Maybe she wanted to be lovers. But how could they take that next step, bonding as much as they could without the benefit of Need, when he couldn't even make himself kiss her now?

He had to get his mind on something else.

"Okay," he said, forcing himself to release her before his hands tightened any more and he bruised Phill's arms. "Now that we have ourselves straightened out, we need to concentrate on Maurice. Did you know he's in love with Angela's friend Holly, the librarian?"

"I guessed, yeah." The sparkle in Phill's eyes and the bright color in her cheeks faded a little. That was to be expected, now that the crisis moment was over.

That was too bad, Will thought, because she had never looked prettier. He shook off that thought and concentrated on explaining to Phill what he had been doing for Maurice. She read through his notebooks on the walk to Divine's Emporium, including the detour when he went through Hunky & Dory's for sandwiches. She admitted she was hungry, and Will gladly ordered enough for a feast. Maybe Maurice would think there was something to celebrate, even though he hadn't finished his research yet.

They were holding hands as they strolled up the sidewalk to Divine's Emporium, and Maurice came flying out to meet them. He flew circles around them three times and came to settle on Will's shoulder.

"So, does this mean you two ninnies got your heads on straight finally?"

Phill laughed so hard she had to sit down. The only likely spot was the wrought iron fence in front of Divine's, and it shook a little from the force of her laughter. Will conjured up a bench for her. She nodded thanks, green and blue and gold tears streaming down her cheeks as she settled into it.

"Okay, should I go for a second career doing comedy?" Maurice said, coming to rest on the end of the bench, with Phill between him and Will.

"You're right," Phill gasped, finally getting her laughter under control. "We've been ninnies. Especially letting our relatives get us all worried and trying to drive us apart. We've both been so worried that Need will hit and drive us away from each other."

"Yeah, and I think you're still ninnies." He jammed his fists into his hips and glared up at them both. "Look, who needs Need when you've got the real thing already? I've been spending enough time trying to help Angela's Human friends match up, I can see when it's real, and for you two, it's real. The way I figure, Need is just to give you that extra hard shove, or maybe some glue to hold you together while you get the rough stuff smoothed out. You two are already together in all the ways that matter, right?"

"Right." Phill turned to Will. Something in her eyes, part fear and part anger, choked him, so he could barely manage to squeak out his own affirmation.

Maurice sighed loudly, shaking his head. "You two are hopeless. It's a miracle you got this far. And to think I was hoping you could give me some answers. Okay, time to speak with a professional. Or as close to a professional as we can get without needing to go to a shrink." He jumped up and spread his wings and hovered at eye-level with Will. "Are you coming?"

"Coming where?" Phill asked, standing.

"Wait and see."

Maurice led them to the offices of the *Neighborlee Tattler*, the local paper. Will had seen Lanie Zephyr a few times on previous visits to Neighborlee. The dark-haired woman hadn't let her wheelchair get in the way of her life. She played wheelchair basketball, had a successful comedy career in the evenings and weekends, and worked as copy editor and advice columnist for the *Tattler* and its sister papers across the state of Ohio.

"What?" Phill said, when Will groaned. Half a second later, the sound was cut off when the door hit him in the backside. They had paused on the slushy entry mat of the newspaper office, looking around at all the chaos that Will supposed was attendant in a twice-weekly paper.

"Wait right here," Maurice said.

"What?" Phill demanded again, as they settled down in chairs and the woman on the phone at the receptionist's desk signaled that she would be right with them.

"Lanie does the *Talk to Terry* column. It's a lot of lovelorn advice," Will said, keeping his voice low. "She doesn't mince words, either. If someone is a moron, she tells him so."

"Ah." She nodded, then frowned. "I assume she can see Maurice?"

"If she's a friend of Angela's, I assume so."

"Will and Phill?" A vaguely familiar female voice came from behind them. Will stood up and turned to see Lanie wheel down the ramp from the next level of the office.

The *Neighborlee Tattler* was housed in four buildings that had at one time been built up against each other in a row. As the newspaper expanded, so had its offices, with walls torn down to make one large building. Ramps were installed where floors didn't match up. Will thought of the early years of Escher and wondered if the architect had patterned the renovated offices after those brain-bending drawings, with the changing levels, up and down.

Lanie Zephyr had a backpack slung over the back of her chair and held a coat and scarf on her lap. Maurice rode on her shoulder and gave them a thumbs up as Lanie slid to a stop a few feet in front of them.

"The timing is good. I was just getting ready to take off for the day," Lanie said. "Want to go for a roll while we talk?"

"Ah...sure," Phill said. She stepped away from Will, reaching for the door.

The door opened before she touched it, and no one was on the other side. Will automatically flung out a feeler of magic and felt the reverberations of power -- not magic, but something akin to it -- holding the door open. He followed those reverberations back to Lanie. She grinned, winked, and swung her coat around to wrap it around herself. Maurice took to the air just before he was knocked from her shoulder.

"That explains a few things," Phill said softly, as they followed Lanie outside and down the short ramp to the parking lot.

Lanie gave her chair a hard push with that power while she pulled her gloves on and finished buttoning up her coat. They all turned down the sidewalk that would eventually lead to the center of town, where the gazebo and playground and Civil War monument all stood.

"Okay, Maurice gave me a general idea of the whole Need problem," Lanie said, when they had reached the next intersection.

"How?" Will wanted to know. He remembered his parents sitting him down and stumbling through his first explanation of Need. He had finally resorted to asking the Ether Lexicon, when his parents weren't around, and it had taken nearly an hour to unravel all the misconceptions.

"Do you know *Star Trek* at all? Heck, any science fiction where there's an inordinate and unnecessary focus on the so-called joys of alien sex?" Lanie grinned and rolled her eyes as she said it. Phill giggled, and that wasn't very encouraging, as far as Will was concerned. "Maurice basically said it's the Fae version of Pon Farr, only a lot more fun. And you two are --"

"Lanie!" A bony, gray-haired man in a late-model Lexus pulled up to the curb where the four of them had paused. "So, what's the word? You're coming, aren't you?"

"Come on, Grover! Ruin my record?" Lanie shook her head. "You know I always have a lot of other obligations --"

"I checked. You don't have any comedy gigs and parties, your church isn't doing anything, and your *Star Trek* club had its

Christmas party Sunday. You don't have any obligations. You're coming to the company party this year if we have to hijack you." He shook his gloved finger at her.

"You point that thing at the wrong people, you could get it bitten off," Lanie growled.

Grover obviously took it as a joke, because he laughed, waved, and took off down the street, heading for the newspaper office parking lot.

"Company party?" Maurice asked. He settled on Lanie's knee. "Those bozos still giving you a hard time about Daniel?"

"It's a situation of 'physician heal thyself,' I guess," Lanie said with a sigh. The grin she flashed them looked crooked, and Will suspected the rosy color in her cheeks wasn't from the icy breeze brushing past them. "Everybody at the office has decided that our owner and I are an item." She shrugged. "I don't know how many times I've interrupted the decorating committee plotting how many bunches of mistletoe they'll have hanging everywhere."

"The thing is, she's good pals with Daniel, her boss," Maurice said, spreading his arms in a helpless what-can-you-do? gesture. "That doesn't help fight the gossip. He's in her *Star Trek* club, they go to Indians games together, they both have the same warped sense of humor."

"We're pals. Why ruin it with all that romantic, mushy goosh?" Lanie finished on a groan. "Who needs it?"

"I do," Will and Phill said in perfect unison. They looked at each other, wide-eyed, for a three-count. Then they laughed. It was much easier for him to put his arm around her this time. Will thought he might even have been able to kiss her, if there hadn't been other people around.

"I'd rather have good, solid friendship with a guy," Lanie said, shaking her head. "Best friends forever. And we certainly aren't to that stage yet. We've faced some of Neighborlee's trademark weirdness, and there's the whole alliance with his grandfather's tribe of gifted folks and … Never mind." She tipped her head to one side. "What you two have already, that's the most important part, what a lot of people take years getting to and making solid between them. It'll kill you to be separated, won't it?"

"That's pretty much how I've felt since we split up," Phill said, nodding. "Like I was dying."

"Isn't that what love is? Not the roses and starlight and violins, but the part about being glued so tightly together it'll tear big chunks out of you if you ever try to separate. Right?"

"Yeah," Will said softly.

"I figure, be happy with what you've got. The gush and mush will show up when the time is right. Besides, from what Maurice has explained about Fae anatomy and adolescence..." Lanie smirked. "You two are still kids. Maybe you're just late bloomers. Be thankful you don't have to go through zits and hormones and your voice changing. Who knows? Pon Farr could still be waiting around the corner."

Will laughed. It meant everything to him when Phill burst out laughing a moment later, still tucked up against his side, safe inside the curve of his arm.

Chapter Eleven

Wednesday, December 19

"How about a goof-off day?" Bethany said, when Harry came in the back door of her father's house that morning.

"Isn't that what we've been doing? All the sightseeing, the Science Center, the Rock Hall, the zoo, the Rainforest, the shopping." He leaned over and took a sniff of the omelet she was making. "Of course, with the way you cook, I need to run around as much as possible to work off all that food. I can't stop eating."

"You're being silly. And adorable." She flipped half the omelet over on top of the filling, turned the heat down on the griddle, and turned to face him as he settled down at the table.

There was something eminently satisfying about seeing Harry sitting at the kitchen table where she had eaten most of her life. And yes, he was adorable, so protective of her and fascinated with things she considered ordinary. She enjoyed showing him the points of interest in the surrounding towns, the places of culture and history throughout northeast Ohio. Harry's honest admiration and gratitude for things like her cooking meant more to her than awards and movie reviews and fan letters.

"Adorable, huh? That doesn't sound like a good bodyguard to me." He grinned at her and reached for the pitcher of orange juice.

It amazed her that Harry had never tasted orange juice until he came out of the Fae Enclaves to protect her. He claimed it was almost as addicting as diet cherry cola or dark chocolate.

"You're the best kind. You see me, Bethany, and not the job or the promotion or the notoriety." She blinked quickly when her eyes got warm and wet, and turned back to take care of the omelet. "Anyway, what I said before. Goofing off. I mean doing nothing. Except maybe sitting around the diner, seeing who comes in, catching up with old friends."

"Uh huh. Have you been thinking about what Angela said? About your mom being a guardian and maybe wondering what kind of powers you have, that you haven't discovered yet?"

"Maybe a little, but I --" She turned around, holding the omelet on a platter and almost ran into him. With a swallowed gasp, she stuck her tongue out at him. After all this time together, she knew she should be used to him suddenly just being there, right next to her or right behind her, close enough to touch. That was part of his job, being able to move quickly, silently, invisible to all the senses.

The thing was, Bethany was sure she was getting attuned to Harry, so she should be able to sense him anywhere and everywhere. She should know when he moved. She should know when he focused those gorgeous eyes on her and stared like he wanted to kiss her. Like he was doing now.

Maybe the problem was that whatever guardian powers her mother had possessed, she hadn't passed them on to her, only that sense of magic-but-not-magic that Harry detected the day they met.

Bethany detoured around Harry and put the platter on the table. The omelet was big enough for both of them.

"If your father cooks like you," Harry said, rubbing his hands in anticipation as they settled down facing each other across the table, "then his place is probably the most popular restaurant in town."

"I cook like Daddy, just barely. He taught me. Breakfast food is my specialty. But Daddy is a thousand times better cook than me." She sighed and bit back a comment.

"What?" Harry rested his hand on hers when she would have picked up the knife to cut the omelet in half. "Tell me. I can see something sad in your eyes."

"I was thinking I didn't inherit much of anything from either of my parents. A sense of magic. Some skill in cooking. But nothing even close to what either of them had."

"That just means you haven't figured out what you're supposed to do yet. Maybe it's unconscious magic, and skills you haven't experimented with yet. And maybe your acting is what your gift is."

"Unless I can take on a role that will change the world, what good does that do anyone? My mother was a heroine. She sacrificed her life for the entire town." Bethany rested her chin in her fist, but didn't tug her other hand free of Harry's grip. She liked the little tingles that came from his touch, fizzy, like those tablet candies she had as a little girl, to make plain water bubbly and sweet.

"You're still young. Give it time. I've been working on my problem for decades. I never thought there was a use for it, until Alexi called me about you. The Fae have a longer view of time. You just need to relax and let things happen. Maybe you're so focused on figuring things out, you're missing details."

"That's easy to say. You're going to live for centuries. I only have eighty or so years left to me, if that much."

"Hmm, maybe."

"Maybe?" She tugged her hand free, but something sparkling deep inside his eyes made her laugh despite the pique that raised her temperature a few degrees.

"Did I tell you about Changelings?"

"Like, kids who get snatched by faeries and faeries are left in their places to be raised by Humans?"

"That's the Human version of the story. What happens is that a Fae and a Human get together and have a baby. If he's raised as a Human, he might not even know he has Fae blood, until something happens to him or his descendants to awaken that magic. It sends off a signal like a tornado siren. When that happens, a Fae comes along, and offers him a chance to... Well, you'd call it gene therapy now, but some serious spell work is done to fully awaken that latent magic and make it the dominant gene. That person becomes a Fae."

"What does that have to do with me? Since I'm not Fae." Bethany busied herself cutting the omelet and serving it to them both, to keep her hands from trembling.

"You have magic. Maybe it needs to be awakened. And even if it isn't Fae magic, maybe --" He looked away and swallowed hard.

He's nervous, she realized, with a flash of insight that made the trembling go away. *Does he feel what I'm feeling, but he's not sure where it's going?*

She wasn't sure how she felt about the concept there was more to this attraction between them than some tingly, experimental kisses that made his invisibility flicker. She did know she liked the breathless, energized, slightly dizzy sensation that flooded her.

Did Harry want her to be with him, forever? He wouldn't bring up the whole topic of Changelings unless he wanted her to become one, would he? Unless he thought it might be possible for her?

"Maybe," she agreed, nodding. "Eat your breakfast before it gets cold. We've been exploring Cleveland and all the big sights to see. Now you're going to see where I grew up."

And maybe, if she was lucky, they would run into Lanie Zephyr and get some answers from her. Her father often said that everyone in Neighborlee visited his diner at least once a week.

~~~~~

"How long has your family run this diner?" Harry leaned in for a closer look at the cluster of photos gracing the back wall of the diner.

"Almost since Neighborlee was Neighborlee." Bethany frowned and looked up from the photo of herself as a baby, asleep in her mother's arms at the long stainless steel counter. "Why?"

"I think there were some Fae around right at the beginning. Which makes sense, with all the power, the dimensional thin spots." Harry traced the definitely pointed ears of the proud man in a white cook's apron, who bore a strong resemblance to Ben. He looked over the long rogues' gallery of photos chronicling the history of the diner. Up until a generation ago, there were pointed Fae ears in every single picture of a Miller.

Bethany got up from the booth in the corner and joined him. She leaned in, almost pressing her nose against the picture after he traced the sixth set of pointed ears. Eyes narrowed, she stared at her ancestor. She gasped, took a step back so quickly she almost tripped over her feet, and stared at him, eyes wide.

"How come I've never seen that before?" She yanked on his sleeve, bringing him closer. "The ears, I mean."

"That's easy. The standard 'don't notice me' spell most law-abiding Fae activate when they venture out into the Human realm." Harry looked around the diner, just starting to pick up traffic as the clock ticked over to 11am, starting the lunch rush. He hooked his arm through Bethany's and led her back to their booth. "It had to be modified when the camera was invented, and we're still having a heck of a time working around digital photography. Basically, the spell remains with whatever permanent images are made of the Fae. With all the errant magic simmering in the background in Neighborlee ..." He settled into the booth again. "Well, the spell probably got mixed up in whatever magic lets people live here with all the weirdness going on without losing their minds. It's easier to conveniently ignore things, rather than think about them and tear your nerves to bits."
~~~~~

"I have Fae in my background, then?" Bethany murmured, staring unseeing at the tabletop. "I thought you said I didn't have Fae magic. But I'd have to, wouldn't I, with all those pointed ears among my ancestors?" She snatched at her ears, holding her hands over them. "Do I have pointed ears, but I never noticed before?"

"Well, put your hands down and let me see." Harry was ready to laugh and tease her, but the words died on his lips when Bethany complied. Sure enough, he saw delicately pointed tips on her ears, for the very first time.

That confirmed his belief that some powerful Fae ancestor had set a spell in motion to protect all his or her descendants, no matter how the Fae blood got diluted by Human. Something shivered deep down in his gut at the sudden realization that Bethany was Fae, even if it was only a tiny fraction of her bloodline. And suddenly her ears raised his temperature a good ten degrees.

"Harry?" Bethany let her hands rest flat on the table. "Harry --"

"Yeah, you do. Not a lot, but enough to see if you're looking for them." He swallowed hard and managed to scavenge up a grin. "You have got the hottest ears ..." He laughed when Bethany turned bright red.

"So how could you say I didn't have magic, when it's pretty clear now I did inherit some?" She lowered her voice and leaned closer to him across the table.

"I have a theory. Let me call up the Ether Lexicon. With something like this, it's better to have facts and a way to get data instead of relying on hearsay."

"Okay, but how good can this thing be, if it hasn't given you an answer for your invisibility problem?"

"Part of the trick is knowing what questions to ask. If you don't ask the right question, it can't give you the answer you really need." Harry decided to enjoy her laughter, rather than be irritated or embarrassed.

Bethany's laughter died when he conjured up the Ether Lexicon out of thin air and it floated down to the table in their booth, accompanied by sparks and miniature whirlwinds the size of his pinky in contrasting neon shades of pink and green and purple. Harry was encouraged to see the Lexicon was only the size of a *For Dummies* book. He snorted when he realized the irony of the comparison.

He was encouraged even more to realize Bethany could see the Lexicon. That said something for the strength of magic in her blood, even if it was battling with the guardian powers, as Angela termed whatever she had inherited from her mother.

That was Harry's theory: the Fae magic battled for dominance with the guardian half of Bethany's genetics. They nullified each other and muddied the trail or the waters or whatever metaphor might be applicable.

"That's a pretty cool trick," a female voice said, coming from just above Harry's elbow height. He looked over to his right and saw a woman in a wheelchair sitting in the aisle, her head tipped to one side, studying the Ether Lexicon.

"Hey, Miss Lanie," Bethany said. She glanced at Harry and waggled her eyebrows, tipping her head toward the newcomer.

"You're Lanie Zephyr?" he asked.

"Guilty. Who's been taking my name in vain now?" She pivoted her wheelchair to face the table, as if she would pull up to the end, instead of gliding past. "Haven't seen you in a while, Bethany. Your dad didn't say anything about you getting home for Christmas."

"We're trying some invisibility this year." Bethany's face turned rosy as she visibly fought giggles.

"Uh huh. Why do I get the feeling you're being very literal when you talk about invisibility?" Lanie tipped her head to the other side and turned her attention back to Harry. "What's with the sudden flood of Fae visiting our town?" She snorted laughter when he choked and nearly fumbled the Lexicon right off the table.

Bethany made the introductions, explaining that Harry was there as a bodyguard.

"So when you say invisibility, that's pretty much reality. Okay." Lanie nodded. "So what's with the cool book that popped in out of nowhere? I've seen some dimensional transference, especially around Divine's, but nothing like this. You can't even see the slit open."

Harry gave a slightly more detailed explanation of the Ether Lexicon, how it provided information, and the size depended on the situation, the question, and sometimes the strength of the one requesting information.

"Cool. Thank goodness none of my students could get at something like this when I was a teacher. There would have been cheating day in and day out. Not that I had to worry about you, Bethany. You stopped just short of being a goody-goody."

"I think that's a compliment," Bethany muttered. Then she met Lanie's gaze and they both sputtered laughter.

"Actually, we were hoping to meet up with you today," Harry said, when the laughter faded out. "Angela said you're a guardian."

"Ah, now that's a word with a lot of meanings, depending on the situation." Lanie pulled her chair up to the table, sliding as far under the surface as her wheelchair would allow, clearing the aisle. She rested her crossed arms on the table. "I have about ten minutes, max, before my lunch date -- I use that word very loosely, and don't you ever repeat it to anyone -- shows up."

"You're scared of people saying you have a date?" Bethany frowned a little.

"I'm meeting the owner of the newspaper chain for lunch, to discuss a charity event we're sponsoring. He wants me to head up the comedy portion. Strictly business. I swear." She raised her hand in the Vulcan salute. "But there are a bunch of people with very shallow lives who keep trying to make something more out of our friendship."

"Since we don't have much time..." Harry wished they did. "What does being a guardian mean for you, specifically? Because we found out just a few days ago that Bethany's mother was a guardian, and she fought down the dimensional...intruder, I guess you'd call it, that Angela says you faced, but she lost."

Lanie's smile flattened to a frown of concentration. She nodded slowly, her eyes hooded, gaze turned inward. "I remember when Stephanie died. There was this feeling in the air. It was the day after we had the celebration canoeing day, down in Mohican. The energy was so disturbed, so uneven, and we felt it even more strongly when we came back into town after being out all day. There was this storm ... Stephanie's specialty was finding the leaks between dimensions and slapping a patch on the hole. That day, though ... it was too much for her. We didn't find out until recently that we have more enemies than we realized, and they were draining the power that not only protects Neighborlee, but helps guardians heal. Your mother died, when she shouldn't have. And I ... well, I didn't die of my injuries, but I didn't heal all the way." She gestured at her wheelchair.

"I remember. A little," Bethany whispered.

"Our numbers are increasing, and as we've identified and fought off our enemies, we're regaining the energy. We've been tracking down all the Lost Kids, going through the orphanage archives. I guess we need to check the descendants of those who didn't show powers. Just in case." She studied Bethany long enough, the girl twitched a little. "Your mother didn't want you to know, so your memories were blocked. Now that you're remembering, maybe your heritage is waking up."

"Heritage? I'm a freak of nature. I just found out Dad has faerie blood, and Mom is from another dimension or whatever." Bethany pouted, but mischief sparkled in her eyes. "I wonder if she knew about him."

"She knew." Lanie grinned, then turned her gaze to Harry. "Something freaky is bound to happen, with all the Fae in town. Have you run into Maurice yet, or Will and Phill?"

"Oh, yeah." Harry shuddered, thinking about Maurice's exile, and scolded himself yet again for indulging in self-pity so often. At least he could live a fairly normal life, with a little concentration and extra alertness.

"Tell you what. I'll get the gang together and give you a good indoctrination. But I gotta go. The Evil Overlord just walked in. Later?"

"Sure. Thanks." Bethany watched Lanie pivot out from the table and head to the other side of the diner. "Wow, just when you think you have your hometown figured out."

"Yeah. As a Fae, you kind of assume there's very little to surprise you." Harry traded grins with her, and flipped the Ether Lexicon open. "We might find some surprises in here, too."

"That's my cue to get us something to eat and leave you to study in peace." She patted his hand and slid out of the booth, hurrying to the kitchen before Harry could reply.

By the time Bethany returned with their lunch, which she cooked herself, Harry had enough general information to confirm his theory. With enough time and research and study, he might have a fix for Bethany's problem or question, and an answer to what she was: Fae or guardian or some new, wonderful amalgam.

"At least you're not a mule," he said between bites of fries drenched in chili, onions and chipotle cheese.

"A what?" Bethany giggled.

"Sorry. A dead end, technically. When two very different species interbreed, sometimes the offspring is unable to reproduce, or inherits no talents at all. My theory is that you have both powers or magics or whatever you call it, and they're sort of fighting each other. Using up energy, trying for dominance in you, so there's no power left over for you to learn how to use them and ... do things."

"Okay, I can be either a sorceress or one of the X-Men, but I can't be both."

"Why not? I think that's what you are, but you have to learn to get completely in the driver's seat and stop the two sides of your heritage from battling and wasting all that energy." Harry closed the Ether Lexicon, with a half-dozen bookmarks inserted to help him return to the spots he hadn't fully studied yet, and willed it into the waiting dimension. "There's a blockage. You need magic or guardian power to get around it. But you can't access that power or magic until you get through or around or destroy the blockage. Catch Twenty-two."

"Like getting an Equity job. You have to be a member of Equity to get a job, but you can't join Equity until you have an Equity job." Bethany nodded slowly, her gaze unfocused, one fry raised and a long string of melted cheese slowly dripping off it. "But miracles do happen. There's always a loophole. I'm proof of that. We'll find the answer."

Harry froze as her gaze focused again and locked with his. Something burst hot and tingling inside him when Bethany said *we*, as if it were the most important thing in the world for them to be partnered in this.

In everything, Harry decided a moment later, mesmerized by Bethany's slowly widening, sparkling, scorching smile. She believed in him. She trusted him. And he would do it for her, no matter what.

Thursday, December 20

Lori wrapped her arms tight around herself, shivering even though she wasn't cold. Then she sighed in pure pleasure when Brick slid an arm around her shoulders and brought her closer.

They stood at the top of a hill in the Metroparks that let them look down on the center of Neighborlee, watching as evening crept in. All the Christmas lights filling the town came on, spreading down the streets like ripples in a pond. This was the result of weeks of hanging lights and planning colors and designs. This was a magic beyond her talents and strength.

"We don't have anything like this back home," she said.

Yes, if she had to stay in the Human realm to be free of the aunties and whichever appropriate husband they had chosen for her, she could be very happy here, with Brick.

He moved his arm off her shoulders and stepped away just enough that a chilly finger of breeze slipped between them.

"I don't believe you." His voice sounded odd. Strained. He didn't look at her as he spoke.

"Believe me." She shivered from something beyond the cold. *What did I just do wrong? Why is he angry?* She felt the buzzing in the air, a storm about to explode across the scene.

"Where do you live? Another planet?" His voice tightened, with a growl underlying it.

"You wouldn't understand." Lori fought the urge to back away.

"Try me. You know all about me, but I don't know much about you. Funny, you're so big on doing everything, helping, experiencing everything, like it's your first Christmas ever. And that just doesn't make sense."

"If I told you, you wouldn't believe me. I wish you could, but despite everything you've said, you wouldn't. And I don't want to lose you." She moved over to stand in front of him, make him look at her, to see how much his words hurt her. Brick just glared through her, like she wasn't there at all, like she was invisible.

"Lose me?" He sneered. "What makes you think you have me? You're too good to be true. You're so excited about things that matter to me, and then you close up. You say things that don't make any sense. You've got holes in your story, sister."

"It's no story, it's the truth. And they're not holes, they're just things that would blow your mind." Lori clenched her fists, feeling magic buzz in her fingertips.

It would be so easy to perform some flashy magic. Lift him to the top of a tree, turn the snowy clearing around them into summertime, open a dimensional slit and take him into another world. But she couldn't. Not if she wanted to protect Brick's sanity. Just because he talked about faeries and his great-grandmother, that didn't mean, when faced with the reality, he wouldn't go insane. She couldn't do that to him.

"Everything just makes me think it's all a scam. A pretty elaborate one, but a scam all the same. Well, guess what? I might be a Willis, but I don't have anything. Tradition and influence and the family name, sure, but no money, no estates. And a lot of responsibility."

The air darkened with the force of his lie. Lori blinked and took a step back, feeling scorched by the anger that spewed from his lips. Why was he so furious? What had she done?

"You didn't do your homework, sister."

"You think I'm here to steal from you? To lie and trick you?" She shuddered and took another step back. "You're not the man I thought you were." She gasped as insight bloomed in her head. "That's why you kept dropping those papers talking about that money, isn't it? To test me."

"Yeah, and did you look at those papers?"

"They didn't make any sense to me. Talking about banks and balances and debts. I didn't understand."

"If you were the rich woman you try to make me think you are, you'd understand all those things. But you're nothing but a fraud. You lasted longer than the others, but you're still a liar and cheat, under all the pretty--"

Brick froze, the air sparkling and buzzing in ten shades of green and orange as Lori halted time around him.

She clenched her fists and gasped through her nose and walked a dozen rapid, nearly blinding fast circles around him. She wanted to pound him. She wanted to turn him into something embarrassing, and have him know what was going on, so he would shrivel up with mortal embarrassment.

"No, no, no," she whispered, her whole body so tight with her fury it stole her breath. Lori shuddered, terrified by the rage that tore through her. She took another step back from Brick, shaking. Tears filled her eyes, as sorrow replaced rage. This wasn't like her at all. She never got this upset. She never got this hurt. What had happened? Why did his opinion of her mean so much? Why did his suspicions and accusations hurt, when they weren't true?

Because she had opened up her heart to him. She felt as if they had started to graft themselves to each other, and he had pulled away, leaving her raw all over, and raw inside.

All she knew in that moment was that she had to get away from Brick. Some place quiet and solitary, where she could think. Where nobody could find her. She slashed at the air with a trembling fingertip, splitting a dimensional slit open, and stepped through. The air flashed as it sealed up again.

The buzz of power lingered and reverberated, chiming off the bedrock of Neighborlee. A light snow fell. A deer tiptoed out from the shelter of the trees, approached Brick and nuzzled his outstretched hand. It didn't like the taste of his leather glove, so it retreated back into the shadows.

Moonlight slowly crept among the trees until it touched Brick's hair. Lori's angry magic expended itself with a soft ringing sound. He gasped and stumbled forward. He closed his mouth, swallowing hard against the dryness and the awful taste, like he had his mouth open for hours. He blinked and looked around.

"Lori?" His voice cracked with the force of the fury that had buzzed in his vocal cords just a few seconds ago.

No, not seconds. He shivered as he looked around the moonlit clearing and saw the ring of tracks from small feet that circled him, multiple times. He knew enough about reading tracks to see the agitation in her staggering steps, despite the light snow swirling around him.

"Thanks a lot, Neighborlee. You've done it again," he murmured, feeling as if he had stood still for hours in the cold. From the darkness and his sense of time, that was exactly what had happened.

The question was how it had happened, and what had happened to Lori. Brick remembered what he had been saying to her. Chances were good she hadn't run off for help.

Had she done this to him? He snorted disbelieving laughter as the idea came clear to his mind. That would explain an awful lot, wouldn't it?

"What? She has magic -- she is magic -- and she's come out of some magical world to experience Christmas for the first time? Yeah, right." Brick shook his head and headed down the hill to his truck. His feet were soaking wet, and if he didn't get those boots off and his feet under a blast of warm air soon, he was going to have pneumonia for a Christmas present.

He couldn't believe what he had just imagined about Lori, even if it neatly explained everything. Despite the "normal" weirdness of Neighborlee, it was just too farfetched.

Or was it?

Deep inside where the cold hadn't quite penetrated, he shivered as something beyond his brain made an enormous, galaxy-spanning intuitive leap, proposing something his conscious mind hesitated to accept. If Lori had done this to him, froze him in time before she vanished, then maybe his theory about her wasn't so off. But what did that imply, for him and her?

Besides the fact he had made an enormous mistake?

And just how was he going to find her so they could straighten things out between them?

Because he knew one thing, just as strong and certain as the ice filtering through his blood: he wanted Lori back. She was right and he was wrong. She did have him, and maybe she hadn't lost him, but he had lost her, and that meant all was wrong with the world.

Chapter Twelve

Friday, December 21

"What do you think?" Holly stepped back from the arrangement she had been fussing over during her dream.

Maurice bit his tongue and just nodded and smiled. That seemed to be all Holly wanted. She flung her arms around him, kissed him on both cheeks, and turned back to the long table. It was loaded with flowers, ferns, ribbons, and those sharp little sticks that went into flower arrangements to hold kitschy little decorations like silver wedding bells and champagne bottles and sparklers. He had never thought there was so much junk related to wedding decorations on the entire planet.

Tomorrow was Jeri and Jon-Tom's wedding, and Holly had been asked to decorate it as well. She had been so encouraged by the compliments and how well her decorations for Diane and Troy's wedding had turned out, she was talking about taking on wedding planning as a sideline business.

Problem: Holly went into blue funks when no one was around except Maurice. He suspected it was because she was surrounded by wedding talk and wedding preparations and wedding details, but none of the details were for *her* wedding.

He didn't know if he was doing her any good by giving her hope during her dreams. When they were together in the dreaming realms, he tried to explain the details of his exile, and she seemed to understand. She sometimes came into the dreams a little depressed, a holdover from her waking time as the girl everyone considered a pal, a confidant, but no guy wanted to date.

It didn't help that she seemed to be getting a lot of sympathy from older women who constantly told her variations of, "Don't you worry, sweetie. Those other girls might be fun for now, but you're the kind of girl a man finally brings home to his mother."

Maurice agreed with Holly's infuriated wail: How could a guy know he wanted to take her home to his mother if he never dated her?

He worried about Holly's balance of mind and soul. The magic that let them meet in her dreams and kept her from remembering or seeing him in her waking hours was effectively splitting her realities, farther apart the longer they were together. Maybe it was splitting her mind and her soul. What kind of damage was the magic doing, keeping her dreams hidden from her waking mind?

"It's perfect," Holly whispered, as she cleared away all the supplies and walked around the flower arrangement she had designed for Jeri and Jon-Tom's wedding. "I managed to remember most of the details when I was working out Diane and Troy's decorations, so I'll remember most of this when I wake up." She bit her lip and turned to Maurice, the first glimmer of doubt darkening her sparkling eyes. "You think?"

"I promise." He hoped Angela wouldn't give him any assignments all day. He would use up most of his allotment of magic manipulating Holly's hand, so she wrote and sketched while still asleep. He wouldn't be able to accompany Holly, keeping disaster away during the following day. He would have to spend most of it sacked out, magic-less and drowsy, until Angela went over to the church to help with decorations that evening. Then he would ride on her shoulder, saving what little energy he had regained, so he could watch over Holly while she climbed ladders and directed work crews.

Fortunately, Diane and Troy were back from their honeymoon, so they could help when he called. And Lanie would be there, so she could use her telekinesis in a pinch.

"I'm turning into a dang administrator, telling everybody else what to do."

Holly woke up and started her day, and Maurice returned to his body, sitting in front of the Wishing Ball. All his discomfort was for Holly, and that made every sacrifice worthwhile.

~~~~~

"So your final analysis is that there's hope, just because I can see and sense magic." Bethany settled back in the sofa in her father's living room. "But you haven't found a way past the block my Fae blood and my guardian blood seem to be creating for each other."

"Just because I haven't found a way yet doesn't mean there isn't a way. Right." Harry closed the Ether Lexicon with a snap and raised his hands, to give it that little toss that would send it back
~~~~~

into the ether.

"Could I?" she asked, catching his wrist and stopping him. She muffled a weary giggle when Harry gave her a confused look. Bethany loved his confused look. It was so innocent and geeky. Then he blushed delightfully, shifting through an entire rainbow.

"Sure." Harry held out the book to her. "Might work this time. You've spent enough time touching the pages."

"And getting my fingers bitten." She wrinkled up her nose in distaste, making him laugh.

"But not so bad, the last dozen times. It's finally used to you. And I think that's a good sign, too. Most people can't even see the Lexicon, much less touch it. It's getting used to you."

She grinned, gloating and not feeling a bit of guilt, at the knowledge that Athena couldn't even see the Ether Lexicon. It sort of made up for all the things she had missed out on, growing up, all the secrets and wonder and magic, because her mother wanted her protected from her heritage. The last week had been fun, and busy. Athena's gang had welcomed Harry with open arms, and none of them blinked for more than a few seconds when Bethany had told them the truth about him. And her own troublesome heritage. Athena, Doni, Wallace and Cosmo had gone through enough strangeness with FlopDrop and London Holiday, and then helping yank the Zephyrs through time this summer. They were used to it. They didn't hesitate to believe Fae were real, even before they saw Harry's ears or how he made himself and Bethany go invisible. This was Neighborlee, of course.

"Let's test. And then let's go for a long walk and get some fresh air." *And maybe I'll take you to the gazebo and trick you into kissing me under the mistletoe,* she added, focusing her thoughts on him. One of these days, Harry was going to hear her thoughts. She was sure of it. For now, Bethany focused on the task at hand. She held her breath and waited for Harry to slide the Ether Lexicon onto her flattened palms.

All that mistletoe woven into the roof of the gazebo, a literal ceiling of the leaves and berries, golden balls, tinsel, and weather-proof ribbons had to have some effect. Harry had explained the magical properties of mistletoe, how it opened the senses to other realms and sometimes persuaded stubborn dimensional slits to loosen up and be pliable for manipulation and travel. Bethany was just hoping Harry would be more pliable to the romantic influence of mistletoe, and give her more than a quick kiss, like a shy little boy who didn't want to be teased by his bruiser pals on the tag football team. The last few times he had kissed her, she had felt increased tingles, like carbonation bubbles. But Harry never kissed her long enough for more than a hint.

"Here we go," he muttered, and set the Lexicon onto her flattened palms, sliding his hands out from under it. "And we have suc -- sorry," he sighed, as the book of Fae knowledge sizzled for a heartbeat, then vanished in a burst of psychedelic rainbow sparkles. "At least you had all the weight on your hands this time."

"Yeah, there's that." Bethany managed a brave smile and popped off the sofa to go find her coat. She wasn't going to pout, and she wasn't going to let herself get depressed. That was progress, after all. The first time Harry had tried to let her hold the book, it had exploded into an angry, snarling red light-and-sound show when her hand was six inches away. At least it didn't snap closed anymore when she read over Harry's shoulder.

Half an hour later, they had strolled down side streets to reach the gazebo in the center of town. Bethany sighed, content with the world -- for now. Harry definitely had to like her, with all the effort he put into finding an answer for her. More than just *like*. She let her hope grow stronger with every day they spent in research and discussing possibilities with Maurice and Will and Phill. Harry was aiming for the golden ring: to make her a Changeling. And that had to mean he really did want eternity with her. Or at least the Fae equivalent of happily-ever-after.

The question was whether she had enough magic in her to be awakened, so she could become a Changeling. Would they reach a point in this search when Harry would have to throw his hands up in the air and give up?

"What are you thinking?" Harry said, as they reached the gazebo. He looked up at the ceiling and his eyes widened, and Bethany muffled a giggle.

So all these years growing up, she wasn't imagining it when she stepped into the gazebo and felt the shiver of power and possibilities in the air. He felt it, too.

"I'm thinking... I wish it could be Christmas all the time, that we could freeze this moment, this season, with all the magic and possibilities and dreams and...there's just so much life and joy in the air at this time of the year. Even if it's dang freezing," she added, earning a chuckle from him.

"There's enough magic gathered here right now to get a good start on that kind of wish." He glanced upward again at the green and gold and red and white ceiling.

"Is it Fae rules, or Human rules, that you have to make the wish and seal it with a kiss?"

"Ah..." Harry looked down at her and blinked several times. "Huh?" When she giggled, he blushed a little, shifting from red to purple to blue, before it faded away. "Kind of dizzying. It's..." He frowned, just as he went semi-transparent from the top of his head down below his shoulders.

Harry closed his eyes and held his breath, and a moment later became solid again.

"It's messing with your anti-invisibility spell, isn't it?" Bethany didn't know whether to pity him or laugh. "We should probably get out of here." She licked her lips from pure nervousness, and was encouraged when Harry's eyes looked dazed again and he stared at her mouth. "But after I get my wish and kiss?"

"Your wish is my command." Harry's voice ended on a rasp.

To her delight, he put his arms around her, instead of just clasping her shoulders like he had the last few times they kissed. Bethany swore she could feel his heart racing against hers, through the thickness of their coats. She slid her arms around his neck and went up on her tiptoes as Harry bent his head down to her level. Just as she closed her eyes, he went entirely invisible.

Buzzes and prickles and fizzing sensations washed over her, lifting her hair under her hat. Bethany ignored it for the wonderful dizzy, warm sensation of Harry kissing her, soft and sweet and deep. And counted the heartbeats as he kept his mouth pressed against hers.

Three. Four. Five. His arms tightened enough she found it hard to breathe. Not that she was trying to breathe.

Six. Seven. Eight. The fizzing, carbonated bubbles sensation faded, leaving a light feeling all over her skin as if a gentle breeze enclosed her, coming between her and her clothes. It was odd, pleasant, but just strong enough to make her aware of it. And it didn't fade.

She kept her eyes closed, even when Harry's lips left hers and he lifted his head.

"Bethany."

That groan in his voice didn't sound good. She opened one eye and saw him looking down at her with growing dismay.

"What?"

"You're ... invisible."

"What?" She leaped out of his arms and turned around, looking down at herself.

Or tried to.

Her first thought was gratitude that it wasn't like some of those ridiculous *Invisible Man* movies, where the flesh was invisible but not the clothes -- necessitating running around in the all-together to make effective use of said invisibility. Her clothes were invisible, too, and still on her body.

Bethany kept turning around, trying to see something, some glimmer, trying to will herself into at least semi-visibility. She kept hoping it was just temporary, just an illusion. Maybe she really was visible, but some magic spell had gone wonky, as Phill had phrased it, and she just *thought* she was invisible.

Then she saw the snow her constantly turning footsteps packed flat. She didn't think optical illusions would let her see what was under her feet so...clearly.

"What happened?"

"Well..." Harry reached out, brushed against her arm, caught hold of it, and felt down her arm until he got hold of her hand. He led her over to the bench outside the gazebo. "I'll need to do some research, but my theory is that between the wonkiness of my invisibility spell, and all that magic coming from the mistletoe overhead, and the fact that you do indeed have magic, plus getting really, really," he blushed green then yellow then orange, "really close for a few seconds ... my wonky spell transferred over to you."

"Okay. Makes sense. I guess." Bethany supposed if it made sense, maybe she had picked up the basic rules of magic. To her frustration, most of it seemed to consist of what a beginner should not do, when starting to learn to use magic. "How do we get it off me, or un-wonk it, or whatever?"

"I don't know yet. But look on the bright side." He brought her hand to his face and pressed it against his cheek. "I think your inborn magic just took the upper hand in the battle with the guardian talents."

"Yeah, but is that a good thing?" she muttered.

Saturday, December 22

Jeri and Jon-Tom's wedding went off without a hitch. Maurice rode on Holly's shoulder and sniffled a few times, until he caught Angela watching him from the corner of her eye. Why shouldn't he be happy? He liked them. They were good people. And they had almost as much standing in their way as he and Holly faced. Barriers from their pasts, people using and hurting them, and distrust that should have kept them far apart.

Jeri should have been the type of woman Jon-Tom despised, but she had bucked her heritage and training, and had chosen to be sweet and giving and simple at heart. She deserved her prince, and from everything Maurice had seen, Jon-Tom was a real prince. He was proud to have been part of Holly's decorating team, even if her waking mind had no idea what he had done. Every single decoration they talked about in her dreams came out, down to the final detail. Maurice had mentioned to Diane and Angela and Lanie what Holly had said about designing weddings on the side. All three had taken her aside at one time or another and given her encouragement and support. Of course, Holly had reacted as if the thought had never entered her conscious mind (it hadn't, of course), but she loved the idea.

"Yeah, kid," he whispered, "you and me, we're a great team, huh?"

Just a few more days and he would have his day of being full-size and visible to the world. He would work hard to impress on Holly that they would indeed make a great team. Someday. When he could be in her life every day instead of four times a year.

Had old Asmondius and the other members of the Fae Disciplinary Council planned on anything like this happening, when they exiled him here? Maurice knew they were strict, but they weren't cruel. Well, most of them weren't. He could guess that they hoped something would happen to shake him up and make him act more responsibly, with more consideration for others' feelings.

What would their reactions be when they found out he wanted to stay in the Human realm? He just had to figure out a way to make sure he and Holly beat the odds for a Fae-Human relationship.

Right now, he thought if he had to sacrifice his magic, it might be worth it.

Pastor Rocky said his final words, his big face nearly splitting with his delighted grin. Jon-Tom and Jeri went into a clinch that Maurice swore turned up the heat in the church about ten degrees, while all their friends clapped, laughed, and shouted approval. When they turned to walk down the aisle, Jon-Tom swept Jeri up in his arms and hurried out of the church amid more laughter.

"I could do that. You think Holly would think that's romantic?" Maurice asked Angela, who sat next to Holly near the front of the church.

I think anything you do to please Holly will be romantic, Angela responded in his mind.

"Great wedding, huh?" Phill joined them after everyone had gone through the reception line and the guests had trooped down the hallway to the church's gymnasium, which Holly had decorated to look like a playground.

The refreshments were picnic fare. The guests had been warned to dress casually. Everyone sat on blankets on the floor or on benches or swings hung from the basketball backstops, or on the bleachers pulled out from the wall. Maurice thought it was great.

"Taking notes?" Angela looked around. "Where's Will? I assume the two of you finally worked things out."

"We're still working things out, but at least we know we want to be together. It's just all the big details, like assuring my family that I'm not dying and assuring his family he's not making a big mistake and... Well, there are some issues that sort of stood in our way all this time."

The gymnasium was large, but the guests came close to straining the maximum capacity. Maurice wondered if they would use up all the oxygen before Jeri and Jon-Tom cut their cake.

He had a good time flitting from group to group, eavesdropping and trying to get clues to what hopeful couples he should try to match up in the coming year. Playing Cupid (without the indignity of the diaper and tiny arrows, thanks very much) was kind of fun. He had some ideas for people to put together, even interfere a little with their lives. With Angela's approval and advice, of course.

Jerry, Jon-Tom's best man, got hold of the microphone and announced it was time to toss the bouquet and the garter. Maurice wasn't sure how it happened, but despite all his protests, Will got pushed to the front of the group of bachelors waiting to catch the garter. Jon-Tom shot it like a slingshot off two fingers. Everyone had their hands in the air, including a good dozen elementary school boys who couldn't be old enough to understand the significance and folklore associated with catching the garter. They were there because they loved Jeri, who volunteered at the schools and took them on adventure walks in the park. They had heard whoever caught the garter got to kiss the bride.

They were wrong, of course. But that didn't matter, because the garter sailed into Will's hands as if guided on a string. Maurice knew he was likely to be accused of that trick, but when he turned to Angela to protest his innocence, she had an interesting little smirk on her lips. She never even looked at him. So he kept quiet.

Jerry next asked all the unmarried women to gather to catch the bouquet. Phill backed up toward the door in response.

"If I did it, you have to do it," Will declared.

"This is ridiculous. It's worse than the running of the bulls," she protested, laughing, while Will and Lanie's two brothers pushed and dragged her over to the huge group of hopeful women.

"We can use all the help we can get," Will told her, as he gave her a final shove into the center of the group and made a strategic getaway before he was crushed or trapped.

"Even if it worked centuries ago, that doesn't mean..." Phill's laughter faded to a thoughtful look, then a scowl.

Maurice followed her line of sight. Several dozen young women all looked at Will with the intensity of sharks following a trail of blood in water. He just stood there with the garter pushed up securely on his upper arm. Maurice gave Phill a mental high-five for realizing all those women recognized Will as their hopeful kissing target in the next five minutes -- and she was jealous.

Phill had no reason to be jealous, but the other girls' interest was definitely good motivation for her to participate in the ritual. It might have lost its prognostication powers through the centuries because newer wedding rituals diluted the process. Still, Maurice firmly believed the garter and bouquet tosses at weddings had some magical zing left in them.

Will was right. He and Phill could use all the help they could get.

Maurice held his breath and closed his eyes and wished and kept his magic firmly wrapped around himself so he couldn't be accused of interfering. Outside magic could jinx the results. Jeri turned her back on the crowd of women, swung the bouquet of daisies and ribbons up and down in front of her a few times, as if pumping up for speed, and let it fly over her shoulder.

"Perfect," Angela murmured. A roar went up from the guests. "You can open your eyes now, Maurice. Holly didn't catch it."

"That wasn't what I was--" He gave up and opened his eyes. "Yes!" He leaped up three feet in the air, when he saw Phill, her mouth hanging open, clutching Jeri's bridal bouquet to her chest.

Several girls scampered away with tears in their eyes, but most of them gathered around to laugh and pat her shoulder and congratulate her. That was part of the oldest magic: everyone had to wish the catcher well, not ill.

"Whew!" Lanie said, wheeling over to join them. "That was a close call."

"You weren't in there, were you?" Angela said, laughing.

"I was on the sidelines, just for appearances' sake. I was mostly worried about Phill getting tackled and someone ripping the bouquet away before she got a good grip on it." She smirked.

"You didn't help things along, did you?" Maurice asked, restraining his chuckles.

"My hands were firmly on the wheels of my chair the entire time." She held her hands up in the air, wiggling them so the multicolored nails decorated with rainbow sparkles flashed in the gymnasium lights.

"It's not your hands I'm worried about," Angela said.

"Hey, playing pseudo-cupid is *my* job." Maurice flew over to Lanie and held up both hands. She high-fived him with her pinky against his palms. Even braced, with his wings fluttering fifty miles an hour, her light tap sent him scooting backwards about a foot. The three grinned at each other while Jon-Tom and Jeri got Will and Phill arranged for the ceremony of placing the garter.

Phill wore a tea-length dress of green lace in multiple layers.

She obligingly tugged the hem up past her knee as she sat down in the chair Jerry and Jon-Tom brought over. Will knelt in front of her and twirled the garter on his finger a few times, earning laughter from the wedding guests. He pretended to struggle to get it over the modest heel of Phill's shoe.

Will's grin faded, the higher he got the garter up Phill's leg, until he looked positively mesmerized by the time he got it up to her knee. He gently tugged her hem down over the garter, stood, bowed, and offered her his hands. Phill moved like she was in a dream, slowly rising to her feet, closing her eyes long before she leaned in to let Will kiss her.

Maurice held his breath as their lips met.

"Uh oh," Lanie muttered, and grabbed her wheels.

The lights went off as a gust of magic wind blew through the gymnasium, moving outward from the center of the vortex that was Will and Phill, locked in each other's arms. Maurice yelped as tidal waves of sparks of every color in the magical and Human spectrums gushed outward from them. Winkies appeared, to dance and spin and toss their magic into the mix.

Wedding guests shouted and stumbled around in the pitch blackness. Some laughed. And the magic-infused maelstrom continued.

"They can't stop!" Angela called through the ruckus. "We have to get them apart. Lanie, can you help?"

Maurice whistled as streamers of visible power shot out from Lanie's head, through the half-blinding light show, and wrapped around Will and Phill. He and Angela pushed against the current that tried to swirl them away, to reach the two who were locked together in a kiss that conceivably could last through the end of time and out the other side into eternity. Good for Will and Phill, but probably uncomfortable for anyone in the magical fallout.

Angela, Lanie, and Maurice reached Will and Phill almost at the same time. Maurice laughed bitterly as he saw the thin streamers of his own reduced magic, wrapping around Will's wrists to try to pull him free of Phill, open his tight-clenched embrace, do something, anything, to break the connection. Angela tried with hands as well as an interesting, kaleidoscopic tangle of strands of power that Maurice likened to seaweed drifting in every direction in the ocean current. Lanie's power flared and then faded gradually as she applied her physical arms to yanking on the two of them.

"We need more help," Angela called.

"Duh!" Maurice shouted with all his strength, until his head throbbed with a hollow sound. *Lori, Harry! We need you. Emergency! Now!*

The air split as Lori and Harry came through a dimensional slide. Harry grabbed Will and Lori grabbed Phill, each around their waists. Lanie and Angela worked on loosening their hands. Maurice worked to slip a wedge between their lips. He made the magical field taste nasty, inserting rancid fish oil into the mix.

Will's eyes came open first, then Phill's. They blinked, they pulled back a fraction, started to grimace, reacting to the taste, then their eyes flared with new heat and they shifted their embrace.

That pause was just enough. Maurice shouted "Now!" and slid a sheet of aluminum foil between their lips. Angela and Lanie pulled Will's and Phill's wrists away from each other's bodies. Lori and Harry yanked hard.

They came apart with a pop that was nearly deafening, and made the punch bowls and their glass ladles chime.

"The hotel!" Lori gasped. "Follow me." She staggered backwards into another dimensional slit, dragging Phill. Harry snagged Will and followed her.

The slit closed with a flash of crimson and green light that left after-images on Maurice's retinas. He rubbed his eyes hard, and when he opened them, the lights had come back on in the gymnasium.

"Okay, that was interesting," Lanie said. "Are they going to be okay?"

"Forget about them." Maurice gestured around the gymnasium. Guests looked at each other with those peculiar half-grins and glances that clearly said, *Did you see that? If you deny it, I'll deny it,* which, he realized, were quite common in Neighborlee. "What are we gonna do about this mess?"

"Be grateful there were no chairs and tables for people to fall over, and it didn't last long enough for anyone to panic," Angela said.

"True." Lanie sighed and looked around. "It's the same old Neighborlee brand of convenient amnesia. People are explaining it away already." She gestured at a knot of high school girls clinging to each other, whispering and giggling. "There's always something weird going on, and easy explanations. Correction: *usually* an easy explanation. Excuse me." She wheeled away, cutting off Officer Gordon Priebe, a hulking man who had stuck a boutonniere in his uniform to dress it up for the wedding.

Lanie had described Gordon to Maurice as a big marshmallow inside a Godzilla-with-a-shave exterior. He was on duty and had gotten permission to attend the wedding with his wife, Mandy, as long as he kept in contact. Gordon was also a member of Lanie's *Star Trek* club, and had been involved in the ruckus two years ago, when that dimensional enemy had tried to break through underneath Neighborlee, creating time slides, and draining people of energy.

"Did Gordon see anything?" Angela asked, when he headed out of the gym, and she returned to join them.

"Not this time. He *felt* plenty. He's getting a little more sensitive to differentiate between ordinary weird, dangerous weird, and out-of-this-world weird." Lanie shrugged. "It helps to be a Trekker. Your brain is already stretched a little bit, so it's easier to wrap it around new ideas. And no, Gordon isn't going to report it to the Chief. He figures it'll all just be gossip and harmless stories by this evening, and nobody will even care in another week."

"Good old Neighborlee protects its own once again," Maurice muttered.

"Then all we have to worry about is Will and Phill." Angela gestured at the refreshment table. "Tomorrow. We are at a wedding, after all."

Chapter Thirteen

Sunday, December 23

"Think we'll ever kiss like that?" Maurice said, as he and Holly slowly skated on the ice that hung in midair over the town. "What?" he said, when she laughed.

"When we kiss, I want to keep kissing. I don't want to blow out the entire power grid of the town and then pass out and lose the entire day." Her smile turned wistful. "Or night."

"True." He shifted his hold on her, unlinking their arms so he could wrap his arm around her waist and draw her closer against him. "It's just ... the look in their eyes, in that split second when we were trying to pull them apart and it seemed like they were coming up for air. It was like 'Yeah, this is it, what I spent my whole life looking for.' Kind of made the misery worth it. And I'm messing up what we've got, right?"

"No. Not really. I think about how long we have to wait until we can be together for real. And I wonder sometimes if this is just a dream after all." Holly rested her head on his shoulder as they skated lazy circles above the town square, where children dressed in red and green built enormous snowmen almost tall enough to reach up to the ice hanging high above them. "Sometimes, when I'm awake, I get fragments of memories of ...this."

"You think? Maybe the spell is wearing thin, or at least shifting a little bit?"

"Since you're the expert on magic, not me, I have no idea." She laughed when he groaned and looked away, his face burning with embarrassment.

"The thing is, Will was looking for answers for me, since I'm denied access to some major Fae information sources." He tugged his arm free, catching hold of her hand and spinning her around in a pirouette that shot off sparks where her skates touched the ice.

Holly laughed. As the spin slowed, she grabbed hold of him, jolting to a stop, nearly pulling them both off their feet. Laughing, they kissed. Soft, quick, sweet kisses that sent rainbow-streaked sparks shooting off from them in all directions and pierced the ice below them.

"We better stop before we melt through," Maurice whispered, and kissed Holly again.

"In answer to your question." She sighed in contentment as he wrapped his arms around her and tucked her head under his chin. "I like every kind of way we kiss. And I kind of feel sorry for Will and Phill."

"How?" His voice cracked with incredulity.

"That kiss ... it's kind of like a fuse finally broke. Or maybe it finally opened up. They've been coming to Neighborlee for years, best pals, but they never realized until now they're meant to be together. They won't be whole without each other."

"That's exactly how I feel about you, Holly Berry, but I don't have a clue how we can get around this big problem," Maurice whispered, and pressed a kiss into the top of her head.

"I'm glad you have this problem."

"Huh?"

She laughed and snuggled even closer, if that were possible. "If you weren't under exile, if you weren't shrunk down and invisible to most people, would you even have come to Neighborlee, much less noticed me?"

"Hey, now that's not -- Well, yeah, I guess it's a fair question. And yeah, even though I thought I was a crusader for the little guy, I guess I was a little shallow." He *oophed* when she poked him in the ribs with two fingers. "Okay, a lot, mega-shallow. I probably wouldn't have, the way I was before."

"Just think of yourself as a world champion runner, the fastest man in the world. You broke your leg, and now you have to limp along with a cast, and you're finally seeing all the scenery you raced past without looking."

"You're more than scenery, Holly Berry."

"I just can't help wondering ..." She sighed, shook her head, and pressed her face against the fuzzy front of his sweater.

"What?"

"Maybe ... maybe you're not there when I'm awake because when you get free ..."

"There's not enough magic in the entire world -- both worlds, Human and Fae -- to make me forget you when my exile is over and I'm back to normal. They could only change my body and limit my magic, but they couldn't change my head and my heart." He pushed her out to arm's length and lifted her so she stood on her toes and had to meet him eye-to-eye. "I had to change my own head and heart, and nothing will make me forget you or walk away. I promise." He swallowed hard. "If I have to, I'll give up all my magic, I'll give up my long life and live a Human lifespan, so I can stay here with you. I swear."

"Really? You'd give all that up? For me?" Tears sparkled in her eyes, turned gold and silver and green, and didn't fall.

"Sweetheart, who says I'm giving up anything? Seems like I'm trading up, big time." Maurice shook her a little, and when she laughed, her voice ragged, he drew her up tight against him. They kissed until streamers of light shot out from them in all directions and the icy fantasy version of Neighborlee melted away.

~~~~~

Holly opened her eyes, curled up in her bed, and sighed, feeling Maurice's arms tight around her and his kiss warm and soft on her lips.

Her eyes popped open. She *did* remember him. Everything about their dream. Gasping, her heart racing, she sat up and looked around. Her bedroom looked entirely too normal. It was Sunday morning, December 23, and she remembered...

What did she remember? Sighing, she closed her eyes and lay back down. Whatever it had been, whatever she had been dreaming when she woke up, it must have been incredible. She could almost cry from the sense of tearing loss. And yet... She smiled and wrapped her arms around herself. Maybe she would have the same dream tonight, when she went to bed?

~~~~~

"Lori? Are you there?" Brick pounded on the door of Lori's hotel room. He gave himself points for waiting until 8 in the morning, so he wouldn't disturb the other guests in the Neighborlee Arms. Or rather, not disturb them too much.

He had haunted the hotel dozens of times each day since she vanished, hoping to catch sight of her. It had taken almost that much time begging, bribing, threatening, finally pleading on his hands and knees, before he found the one person on staff who pitied him, and had seen him with Lori and thought they made a good couple. That person had called last night and reported that Lori and another male guest were holed up with Will and Phill, taking care of them.

Brick was reassured, knowing Lori was busy taking care of Will and Phill. He had heard about the light show and power outage at Jeri and Jon-Tom's wedding. He was also worried. Who was the other guest at the Neighborlee Arms, who knew Lori well enough to team up with her to take care of Will and Phill?

He kicked himself a dozen times over for not attending the wedding. He could have caught up with Lori there. Who was this man with Lori? Brick imagined her being so hurt by his stupidity, she had turned to someone for comfort. He couldn't imagine her doing it just to punish him.

"Yeah, and how did you come to that conclusion after accusing her of only being after your money?" he snarled, even as he clung to that belief. He raised his fists and pounded them against her door again. "Lori? Please? Talk to me?"

She was there. She had been there all night. Brick's contact at the hotel assured him that she hadn't left.

Of course, that really wasn't much assurance, considering how Lori had vanished into thin air when he was with her.

"Do you mind?" Lori whispered loudly. From the room across the hall and one door down. She glared at him, when Brick whipped around so fast he nearly fell off his feet, and stared at her. "There are people trying to sleep. I have sick people here."

"Lori. I've been worried sick about you. I'm sorry. I was a total jerk. I shouldn't have said it. I shouldn't even have been thinking what I was thinking." Brick stumbled down the hall and grabbed at the hand that held the door open.

He wasn't ashamed to admit that he looked over her shoulder, into the hotel room, and saw Phill sprawled across the bed, white-faced, with a green Neighborlee Arms monogrammed washcloth on her forehead. And no one else in the room.

"You're right, you shouldn't have." She sighed, and some of her sternness faded. "And I'm to blame for some of that."

"No --"

"I've been keeping secrets from you. Big secrets." Lori rubbed at her face with the hand Brick wasn't holding. He gave himself points that she didn't tug her hand free. Or worse, slap him with it.

"We need to talk. But I'm busy with Phill."

"I heard a little about the wedding yesterday. How is she? How's Will?"

"If you could help Harry with Will, that would be great. I think they'll both be awake soon, and hopefully sitting up by lunchtime." She shook her head and glanced over her shoulder at Phill. "I've never seen anything like it before."

"What happened?" He offered an apologetic grin. "Or is that something I shouldn't ask?"

"You should be able to ask and get honest answers," she said softly. "If we're going to...to make anything of what we've built up between us these last few weeks, we have to talk. But later, okay?"

"Sure. You got it. Anything you want." He looked up and down the hall. "Umm, you said to take care of Will? Where is he?"

"I asked you to help Harry with Will. And he's in the next room." She pointed up the hall. A tiny spark shot off the tip of each finger of that hand. "Harry will be expecting you. In fact, I think he's kind of relieved. He has someone he needs to take care of."

"Can I ask who Harry is?" Brick took one step backward, heading for Will's room.

"Harry is from back home. And from what I've picked up, he's head-over-heels with someone who lives here in Neighborlee."

"If that's your diplomatic way of telling me I'm a moron for being jealous, thanks."

"I don't let anybody call the man I love a moron," she said, trying to be stern, but only managing a teary, trembling smile.

"Did you say --" Brick stepped back toward her. Lori stopped him with two fingers pressed against his lips.

"We'll talk tomorrow. All day. I promise. Now go help Will."

"Ma'am. Yes, Ma'am." Brick saluted, earning a giggle from her, and hurried down the hall.

The door opened when he was two steps away. He realized he had seen Harry before, when he was driving around with Lori. Harry looked up from where he bent over Will, pulling back one eyelid. He grinned and nodded to Brick.

"You're saving my life. Bethany's been waiting since last night, and I hate leaving poor Will alone like this. Thanks." The jacket that had been lying tossed across the other bed, and the shoes that had been on the floor on the other side of the room, suddenly appeared on Harry. He grinned when Brick's mouth dropped open. "Lori says you're getting the full truth treatment tomorrow, so I figure, save myself some time. Thanks!"

Harry vanished with a soft popping sound and a blip of green light, just at the moment Brick realized his ears had definite points.

"Okay, that explains a few things." He swallowed hard, wishing he hadn't braced himself with the lumberjack breakfast special at Hunky & Dory's. He sat down on the end of the bed where Will was a limp, pale lump. "Magic, right? Real magic. Or else I'm drugged." He swallowed hard again. "Hey, how did Lori tell him when there wasn't time for her to call ..."

Will groaned, rolled over, and let out a long, rattling snore.

Brick decided to take that as a good sign.

~~~~~

"Thank goodness this happened in Neighborlee, instead of somewhere else where we'd have the FBI, CIA, CTU, NCIS and real-life Mulders and Scullys coming down on us," Phill grumbled. She sat up in the bed, letting the damp cloth slide off her forehead. It hit the mattress and tumbled to the floor with a soft, sodden plop.

"Angela assured me that Neighborlee's resident mass amnesia field would smooth over memories and questions." Lori held out her hand and a glass of fizzing magenta liquid popped into it. "Here. This will cure what ails you."

"What does ail me, exactly? And is Will okay?" Phill reached for the glass. Missed. Closed one eye and tried again.

"I haven't checked the Ether Lexicon, but I don't think I have to. Not with all the research I've done, bracing to fight against my relatives." Lori settled on the end of the bed and frowned, waiting until Phill tipped the glass back and drained it.

"Oh, that's awful."

"It is not. I made it your favorite flavor and twice as strong as necessary."

"Not the taste." Phill stuck her tongue out, then winced and pressed her hand against the back of her head while holding out her other hand with the glass. "The feeling of all those bubbles going to work inside my head." She sighed. "So, is Will okay?"

"The last I checked with Harry, he was pretty much progressing like you."

"So what's wrong with us?"
~~~~~

"My diagnosis is a massive case of Need denied."

"Huh?" She stuck her tongue out again when Lori giggled. "We don't have Need."

"Think about it, you dope. Need is there to draw two people together. You and Will have always been together. You want to be together. Right?"

"Absolutely."

"Need is to glue people together until they can make the soul bond, but you and Will are bound together already. My theory is that you never went into identifiable, physical Need because Will has always been there, and hasn't been resisting at all. So there was no Need to turn on the superconductor magnet, to use some Human terminology."

"And use it badly." Phill rubbed once more at the back of her head and sighed. "Considering what you did for my aching head, I'm willing to consider you a doctor and take the diagnosis. So, what about last night?"

"A long overdue linkage, to put it simply."

"To put it mildly, and understate it to the hundredth power. Wow. Did we really knock out all the lights?" A slow smile unfroze the aching muscles in her face.

Lori rolled her eyes and grimaced, and a moment later they both burst out laughing. Phill snuggled down in the blankets again, after plumping her pillow.

"Okay, then we get our happily-ever-after, despite all the dire predictions of both our relatives. Can you believe, that ninny was ready to walk away, because someone convinced him that since I hadn't gone into Need, he must be interfering, and that meant I might die?"

"True love?"

"I can accept that diagnosis, too." She stretched luxuriously. "I'm wiped, but a thousand percent better already. So... Now that my problems are all solved, we need to concentrate on you."

"Hmm, maybe."

"Maybe?" She snatched at Lori's hand when her friend got up to walk away from the bed. "What's that smirk for?"

"Brick was here."

"You were making out with him while I was lying here, dying?"

"We did not make out, and there was no chance of you dying." Lori pouted, eyes sparkling with mischief, and sank down on the end of the bed again. "He came to apologize and beg me to forgive him and... I promised I'd tell him everything tomorrow."

"Everything? As in ...*everything*?" Phill whistled softly and low. "You think he can handle it?"

"He has to, if we have any chance. At least the fact that he's from Neighborlee and he's kinda-sorta used to this kind of thing should... Well, not prepare him, but cushion the shock a little."

"A little." She sighed. "I hoped it works out for you two. Really. He's a great guy. And you need someone spectacular."

"As in... Need?" Lori giggled when Phill grimaced at her again, and squealed the next moment when the pillow slipped out from under Phill and swung at her. She ducked and called up a pillow three times bigger from her bedroom back home. In moments, a pillow fight reigned, augmented with swirls and sparks and streamers of magic in every color conceivable.

~~~~~

"Take my advice. If you're as stuck on Lori as I am on Phill, you can't let anything get in the way. Grab the one who's right for you, no matter what, and hold on tight." Will levered himself upright, then slid out from under the blankets and tottered across the floor to the bathroom.

"I already figured that out." Brick tapped the coffeemaker, willing it to brew faster. He needed coffee just as much as Will seemed to. "So, Lori said she'd tell me everything tomorrow."

"Everything? As in...*everything* everything?" Will paused in the doorway of the bathroom. His color looked better, just getting upright.

"Everything that she's had to keep secret from me. Is that bad or good?"

"Good. Definitely. I think, living in Neighborlee, you might just be able to handle it."

"Handle what, exactly?" Brick thought back to what he had seen Harry do, what he had heard about the power outage last night. "Will, is magic real?"

"There's magic, and there's magic. What kind are you talking about?"

"Will!" He regretted making the ceiling light vibrate, but didn't
~~~~~

apologize, even when Will winced and bent over slightly, holding his head between his hands as if it would burst open.

"Okay, crash course. Give you something to think about." Will straightened and held out his hand. A giant Slurpee-sized glass filled with a fizzing, violent purple liquid appeared in his hand. He drank it down, though it took nearly two minutes to chug it all. Sparks spun out from his ears and the ends of his hair and Will turned that same shade of purple before a burst of steam exploded from seemingly every pore in his body.

He sagged, smiling in relief. "Yeah, that did the trick." He opened his eyes and his smile turned to a smirk. "And yeah, there's magic. Phill and Lori and me, we're magic. It's in our blood. We're Fae. And there's a lot of magic soaked into the ground and air here in Neighborlee, so that might just make things easier on the two of you. If you want to be together."

"Yeah. Together. Forever." Brick swallowed and finally let out the breath he had been holding since the glass appeared in Will's hand. "Tell me everything."

"Everything. Okay. Got all day?"

"I got all the time in the world, when it comes to making sure Lori and I are together, permanently."

"Is that your final answer?" He grinned, snapped his fingers, and the next moment appeared fully dressed and sitting at the table on the other side of the room, with plates full of every breakfast food imaginable covering the table. "Pull up a chair. We got a lot of talking to do, and you're gonna need all the energy you can get."

~~~~~

"Anything?" Ben said, when Harry popped into the living room. The expectant look fell off his face a moment later. "Are you all right?"

"I've been up all night taking care of a sick friend." Harry shrugged. "How's Bethany?"

"I'm fine," Bethany said.

He narrowed her location down to somewhere in the far corner of the living room. Judging from the slight depression in the couch and the decimated bag of peanut butter M&Ms, Harry guessed she had curled up there to watch TV and drown her sorrows.

"The problem is," she continued, "I've run out of witty euphemisms for being invisible."
~~~~~

"I swear, honey, if it wasn't an emergency last night, I would have been here the whole time. I did get a lot of reading in while Will was unconscious. Which was a lot." Harry gave Ben a pleading look.

"Give the boy a break, Bethy." He got up and gestured at the kitchen. "I'm gonna whip us up some lunch, then I recommend you let him get a good chunk of sleep. I may not know much about magic, but it makes sense that he won't do you a lick of good if he's dead on his feet."

Harry thanked him with a nod and a grin and started across the room. It made his head ache to call up enough magic to find Bethany and throw his anti-invisibility spell around her. Then he thought of something before he did it.

"You are dressed, aren't you?" He halted just in front of the coffee table, with it between him and the couch.

"What kind of a question is that?" She laughed. The sound came from his right. So she had gotten up from the couch.

"I'm going to make you visible, and I don't want to embarrass you."

"No. Whatever this is, it's a field around me so everything I'm holding and wearing becomes invisible with me, but anything I let go of becomes visible again. Which could be convenient if I wanted to become a cat burglar, and when I couldn't care less about fashion."

"Bethany, I'm so sorry."

"You look awful. How much energy does it take up to make yourself visible?"

"I don't know. It's unconscious now. Except when I'm actually unconscious, rather than sleeping. Then everything gets reversed and I'm visible until I wake up and think about being visible and then the invisibility sets in again."

"And when we kiss. Then that negates... Hmm." She grabbed hold of his arm.

Harry let her lead him to the couch. He was about to protest that she had shoved him down into her seat, but then Bethany settled herself on his lap.

"Is that better? You know exactly where I am, and I feel a little more real and... Ah ha!" She giggled as she became a transparent, Bethany-tinted and Bethany-shaped mist. "I thought so. If the invisibility wrapped around me when we were close, then I figured the anti-invisibility would work just as well."

"You're a genius. You do the thinking for both of us from now on." Harry wrapped his arms around her and sighed in complete contentment when Bethany rested her head on his shoulder. Snuggling together for the rest of their lives, just like this, suited him just fine.

"Just how much energy does it take up, fighting the invisibility?" she asked after a few minutes of blissful, restful quiet. The sounds of her father opening cupboards and the refrigerator and chopping something came clearly from the kitchen.

"I don't know. It is a drain, I know that. Why?"

"You could just let yourself become invisible while you're indoors. Turn it off completely when you go lie down after lunch."

"Uh huh. And you wouldn't feel so alone?"

"I'm not alone. You're here," she said in a very quiet, small voice.

"Bethany... Okay, I'm gonna have to back up a little and explain all about the emergency that dragged me away last night before I can say this right. I came to a realization last night. I'm probably moving too fast, but after I saw how miserable Will and Phill made themselves and what happened last night ... Okay, here goes."

"Wait. Will and Phill? That emergency last night was them? Dad's been getting bits of gossip. Of course, the way things work in Neighborlee, whatever explanations people are coming up with aren't anywhere near the truth. What did they do? What happened to them? Are they okay?"

"They're fine. Or they will be, when they wake up." Harry pressed two fingers against her lips, stopping her when she opened her mouth to speak again. He could see dozens of questions in her eyes. "Just listen, okay?"

Bethany glared at him, teasing, then nodded. He didn't realize until that moment how glad he was to be able to see her glare at him. Harry took a deep breath, scooched around on the couch to get a little more comfortable, and let spill the whole tale of Will and Phill's explosion at the wedding reception. Then he explained the theory he and Lori had batted back and forth while they tended their unconscious charges.

"So I figured, no matter what people say, no matter what

stands in the way, no matter how weird the circumstances --"

"And in Neighborlee, everything is weird, at one time or another," Bethany interjected. She giggled when he pressed four fingers against her mouth this time.

"When you find the one and you can't imagine living life without her, you tell her and hope she's willing to put up with all the trouble and work, because it'll be worth it in the end. So I figure, you're the one for me, Bethany, and I'll spend the rest of my life proving I'm the one for you." Harry braced himself, took his fingers off her lips, and waited.

"So..." She tipped her head to one side. "Are you sneaking up on saying you love me?"

Harry groaned, closed his eyes, and let his head drop against the back of the couch. "This is why I've been in this mess all my life with the invisibility. I forget the simplest and most important part of everything. Yes, I love you. Forever and always. Even if you can't become a Changeling. Even if we have to use an anti-invisibility spell for the rest of our lives. I'll stay out here in the Human world with you, if you want. Or I'll take us to the Fae realms for the rest of our lives, if you want to get away from Hollywood and the paparazzi. Or we can settle here in Neighborlee. Whatever you want to do."

"What about what you want, Harry?" she whispered, pressing her little hands against both sides of his face and looking into his eyes.

"I want to make you happy." He laughed. "I want you all to myself until the end of time, but that's pretty selfish, so --"

"Not selfish. Because that's how I feel about you, too. Despite everything." She giggled as she tipped her head slightly to the left and brought her lips to within a sixteenth of an inch of his. "Oh, yeah. I love you, too."

Harry thought maybe he had a small taste of that magical sonic boom that shook Neighborlee yesterday when Will and Phill kissed for the first time. Bethany's taste and scent and the feel of her in his arms and the rhythm of her pulse sank into him. All that mattered was Bethany safe in his arms and the sweetness of her spirit flooding into him, merging with his, melting together.

If this is what happens with a true love kiss... I am a dead man when we get to the stronger stuff.

"I can hear what you're thinking," Bethany whispered against his lips.

"You two want to wait until after there's a ring on her finger before you go any further?" Ben called from the kitchen.

"Sorry, Daddy!"

"Uh, sir, I should have probably --" Harry began.

"If you're asking my blessing, you have it." Ben laughed. "Lunch is ready. Why don't you two come up for air and come get something to eat? Bethy, go out to the spare fridge and get my homemade pickles and corn relish, okay?"

"Oh, that's a good sign." Bethany slid off Harry's lap. It took all his self-control to open his arms and let her go. "Daddy's homemade stuff is only saved for special occasions. He wouldn't feed it to you unless he approved."

She winked at him and scurried out through the kitchen. Harry couldn't quite lever himself up from the couch until he heard the door into the garage open and close. He felt good, but kind of hollow at the same time. He knew he was tired, but there was a buzzing tingle or a fizzing in his blood that made him think he could keep going for a few more hours before he collapsed into a coma. That was Bethany's own brand of magic, he was sure.

"Welcome to the family," Ben said, as Harry shuffled into the kitchen. He glanced over his shoulder at him and nodded toward the kitchen table. "Better sit down, son, before you're face-down."

Bethany screamed, and there was a crash of breaking glass and the splat of something liquid on cement. Harry and Ben nearly got jammed up in the garage doorway in their struggle to get out to her first.

She stood in the middle of a puddle of broken jars and dill pickles and yellow-and-green-and-red bits, holding out her arms and staring at them. She wore a ratty pair of blue sweatpants with holes in the knees, and a faded, bleach-spotted matching sweatshirt, and holey sneakers on her feet. Harry wasn't sure why he made note of what she was wearing. He was probably too exhausted to think clearly.

"Bethy -- I can see you," Ben blurted.

Oh, yeah, that was it. She was visible, and she wasn't inside Harry's anti-invisibility field.

"The kiss," Harry said. "The kiss cured you."

"Uh, yeah." Bethany took several cautious steps out of the puddle of glass and spilled preserves, and let her father wrap his arms around her. "That kiss could raise the dead."

They found out some time later that his announcement wasn't quite accurate. By the time they got the corn relish and pickles and broken glass picked up, and they sat down to eat lunch, Bethany grew transparent around the edges. The transparency had gained dominance by the time they finished eating. Harry realized the same thing was happening to him. He gave himself a headache trying to give his anti-invisibility spell a boost.

"I think maybe we're in synch," Bethany said. "Let's see how visible we are after you've had your nap and you're back up to strength."

"If that's true." Harry wobbled a little as he got up from the table, and nearly dropped the dish he was trying to take to the sink.

"Off to bed with you, son," Ben said. "You're no good to me here. In fact, you're a hazard. Both of you. We'll be tripping all over each other with you two invisible."

"If that's true," Harry repeated, slower this time, because even his tongue felt thick and heavy and half-asleep, "then you gotta marry me."

"Marry you?" Bethany blushed. And interestingly enough, that fought the transparency, washing color through her from head to foot. "Are you--"

"Very serious. Marry me, Bethany Miller? I love you more than anything or anyone in the entire world. In both worlds. In the whole universe. In --"

"The boy's loopy with fatigue," Ben scolded, turning around from the sink, where he was up to his elbows in suds. "You've caught him, Bethy. Nice and secure. Now take care of him."

Harry liked the sound of that: Bethany taking care of him. He could barely stand up straight, but that was all right, because she wrapped an arm around him and led him to the guest bedroom. He collapsed like a house of cards in a stiff breeze when she pushed him onto the bed. He wanted to tell her he loved her, just to be sure, but there were two, maybe three or four of her in the room now, and he wasn't sure which one he was talking to. Bethany leaned down to kiss him goodnight. He closed his eyes, sighed, and thought about complaining that there was only a fizzy tingle as their lips met. He fell asleep before the thought finished.

~~~~~

"That's for you," Phill said, when Lori came out of the bathroom.

"What's for me?"

A knock came on the hotel room door. Phill patted her on the arm, winked, then the next moment changed her pajamas and robe into ski clothes.

"We're heading to the Alps. It's beautiful this time of year. Merry Christmas!" Phill added, and blinked out before Lori could say more than, "We?"

The knock came on the door again.

"Are you gonna get that?" Will said, his voice echoing slightly as it slid through several dimensional doorways.

Lori muffled a few choice words on interfering half-wits who couldn't see what was obvious to everyone else in the known universe. She stomped across the room to answer the door.

"I'm coming!" she shouted, when a third knock came, a little louder and faster this time. "What's the --" Her voice caught in her throat as she yanked the door open and found Brick standing there, looking a little frantic.

"Look, I know it's not tomorrow, and I know you can zap me into next week, literally, but --"

"How do you know?" Lori backed up. He followed her into the room and kicked the door closed behind him.

"Will spent the entire afternoon giving me an education on the Fae facts of life. I sure hope that's what you were going to explain to me tomorrow."

"Uh ... yeah. Kind of slowly. Sort of take it one step at a time, to see how well you could take it."

"I think I took it okay." He caught hold of her hands, effectively stopping her from backing right into the bathroom. "A couple times I wanted to go running for the hills, but yeah, I get the whole picture."

"What stopped you?"

"From running?" Brick tugged hard, effectively yanking her off balance so she fell forward, right into his chest. He wrapped his arms around her. "You."

"Yeah?" Lori decided she'd be an idiot to struggle, even if it was
~~~~~

a matter of pride. Caught in Brick's arms was exactly where she wanted to be. She and Phill had spent the afternoon talking about all the problems she would have, especially if Brick didn't have any Fae blood in his background, and how to resolve or at least work around those problems. Then the last hour, they had discussed how to break the news to Brick and what she should do if he proved hard to get.

Obviously, he wasn't going to be hard to get at all. Judging by the tightness of his arms around her, he was "got" already, and he was worried about "getting" her.

Lori considered making him worry, just for a few seconds, then tossed the thought aside.

"Good. Because I'd chase you wherever you went. Even to other worlds."

"Let's talk about our travel plans later." Brick lifted her up against him, so she stood on her toes, and kissed her.

Lori was pretty sure she heard a few muffled magical sonic booms, but that could have been the thudding of her heart. She was definite about the buzzing of magic that shot out through her feet and sank down roots into the magic-soaked soil of Neighborlee, and then came up again to meet Brick's magic roots. Yes, he had some Fae blood. Faint to the point of being nearly invisible, but it was there. That solved a few problems, and any legitimate complaints and roadblocks her conniving, matchmaking, dynasty-building relatives might throw in her way.

"Stay here," Brick whispered, when they came up for air a good ten minutes later.

They were also hovering a good ten inches above the floor, more proof he had some magic of his own, latent up until this point. Lori put that little lesson aside for later.

"Stay here in Neighborlee. Will explained all your problems back home. Stay here and be part of our magic. Please? Oh yeah." Brick grinned, but just for a second Lori saw panic flash in his eyes. "I love you, Angeloria."

"What a coincidence," she whispered, and tipped her head to the side for a better angle. "I love you too."

Stay? He flinched only a little when his thoughts slid up against hers.

Forever.

~~~~~

"Someday," Maurice whispered, holding Holly close as they listened to the clock in the center of town make the first strike of midnight and reverberate through her dreams. "Someday we'll have forever."

"All I care about is making sure we do everything today that we planned," she said, and glanced up at the mistletoe and holly filling the roof of the gazebo in the center of town. "Add this to our list? We'll come back here tomorrow when I'm awake, and kiss for luck?"

"If you let me. After all, we've only met a couple times while you're awake. If I try to kiss you, you might punch my lights out."

"Then I'll kiss you right now," she said, and went up on her tiptoes to kiss Maurice as the clock hit the ninth stroke. She dug her fingers into his arms and kissed hard on strokes ten and eleven.

Maurice vanished, feeling her fingers still gripping his arms, on the stroke of midnight.

Monday, December 24

"Holly," Maurice whispered, as he woke on the couch in the furniture room at Divine's Emporium.

The last chime of midnight still hung in the air.

That had never happened before.

Usually, no matter how hard he tried to have the entire twenty-four hours of his day of having a full-sized, see-able body, he always woke up around dawn.

Trembling, Maurice vaulted off the couch and reached for his clothes. No, wait. He hadn't put his clothes out last night before he went to visit Holly's dreams. Wasn't that stupid?

But a second later, his hand closed around his clothes. New clothes, a thick black sweater with holly and mistletoe embroidered around the collar and cuffs, black slacks, boots, even a hat and gloves and snazzy leather jacket.

"Thanks, Angela," he muttered as he struggled into the stiff new clothes.

His stomach growled. Hunger was a natural result of having his body expanded from five inches tall to six feet. He made his way
~~~~~

upstairs as quietly as he could, to raid Angela's kitchen. After all, it was midnight. Nobody would be awake for a few hours, at the very least.

Correction: Angela was awake, making a massive breakfast. She gestured at the big red teapot sitting in the middle of the table, set for three.

"Expecting guests?" Maurice asked. He lifted the lid of the teapot. The heavenly aroma of Angela's special recipe, triple-chocolate hot chocolate rose up to tantalize his nose.

"Hoping. No assurances. But considering your record and how many times I've pestered the powers-that-be..." Angela shook her head and bent to open her oven and bring out a pan of cinnamon rolls.

Maurice poured for both of them. They toasted each other and silently sipped their first cupfuls while Angela finished cooking the last few strips of bacon.

The magic guarding the house shivered. Maurice grinned, delighted he could sense even that much magic. Usually he was an ordinary Human in the total sense of the word on the days he got a full-sized body. Angela quirked up an eyebrow.

"You felt that?" Her look grew smug when he nodded. "That's a very good sign. Our guest has a key, but maybe you want to go downstairs and meet her, just in case she's having a hard time navigating. Or maybe she's afraid to come the rest of the way."

"Her?" Maurice didn't want to hope, was afraid to hope. He put down his cup, nearly missing the table, fumbling so it hit with a cracking sound. He almost tripped over the chair in his hurry to get away from the table, out of Angela's quarters, and to the stairs.

Holly stood in the main room, arms wrapped tight around herself, staring at the Wishing Ball on the counter. It glowed and swirled with more magical light than Maurice had ever seen before. He stood in the doorway behind her, drinking in the sight of her, afraid she was just a dream.

He cleared his throat, not sure what he would say first.

"Maurice?" Holly turned around, pale and gasping. "I remember."

"Me? You remember me?"

"For good behavior." Asmondius's voice came from the Wishing Ball. "The terms of your exile still stand. One more year in reduced circumstances, but because of your good behavior and efforts toward reform, and because of the recommendations of your parole officer, the block on your sweetheart's memory is lifted." The Wishing Ball's light started to fade, then flared brighter. "Merry Christmas, lad."

"Thanks, Asmondius," Maurice said. He staggered only a few steps toward Holly. That was all right, because she staggered toward him and they met halfway and clung to each other. "So ... you won't punch my lights out if I kiss you under the mistletoe?"

"I will if you make me wait for the mistletoe," Holly whispered, and slipped one hand around the back of his head, to bring his lips down to meet hers.

THE END

Neighborlee, Ohio

(Title, Original Title, Release Date)

Confessions of a Lost Kid (Growing Up Neighborlee) 05/20
Semi-Pseudo-Superheroes (Dorm Rats) 07/20
Virtually London (London Holiday) 09/20
Living Proof (that no good deed goes unpunished) (Living Proof) 11/20
Night of the Living Proof, 01/21
Quitting the Hero Biz (Hero Blues) 03/21
Bride of the Living Proof, 05/21
Shrunk: The Exile of Maurice (Divine's Emporium) 07/21
Return of the Living Proof, 09/21
Allergic to Mistletoe (Have Yourself a Faerie Little Christmas) 11/21
Dawn of the Living Proof, 01/22
Angela's Knight (Divine Knight) 03/22
The Living Proof Gets the Blues, 05/22

About the Author

On the road to publication, Michelle fell into fandom in college and has 40+ stories in various SF and fantasy universes. She has a bunch of useless degrees in theater, English, film/communication, and writing. Even worse, she has over 100 books and novellas with multiple small presses, in science fiction and fantasy, YA, suspense, women's fiction, and sub-genres of romance.

Her official launch into publishing came with winning first place in the Writers of the Future contest in 1990. She was a finalist in the EPIC Awards competition multiple times, winning with **Lorien** in 2006 and ***The Meruk Episodes, I-V,*** in 2010, and was a finalist in the Realm Award competition, in conjunction with the Realm Makers convention.

Her training includes the Institute for Children's Literature; proofreading at an advertising agency; and working at a community newspaper. She is a tea snob and freelance edits for a living (MichelleLevigne@gmail.com for info/rates), but only enough to give her time to write. Her newest crime against the literary world is to be co-managing editor at Mt. Zion Ridge Press and launching the publishing co-op, Ye Olde Dragon Books. Be afraid … be very afraid.

www.Mlevigne.com
www.MichelleLevigne.blogspot.com
www.YeOldeDragonBooks.com
www.MtZionRidgePress.com
@MichelleLevigne

Look for Michelle's Goodreads groups:
Guardians of Neighborlee
Voyages of the AFV Defender

NEWSLETTER:
Want to learn about upcoming books, book launch parties, inside information, and cover reveals?
Go to Michelle's website or blog to sign up.

Also by Michelle L. Levigne

Guardians of the Time Stream: 4-book Steampunk series
The Match Girls: Humorous inspirational romance series starting with **A Match (Not) Made in Heaven**
Sarai's Journey: A 2-book biblical fiction series
Tabor Heights: 20-book inspirational small town romance series.
Quarry Hall: 11-book women's fiction/suspense series
For Sale: Wedding Dress. Never Used: inspirational romance
Crooked Creek: Fun Fables About Critters and Kids: Children's short stories.
Do Yourself a Favor: Tips and Quips on the Writing Life. A book of writing advice.
Killing His Alter-Ego: contemporary romance/suspense, taking place in fandom.
The Commonwealth Universe: SF series, 25 books and growing
The Hunt: 5-book YA fantasy series
Faxinor: Fantasy series, 4 books and growing
Wildvine: Fantasy series, 14 books when all released
Neighborlee: Humorous fantasy series
Zygradon: 5-book Arthurian fantasy series
AFV Defender: SF adventure series
Magic to Spare: Fantasy series
Book & Mug Mysteries: cozy mystery series starting in April 2022

"Unsure what's going on in contemporary speculative fiction? Learn about modern voices in genre, both through their own words and criticism. Interstellar Flight Magazine's first Best of Year One collection covers a wide variety of topics from today's authors."

Review by Warp Speed Odyssey